NO MORE
TEA and TOAST

RICHARD JOHN THORNTON

NO MORE
TEA and TOAST

THIS STORY IS DEDICATED TO LOVERS.

PROLOGUE

If truth be known, Sandra Bancroft wasn't aware she needed a source of exhilaration when it crashed completely uninvited into her life.

At forty-two years of age and after twenty-one years of what she believed was an altogether happy marriage, she had contentedly succumbed to the stable schedule supplied by work and home.

It was a comfort zone that she felt familiar with, and the abiding sense of security was generally rewarding, if hard earned at times.

Most aspects within her realm of domesticity were of a positive nature. Her two adolescent children - one of each - were thriving as blossoming individuals, besides performing well academically.

She enjoyed her full-time job at the local bakery come café in town.

And despite having recently entered her fifth decade, her feminine attributes had waned little since her early twenties.

Sporting a curvaceous figure and blessed with a dark complexion, Sandra effortlessly belied her true years to the casual observer.

Her fifty-one-year-old husband, Stuart, had climbed aboard the bottom rung of the banking ladder on leaving school at sixteen, and his long-held occupational ambitions had reaped due reward.

He now sub-managed a High Street branch in the city, complete with healthy annual bonus and a big three-litre engine silver company car of which Sandra could never remember the make or model.

Being a devout non-driver, and hence a time-honoured pedestrian and employer of public transport, a ride in the family limousine was a rare treat reserved for the occasional weekend visits to the garden centre.

However, such excursions were strictly for Stuart's benefit, not hers, as aside his financial acumen, he was also the green-fingered magician within their particular union.

One or two loyal friends distracted Sandra from the humdrum groove of her normality from time to time, readily littering her existence with humour. A commodity that she secretly craved daily.

Yet it seemed to be in woefully short supply of late.

7

Laughter had become an invaluable medicine over time.

An element of life she had become increasingly dependent upon.

Especially on those days when she had to visit her cantankerous elderly mother, to indulge in her cleaning and shopping whilst partaking in the dutiful bickering, debating, and sympathising.

Whilst being widowed, partially infirm and infrequently incontinent, Phyllis Baxter was also completely sane of mind with a full set of marbles.

As a classic matriarch she maintained an overly keen eye on her daughter's comings, goings, outgoings, and shortcomings.

Having never been an avid fan of Sandra's safe and loyal other half, Phyllis would rarely miss the opportunity to throw the critical knife into his back regarding any arising issue in the Bancroft household.

This was usually in an unsubtle attempt to incite thoughts of a sudden divorce on behalf of her daughter, so Sandra might become official benefactor of any perceived post-nuptial reward that she may be due through a fifty-fifty split of the estate.

Phyllis had resigned herself to a long wait for this dream to flourish.

But her son-in-law was not alone in suffering Phyllis's disapproval.

Now that the grandchildren hardly ever visited her due to the hectic demands of their frantic social lives, they too were regularly lined up to be lashed by their grandmother's mildly poisonous tongue.

Phyllis, although unconditionally bitter regarding the hand that fate had seemingly dealt her, was indeed made of stern stock, and presented a worthy foe to any unwitting opponent.

At eighty-one years of age, she was still capable of punching her weight - if not physically, then certainly verbally - particularly regarding her daughter's marriage and its presumed frailties therein.

Though, whilst her views were not very often requested by Sandra, they were readily offered, anyway.

The worrying aspect to such unwarranted contributions was that Sandra would occasionally find herself sitting in silent agreement with some of her mother's opinions.

Even those about the man she had married.

But Sandra was also fiercely loyal when it came to her family.

She knew where she stood with them and who she could depend upon.

Daily routine was her personal anchor and possibly her mantra.

The ritual of domestic grind was never likely to be altered by outside influence.

Not even Phyllis Baxter could thwart Sandra's obligation to regimental duty as a mother and spouse.

Nothing would sway her from her designated missions.

Especially the unexpected or the unpredictable.

And in all truth, like many other housewives of her peerage and position, that was exactly how Sandra preferred it.

Adventure was certainly not on the agenda.

But nevertheless, adventure lay in wait.

Whether she was ready for it or not…

1
MEET THE BANCROFTS

Nineteen-Eighty-Seven.

Thursday the fourteenth of May.

Seven-thirty-five, a.m.

Orchard Road; an ordinary suburban street.

Number Twelve; an ordinary semi-detached house, in that ordinary suburban street.

And residing within the walls of that ordinary semi-detached house, a *reasonably* ordinary, suburban family.

Sandra had just commenced the morning analysis of her physical form in the bedroom dress mirror. A nagging habit that had recently been implanted in her head by a medical scientist guru fella on TV-am, who implored all females of a certain age to introduce self-examination as part of their daily schedule.

Sandra had long forgotten her initial reasons for buying into such a fad, and it wasn't an aspect to her day that she relished or often derived satisfaction from.

And she supposed that most other verging middle-aged ladies who had been persuaded to jump on the bandwagon also felt the same, such was the penchant of most women to uphold negativity regarding their individual shapes and sizes.

Surprisingly, today she was not overly depressed by the sight of her reflection. With the curtains closed and the lights off, the uncertain outline of her legs and hips appeared relatively taut and blemish-free albeit in the murk of the bedroom.

And after studious consideration, rather than mournfully deciding that her silhouette resembled an egg cup with boiled egg inserted, her general form veered more towards that of an egg *timer*.

Yes, today she adjudged her figure as being positively hourglass, as opposed to pint glass. But as per usual, it was all a case of mind over matter, whatever story the reflection conveyed.

Within the space of twenty-four hours since the last inspection, she had mentally transformed herself from a retired member of the Roly-Polys and back into Madonna.

Conceivably, all sass, frontage, and attitude.

Yes, today she was back in the halcyon days of the mid-sixties, when she was perhaps lithe, energetic, and dynamic.

Fearless, opportunistic, and eye-catching.

This was all before becoming a wife, of course.

And then becoming a mother.

The conflicting images reigned in her mind until vaguely disturbed by the sound of Stuart rummaging around downstairs in the hallway. However, it was not quite the right time to allow the spring sunshine to illuminate proceedings and spoil the illusion.

The physical examination was not yet completed.

Having reluctantly removed her Paddington Bear nightdress and faded sky-blue bra, Sandra pushed back her shoulders and offered her breasts a chance to lift by a centimetre or so.

Quickly becoming frustrated by the futile procedure, the ever-nagging thought recurred.

They could do with being a little bigger.

So, what else was new for women the world over?

Whilst being a size thirty-six-A in reality a thirty-eight-B was only temporarily convincing if she briefly glanced at them sideways on, folded her arms and gave a little wiggle.

But alas, the inward sigh of resignation was never far away.

After all, who was she trying to fool?

Even more demoralising - who else was bothered, *anyway*?

Certainly not Miss Jones, the family cat, who sat patiently through the tedious exhibition every morning whilst nurturing a grumbling stomach.

An unkempt fusion of long black and white fur, Miss Jones could offer little in the way of opinion on the jiggling images of her maternal human owner in the mirror, but there was method in the madness.

Sandra was always the most likely candidate to refill the cat's food bowl should it become empty at any time. Mornings were an absolute dead loss regarding the rest of the family's acknowledgement of their famished pet.

In their hasty preoccupation to get ready to get wherever they needed to get to, everybody else in the household either wilfully shunted Miss Jones out of the way with their feet, or stood on her accidentally, or when really pressed for time, shut her out of the house completely and pretended she didn't exist.

So as far as a hungry feline was concerned, observing the sole provider of sustenance vainly observe herself in the bedroom mirror each morning did guarantee to eventually bring its rewards.

Besides ensuring that she avoided the alarming experience of being inadvertently - or maybe purposely - kicked downstairs.

If achieving nothing else, biding her time secured the first meal of the day and it was always well worth the wait. Miss Jones yawned and settled on the bed as Sandra altered her posture for the umpteenth time.

Sandra had always liked her legs. They had remained shapely and toned since girlhood. Dance lessons and gym club as a youngster had certainly assisted this cause.

Thankfully, cellulite was not an obvious affliction, especially with the curtains closed.

Sandra then reluctantly faced away from her reflection to try and catch a profile of her bottom which this morning was adorned in large white cotton pants.

Straining her neck to obtain the merest of viewing angles, she declared it quite passable to the untrained eye.

Now it was time for the real acid test.

Looking toward the mirror once more, she flicked on the dressing table lamp.

Magnifying the analysis to her face, she began to pull it hither and thither, ironing out one or two minor wrinkles and stretching her minimal crow's feet to create the appearance of smooth skin.

There were no dark rings around her eyes, but then it was tricky to identify dark rings in the semi-darkness. She played with her shoulder length brown locks, which amazingly, were still free of any greying strands.

Gently scraping it back to the hairline revealed a spotless forehead that sported what could only be described in absolute exaggerated cruelty as two-and-a-half mild frown lines. Certainly, no more than that.

Yes. Today Sandra passed herself off with flying colours.

But there was no need to allow natural light into the room just yet.

Such an ingredient only served to detract from the temporary sense of appeasement. But of course, her psychological bubble of perfection never took long to burst.

'Sandra, dear! Put some bloody clothes on, will you! The kids are getting up!'

Bolting upright from her crouched position at the mirror, Sandra felt a twinge in her back as Stuart retrieved her pink towelling night gown from the bedroom floor and threw it across the room to his startled other half.

'*Jesus*! You didn't half make me *jump*! Don't you ever knock before entering?'

Stuart gazed at his wife through a mask of puzzlement.

'No need to call me Jesus, dear. Stuart will do just fine in the bedroom. Anyway, why should I *need* to knock? I do live here too! I know who's likely to be in here after all these years. By the way, what the hell were you doing?'

Suddenly rendered self-conscious and mildly embarrassed, Sandra replaced her bra and topped off the unalluring effect with the flannelette night gown.

'It's called self-assessment. All modern women should do it every day, apparently. It encourages you to feel good about yourself. That's if you're not afraid of looking in the first place.'

Stuart chuckled as he threw off his own bathrobe, revealing a particularly unappealing set of matching white vest and y-fronts.

14

Sandra noticed that this underwear combo also brilliantly served to accentuate her husband's carefully nurtured pot belly.

She heard his voice resonate once again as her eyes continued to study his rounded stomach.

'Where did you read such codswallop, anyway? One of your women's magazines? I don't know. I never thought my wife would feel the need to join the Jane Fonda fan club. Have you seen my onyx cufflinks?'

Mildly frustrated at the intrusion on her portion of privacy, Sandra shoved her bare feet into her favourite white fluffy slippers and made for the landing.

'No, I haven't seen them. Why *would* I have? Anyway, I thought you said the kids were getting up? It's like a cemetery out here!'

Stuart emerged from the bedroom with a clean beige shirt draped over his arm.

'Well, they'll be up soon! Just as well they are still in their pits, isn't it. We don't want them seeing their mother sprawled naked all over the furniture, do we?'

'No. *You* don't…*do you*? Not these days, *anyway*! Should know better, shouldn't I? The usual for breakfast then, is it?'

Smirking at the sight of his wife's feigned expression of annoyance, he gave her a peck on the cheek and scampered downstairs.

'Yes, please, dear. Has the paper boy been yet?' he shouted back up the stairwell.

Sandra leaned over the top banister and conveyed a cheeky repost.

'I've no bloody idea, darling! I've been far too busy examining my bosoms!'

Feeling genuinely smug with the retort, Sandra's sense of victory was however woefully short-lived.

'Morning, Mum.'

With imperfect timing, her son Daniel appeared at his bedroom doorway, his gangling form hovering behind her adorned in a pair of ridiculously long boxer shorts.

He was the archetypal, cheeky fifteen-year-old. Full of self-confidence, unflappable and perilously quick-witted. As such, Daniel never failed to pick up on any aroma of mild adversity that may have been left trailing around the house.

And if he couldn't follow the scent and gleefully add fuel to the fire, then he felt it his rightful duty to initiate conflict from the off.

'How are your bosoms then, Mum? Alright?' he yawned.

Lightly shamed by his sarcastic commentary, Sandra mockingly clenched a fist in her son's direction.

'You're not too tall for a clip around the ear, you know! And it's traditionally rude to listen in on people's private conversations!'

Daniel yawned loudly once more, scratched his crotch, and stretched his arms as his mother descended the stairway.

'Mum! That was hardly a private conversation, was it? You two woke me up shouting about your boob inspection! Barely discreet, is it?'

She did not respond as she grasped the banister rail. Now forced into silently conceding defeat to her youngest offspring, Sandra made for the kitchen and began to drag the relevant pots and pans from the cupboard as Stuart reclined at the table with the Financial Times.

He mumbled as he read, not really addressing anybody in particular.

Certainly not his wife, who knew as much about the stock market as she did about his two other great loves - cricket and gardening. He continued to scan the page to a backdrop of clattering kitchenware and then the highly audible, yet vital contribution of the radio.

Right on cue, Miss Jones glided silently into the room and was immediately greeted by the welcome vision of a full bowl of beef chunks in jelly.

'*Shit*! Marko shares have dropped. But, oh…very interesting… Insignia have risen. Should put a smile on Guy's face this morning…'

Sandra's priorities lay elsewhere at that moment as she began to enjoy the latest pop sounds courtesy of the kitchen stereo.

'Scrambled or fried, dear?'

Stuart's concentration continued to remain centred between the pages of the newspaper.

'Wow…Dean's totals have steadied. Erm…scrambled please, dear.'

'Tomatoes or beans?'

Sandra commenced a singalong to Johnny Hates Jazz, accompanied by a semi-rhythmical jig in front of the tin cupboard.

'Down two points on Tuesday's mark. Oh dear. Erm…beans please.'

'Fried or toast?'

'Toast please, dear. And can you turn that racket down?'

And so, the fractured conversation ensued.

A well-rehearsed interaction of breakfast requirements, pop music and economical overview. The dialogue was in evidence, but as usual, there was little meaningful communication between man and wife.

'You know as I'm serving people food all day, I might make it a new rule that *you* have to cook breakfast for *me* in the mornings.'

Stuart did not even look up from his read.

Now dressed in a significantly creased t-shirt in addition to his unlaundered sports shorts, Daniel meandered to the table, slumping heavily onto the chair next to his father.

'Mum, have you washed my gym stuff? I'm going to footy training with Ady after school.'

Sandra spun around from the stove with frying pan in hand and looked confusedly at her son.

'I haven't seen your gym stuff for days. If you don't bring it down then I can't wash it, can I? How many times do I have to tell you? It's not going to get cleaned if you hide it under your bed, is it?'

Promptly rising from the table with a heavy groan of disgruntlement, Daniel disappeared once again to search for his missing kit.

As he got to the bottom of the stairs, his seventeen-year-old sister Laura was in mid-descent and fronting her typical early morning mode.

Namely, half asleep and half in a ritually bad mood.

Mascara stains streaked from either side of her eyes.

Her blonde hair resembled a burst mattress.

This was far too good a chance for a doting brother to resist.

Laura was a sitting duck.

Ever ready for the opportunity, Daniel opened fire as he recoiled in mock horror.

'Christ! Weren't you in the sequel to Nightmare on Elm Street? It's a *really* authentic *likeness*! Can't you cover your face up? There are elderly and infirm relatives in the house! You'll scare them to death!'

Laura offered her brother a look of genuine scorn and a supplementary pair of middle fingers as she passed him in the hallway. The daily sibling altercation began in earnest as she finally murmured a suitably cutting reply.

'Well...I see you've still not woken up with a sense of humour. Don't panic, though. It'll happen one day. Probably quicker than your entry into puberty, too!'

Daniel had by now reached the top of the stairs, requiring a slight increase in volume to adequately convey his ill-conjured response.

'Naff off, Laura! Had a row with that cabbage of a boyfriend of yours again last night, did we?'

Her return of serve promptly resonated back up the stairwell.

'Piss off, Dan! And another thing, have you been using my lady-shave?'

'No, I have *not*! Why the hell *would* I?'

Now re-positioned at the bottom step, Laura's raucous tone also increased in ferocity.

'Well, it wasn't where I left it at the weekend. And it's hardly cutting at all now!'

An easy win upcoming for the brother.

'I'm not surprised with the bristles on *your* legs!'

Daniel commenced chuckling on the verge of his triumph.

'Bollocks to ya! Mind, you wouldn't need a shaver anyway yet, would you? Little boy!'

Daniel disappeared on the landing as Laura turned to see her mother standing silently with hands on hips in the lounge doorway.

However, the hiatus in conversation did not last long.

'Do I honestly *have* to listen to this every morning? Can't you two grow up for one day? Just *pretend* to be a little mature…just for *me*…just for five minutes?'

'Tell *him* then, Mum. *He's* the idiot with the big mouth!'

Sandra slowly shook her head as she swivelled in her fluffy slippers.

'Well, from what I've just heard your gob isn't far behind *his*! Laura…you're *seventeen*…rise above it!'

Eventually, as the inmates of Number Twelve, Orchard Road began to fully rouse themselves from slumber and exhaust their inherent need for antagonism, the cooking was eventually accomplished to order.

Daniel was last to the table, purposely brushing past his sister whilst making sure she received a face full of his dirty shorts and football shirt.

'You're a disgusting twat, Dan! I'm trying to eat!'

Sandra looked across the table to the supposed man of the house, who continued to scrutinise his broadsheet in between forkfuls of bacon and egg.

He was seemingly oblivious to the ongoing commotion between his offspring, so she adopted the mantle of chief controller once more.

'Please don't swear, Laura. It's not very lady like.'

'She's not a lady. She's my *sister*!' piped Daniel, dropping his gym kit in front of the washing machine.

Laura's response came in the form of another well harnessed middle finger. But her brother was far from deterred.

Instead, he altered his target as he dropped his string bean form onto the chair.

'Hey, guess what Mum was doing this morning, sis! You'll never get it! Bet you a *tenner*!'

Laura looked to her brother, slightly bemused by the inane grin that had spread across his features, before glancing to her mother for an explanation.

19

But Daniel could not restrain his mischievous whim, albeit conveyed in whispered tones with a hand playfully held to his mouth.

'She was only inspecting her...'

Finally, Stuart decided to reclaim a semblance of supreme paternal authority over the situation.

'Daniel Bancroft! Can you just eat your breakfast! Everyone's getting a headache thank you! It's far too early for us to listen to such rubbish! And why do I sound like one of your teachers! Honestly you drive me and your mother mad at times!'

Brother and sister grimaced lovingly at one another as an unsteady peace resumed for at least two and a half minutes.

'You'll have to come home for your gym kit after school, Daniel. I haven't time to get it ready before you go.'

Daniel frowned at his mother with a mouthful of bread and butter then duly affirmed her declaration through the same mouthful.

'Don't worry, Mum. I'll wait for you. I'm in no hurry.'

'No, you won't wait! You must have been late for school every day for the last month!'

'Okay...I won't go to school at all then!'

'Oh yes you *will*!' snapped Sandra.

Laura chuckled inwardly as Daniel's feeble argument crashed and burned. Aside to the shenanigans at the table, Miss Jones contentedly licked her bowl clean before making her way back upstairs and the welcome sanctity of one of the three vacant bedrooms.

Sandra made the most of the temporary resumption of near silence and turned up the radio volume slightly before emptying cornflakes into a bowl. Whilst not officially dieting, the earlier scrutiny of her figure, whilst mostly satisfying, also now prompted her to err on the side of caution.

Eggs and bacon were a scrumptious and infinitely preferable option, but potentially damaging to a borderline size twelve.

Stuart cleared his plate and checked his watch.

'Are you visiting the dragon's lair today, dear?'

In reference to his mother-in-law, Stuart almost spat the words from his lips in time-honoured distaste.

He was aware of Phyllis Baxter's dislike of her daughter's choice of husband.

The animosity had quickly become mutual well before the day in church.

Inwardly frustrated by the persistent and seemingly insolvable feud, Sandra maintained her habitual dignity as unwitting and unwilling diplomat.

'No, dear. I spend my day off with her. Which is Wednesday. As it has been for the past seven years! Wednesday was *yesterday*. It is also the day *before* Thursday, as it has been since time began.'

Mildly puzzled by his wife's flippancy, Stuart offered a smile as he folded up his newspaper.

'Oh yes…I always forget. *Wednesday* is Gorgon Day.'

'Yes. Very convenient memory loss. Well…no matter. So long as you remember what's important to you. The Test Match. The Stock Exchange. That's all that counts, isn't it? That goes for all of you! Just you worry about yourselves! I'll mop the bloody mess up when you've gone, as usual!'

Daniel and Laura looked at one another in mild astonishment at their mother's untypical outburst, even prompting a concerned query from the former as half a rasher hung from between his lips.

'You okay, Mum?'

'Yes! Of course! I'm *Fine*! I've got to be, haven't I? To make sure that you lot are alright every bloody day of your lives!'

Stuart had now vacated the table and proceeded to button up his clean, ironed, beige shirt.

'Erm…don't worry about those onyx cufflinks, dear. I'll just wear the gold ones. It doesn't really matter!'

Sandra dropped her spoon onto the table and rose to her feet, pretending to feint. She was now more than ready to employ her own brand of fully fledged sarcasm.

'Oh, my darling husband! Thank God you'll be okay! I was about to lose sleep over those bloody cufflinks, as well! Can you truly cope? Are you sure, dear?'

Stuart now observed the amused expressions on the face of his son and daughter. Again, Daniel could not resist the unspoken invitation to contribute.

'Erm…Mum! Swearing! Not allowed! Remember?'

A disconcerted father attempted to steer the situation back into the realm of amiability.

'Okay, Dan! No need to encourage your mother in her moment of unleashed fury. She'll love us all over again by this evening!'

Daniel shook his head as he too decided it time to depart the kitchen.

'Well…as long as she's not going mental. I was a bit worried.'

Again, Sandra was spurred into commentary.

'Oh…I *was* going mental, but only for a minute, my dearest son! Heaven forbids that I should concern you for more than sixty seconds of your vitally important day. Please, pardon the intrusion on your inner concentration! By the way, I'm about to wash your smelly gym stuff after all! You can rest easy now!'

Now Daniel was genuinely perturbed by his mother's peculiar diatribe. He simply shook his head and muttered a 'thank-you' before sloping off upstairs to get ready for school.

Sandra dropped the breakfast pots into a sink full of bubbles and began to wipe them furiously.

Laura opted to say nothing and disappeared before attentions could be returned to her and her unstable love life, the latest episode of which had played out at the front door at one-thirty that morning.

Finally, Sandra was alone and at peace once again.

Much solace can be attained from washing the pots to the melodic accompaniment of Erasure. It was a soothing distraction.

Inspiring music for women performing uninspiring chores.

For a wondrous moment, she closed her eyes.

Suddenly, Sandra was a sequinned diva in Vegas.

Adored by millions.

Then Stuart re-appeared trousered and booted, in full readiness for another day behind the money-counting desk.

His tentative peck on Sandra's cheek was received with dubious acclaim.

'Goodbye then, love. See you later.' he muttered somewhat cautiously.

Sandra dropped the tea towel on the work surface.

She presented her husband with his sandwiches, which were neatly wrapped in cling film and boxed in their usual plastic container.

'Tuna and tomato. Just how you like them. And an apple for the teacher.' she smirked.

Stuart sniggered as his wife returned the gesture of a kiss on the cheek. She followed him to the front door and watched as he hung his black pin-stripe suit jacket in the back seat of the big silver three-litre car.

'Oh, by the way, darling. I've got that Grower's Association meeting on Saturday afternoon. No doubt you'll be wandering the streets shopping with our daughter? I just wondered if…'

Sandra smiled inwardly at her husband's thinly veiled extension for her to attend the local home agriculturalist's orgasm-thon.

'Don't worry, dear. You can go alone. I'm sure I'm not missing anything.'

Visibly appeased, Stuart opened the driver's door.

'Fine! But it may mean a secondary meeting on the Sunday. So, I don't know if I'll be around for Sunday lunch! Have a good day. Play nicely with the customers!'

Sandra watched the big silver three-litre car reverse off the driveway and she confirmed its departure with a wave.

Behind her in the hallway, Daniel suddenly re-materialised.

'Right then, Mum. I'm off! I'll fetch my kit after school.'

'Okay. See you later. I'll leave it in the tumble drier, alright?'

The son kissed his mother in a timely act of affection.

23

'Brill, Mum! Love ya!'

Daniel bounded off up the street never thinking to look back and behold the vision of his tired and frustrated mother.

At last, tranquillity could resume once more within the walls of Number Twelve. Sandra returned to finish up in the kitchen as the eight-thirty news blared from the radio.

After a quick wash, it was upstairs to make the beds.

It was then that Laura revealed herself on the landing, looking more than a little distressed.

'You okay, love? Got a free period this morning? I don't know…you Sixth Formers…life of Riley!'

Laura nodded, evidently on the verge of upset.

Then, as most vulnerable children tend to do in the presence of their mothers, she buckled, and the avalanche of tears ensued.

Sandra placed both arms around her daughter's quivering shoulders and whispered gently into her ear.

'Whatever is the matter my sweet? Come on downstairs. I'll make a drink and you can tell me all about it.'

Back in the kitchen, mother and daughter convened around the table. It made a pleasant change to have the house to themselves without the typical noise and bustle contributed by felines and males.

As Laura disclosed the cause of her troubles, a small selection of used tissues gradually amassed next to her left wrist. A box of clean ones lay in readiness to her right.

Sandra placed a sweet mug of tea in front of her trembling seventeen-year-old, turned the radio volume down and sat next to her.

'Now, then. Is this about that row you had with Craig last night?'

Laura nodded quickly and wiped her nose.

'So then…what's he done now?'

Sniffling and taking deep breaths, Laura struggled to compose herself. Sandra looked at the clock on the kitchen wall. It was getting on for a quarter to nine. She had to be at work for ten.

There were many chores to attend to before leaving the house was even a consideration.

24

'Come on, love. Whatever it is, you'll make it up between you. I'm sure. It's just a little tiff. We all have them.'

Sandra engaged with the moistened gaze of her beautiful little girl in anticipation of listening to a replay of some unimportant quarrel that had gotten out of hand.

She waited as her daughter continued to sniffle and bubble in rhythmical motion.

Then she checked the time once more.

Impatience was now getting the better of Sandra.

Although like all concerned and well-meaning parents, she maintained the pretence of deepest compassion.

Finally, to a mother's eternal relief, Laura spoke about her plight.

'He…he…he thinks he…loves…somebody else…'

With that scant revelation, the tears reappeared in veritable floods.

Again, Sandra offered a sliver of maternal consolation. Again, she checked the clock. Her bus would be due around the corner in thirty minutes.

Finally, as the storm of emotion subsided, Sandra looked her daughter squarely in the eye.

'Now listen here, my girl. If he's honest and true and you love him and trust him…then you haven't got a problem. Have you?'

Laura was not convinced by the simplicity of her mother's logic.

'But Mum…he says he also fancies other girls, apart from me.'

Sandra shuffled herself closer to her daughter and whispered.

'ALL men fancy other women, Laura! It's how they're *born*! They can't help it. They think with their trousers first and their brains last!'

Genuine astonishment quickly eclipsed the mask of romantic unease as Laura looked to her mother for an explanation.

'What? Even *Dad*?'

In an instant, such unexpected yet pertinent logic rendered Sandra's argument unstuck.

It was a very fair point, in truth.

Stuart Bancroft was acutely *disinterested* in the wares of other females.

25

'Well…okay…maybe your father's a bit unusual…but no, alright…I'm fairly sure he's never even *looked* at another woman in his life! No chance! He's far more interested in his vegetables!'

Laughter echoed around the kitchen at last, serving to drown out the nine o'clock news.

'Listen Laura, love. You'll just have to talk to Craig and get the answers you need from him. If he says he still loves you…then great!'

Laura blew her nose again as the clock ticked on.

'And what if he *doesn't* love me anymore, Mum? Then what do I do?'

There was a pause as Sandra thought on her feet.

This answer needed to be good.

And conclusive enough for the pointless conversation to end.

'Then…you…well…you *dump* him! Find someone who *does* love you! There are plenty of young men out there who would jump at the chance to take you out!'

With her fears allayed, smile restored, and thirst quenched, Laura dashed back upstairs and readied herself for school.

Within minutes, both mother and daughter stood outside the front door, fully prepared for the day ahead.

'Now you tell him straight, Laura! Don't let him mess you around. You aren't a doormat! Give him something to think about, aside from other girls of course!'

A final embrace preceded departing goodbyes.

'Thanks Mum! You're the best!'

'I know. I know! See you tonight, my love.'

Miss Jones watched covertly from the front bedroom window as Sandra and Laura headed in different directions to face their individual destinies.

With a relieved lick of her paw and a wipe of her face, she turned to the unmade bed behind her. It looked like she would have to sleep on her owner's pink towelling dressing gown and run a gauntlet of abuse for covering it in fur.

After a quick drink, that is.

Gliding down to the welcoming tranquillity of the kitchen, Miss Jones navigated her way around Ashley's pile of dirty gym kit that Sandra had forgotten to launder after all.

Finishing off the remaining milk from her saucer, she relished embracing the prospect of a few hours undisturbed slumber among the bedclothes.

2

A FAMILIAR ROUTE

The late spring breeze carried a strand of very welcome warmth as Sandra loosened the zipper on her jacket.

The bus stop was a mere five-minute walk from Orchard Road and as she approached, the regular faces could be seen standing under the blue painted shelter in an orderly yet typically uncommunicative line.

Sandra didn't particularly mind being transported by bus, but the tedious nature of the business often came to the fore through the varying characters that travelled with her on frequent occasion.

Even from a considerable distance, she could hear the two old ladies - donned in their traditional uniforms comprising violet-coloured overcoats and matching hats. Their forte was nattering quietly to one another about anything and everything to do with anything and everything.

Sandra had never summoned sufficient motive to ask them where they went each day. They were obviously too old to still be at work. So, she presumed it might be some social club or volunteer group that was the only plausible destination of their jaunts together.

It amazed Sandra that two people could spend so much time in one another's company and still un-earth something to talk about. Yet the almost whispered conversations between the pair never faltered even to catch a mutual breath.

Whether the subject being covered was the unpredictable weather, stress whilst shopping, favours for friends, fallouts with family, nosy neighbours, paltry pensions, the pomposity of politics, over-spilling litter bins.

Every day they would stand and gossip as if their lives depended on it.

Yet in all honesty, they were even more likeable for the fact.

'Morning, ladies!' chirped Sandra, expectant of the same upbeat response she always received.

'Morning, my dear.' they squeaked. In harmony.

'A little warmer today, isn't it?' Sandra strove.

'Oh yes. Soon be summer, my dear. Soon be time to leave the coats at home, hopefully!'

Sandra forced a hearty smile, already becoming bored by the ritualistic exchange.

Thankfully the bus was on time for once, which offered some inner relief from the struggle to be pleasant to people to the point of monotony. It was a terrible attitude to uphold really, but that was how Sandra truly felt inside.

However, soon enough there would be an earnest reason for feeling downbeat. As the bus drew ever closer, she recognised the bulldog-like expression of the driver, who was possibly the most curmudgeonly example of human existence in the entire history of the species.

Another imminent chore of her routine awaited in attempting to get him to lighten his glum visage for even a split second. A personal ambition of Sandra's that had yet to be successfully sated.

Filing onto the bus after waiting for the brakes to cease screeching, the old ladies displayed their passes and perched in their usual seats. They always sat closest to the driver as possible. Nearest as they possibly could to the front.

Half a dozen or so other impatient passengers climbed aboard and one by one encountered the misery-guts behind the steering wheel.

Then it was Sandra's turn to engage with the grinch.

With her teeth now grinding in protest, she sensed the driver glare through her, as though she had just boarded the vehicle accompanied by a pack of slavering rottweilers. It required a sustained effort to feign even the smallest of pleasantries with the man.

But being polite by nature, Sandra would always persist in the fading art of sociability. Yet this guy would wittingly test the abiding patience of a country vicar.

The typically sullen expression he carried made him look as though he was chewing on a nettle.

An unusually thick mop of black hair was underscored by unusually bushy, black eyebrows and a pocked nose, with contrasting thick white hairs protruding from either nostril.

Two sour-looking cherry lips turned downward at the edges as though weighted either side by lead shot. The rings under his eyes were the colour of fresh plums and vaguely reminded Sandra of used tea bags.

He was an altogether unappealing specimen, and that is before he even attempted to offer the vaguest semblance of conversation.

Which he rarely did.

'Good morning!' Sandra beamed, painfully.

The driver's joyless reaction materialised in the form of a merest nod of the head as he stared and sneered at her six-monthly travel pass, which was decorated with a mug shot that Sandra now begrudged showing him every single day.

It wasn't a particularly uncomplimentary photograph, but the driver had taken her into town at least one thousand times in five years. Surely the charade of personal identification could be argued as becoming even slightly contrived by now.

Even so, the melancholy fellow in charge of the helm studied the picture for a full five seconds before making a visual comparison via another vacant, yet suspicious glare.

His affirming bob of the head was final confirmation that Sandra had again satisfactorily proved who she was and could now take a seat on the bus which she had paid for in advance several weeks earlier.

She made her way down the aisle, clenching her fists, wishing she could have the opportunity just once of throwing one of them in the direction of his sullen pudding muncher.

And as per usual, Mister Charisma behind the wheel took the option to put his foot down and pull away from the curb side, just as Sandra was about to locate her seat, causing her to lurch into it like a drunkard on a party dancefloor.

Fellow passengers quickly turned in her direction, possibly stifling their amusement or possibly not.

Mildly embarrassed, she re-adjusted her posterior onto the orange chequered cushion and grimaced forward to the front of the bus, hoping to catch the driver's eye in the rear-view mirror.

This was a game she liked to play every time he picked her up. But she never did catch his devious reflection. Yet she was sure he was always laughing inside.

Just once she hoped to catch him sneaking a cheeky glance at her stumbling attempts at sitting down. After all, how could the man *not* be enjoying himself? Under his feet he possessed the power to make any of his passengers look foolish with minimum effort.

Gliding gloomily through the local estate, Sandra gazed vacantly beyond the window in the hope of seeing something vaguely more interesting than the passing views she had become overly accustomed to over the years.

Seeing the local infant school was always a pleasurable aspect to the trip. By the time she passed it by the children had long-since entered the hallowed territory of the school building of course.

No doubt, as Sandra did herself, the small group of mothers still gathered outside was anticipating the possibility that their tearfully distressed young ones may burst forth from the large glass doors in the hope that mummy will take them home again.

Or maybe they were wilfully passing time by gossiping, as it staved off having to tackle the mountain of housework that awaited them on their return home.

Sandra always thought of Laura and Daniel as the school honed into full view. That supposedly idyllic era when she used to take them to the playground gate at nine and pick them up again at three-thirty seemed like only yesterday.

Laura loved school and never played up. Unfortunately, Daniel hated his formative years in education and never failed to scream the place down on entry. The only way the nursery supervisor could stop him crying was to offer him a constant supply of biscuits.

Not much had changed on that score, either.

Such happy days. How did they fly by so quickly?

Now over a decade ago, but the rightful memories of a proud mother still burned as brightly as the Christmas star she used to tell them about so lovingly.

Sandra's nostalgic inflation was a temporary experience, however.

The bus pulled up at the next stop with another disconcerting sequence of stamps on the brake pedal.

And waiting under the shelter was the town tramp, Oscar.

His Christian name was the only fact that anybody knew about him.

And all they *wanted* to know about him, for that matter.

Indeed, some bus drivers didn't even acknowledge Oscar's unsteady presence at the shelter and often drove straight past him on purpose if nobody else needed the stop.

Whilst probably a crude and ignorant gesture to the casual observer, there was usually at least one good reason to ignore the dishevelled looking figure that hunched against the windowpane of the shelter.

Firstly, he was renowned for never having any money to pay his fare. So of course, the customary debate with the driver would ensue when he did occasionally amble onto the bus.

Not to mention the uproar that brewed among other passengers when Oscar occasionally managed to encounter a driver with a kind heart who *would* taxi him for free.

Secondly, he was always drinking export lager and made no effort to conceal the half-empty beer can that was perennially clamped in his dirt-encrusted fist.

Yet again, the driver would try and explain the law of the land, but usually to no avail. The tramp would never listen to common truth and would usually slur his feeble excuses about it being a free country and the like.

Thirdly, he smelled.

A fragrance that turned Sandra's stomach should she come within ten feet of the guy. This of course was not difficult to achieve if he happened to be sitting in the same vehicle.

It was not the typical stench of body odour, though. It was a vile, pungent aroma, the ingredients of which could only be surmised.

Yet this proved its worth as another game that had served to pass the time for Sandra during many journeys. It presented itself as a kind of memory test for bored housewives on their way to work.

So once again, Sandra indulged herself in guessing the contents of Oscar's germ cloud.

Urine; convincingly.

Stale booze; undoubtedly.

Dried sweat; went without saying.

Unwashed clothing; evidently.

Wet dog; potentially - if indeed he had a dog.

Tobacco; likely judging by his yellowed fingers.

And Oscar also possessed the breath that carried the stench of an elephant's. This was however a completely unsubstantiated and wild rumour that Sandra could not sustain, solely based on her complete ignorance regarding what an elephant's breath truly smelled like.

The list of items in the halitosis recipe were unlikely to be exhausted, but Sandra had never been able to positively identify any further constituents of the stinking vapour that enveloped Oscar's unpleasant form.

Considering all the above, it was even more puzzling and ironic then, that willingly engaging the tramp in dialogue at that moment, was the most impatient, intolerant, and unsociable bus driver in the whole wide world.

Why he should feel any inclination to offer the unkempt drunkard even one of his sternest stares - let alone actually physically stop the bus beside him and communicate - was a lifelong mystery.

There was an atmospheric intake of apprehension throughout the vehicle as the doors hissed open and the vagabond boarded at the second attempt, after the first try saw him stumbling back into the gutter.

All eyes were fixed perilously to the front as Oscar staggered to attention adjacent to their uncharacteristically cordial chauffeur.

33

The men exchanged smiles, but nothing was said for a moment or two as the scruff rummaged around in his trousers. For seconds on end, the rest of the passengers studied the display, checking their watches and anticipating the whiff of walking death to begin drifting its way down the aisle.

For such a historically uncooperative personality, the driver strangely exhibited an unprecedented capacity for patience at the behest of the penniless individual wavering before him.

The tramp duly belched before listing backward, nearly causing him to fall out of the bus once again and back into the shelter.

Finally, much to the collective telepathic relief of his passengers, the driver presented Oscar with his solitary option.

'Thirty pence to town. No money…no ride. Sorry. Not my rules, mate.'

For some unfathomable and perverse reason, the name suited the un-cleansed hobo in the grey mackintosh. It was a distinguished and yet uncommon moniker, for sure.

The grimy gentleman muttered something that sounded like 'fishing baster', but Sandra must have misheard as the conversation between the men developed into something rather more upbeat.

She subconsciously gripped her handbag tighter as if to ward off any possibility that Oscar might request a whip round from his quietly seething audience.

'I'll pay you tomorrow…' declared the ever-hopeful scruff.

'Okay. Then I'll pick you up tomorrow.' recoiled the driver.

'But I need a lift today!' explained the tramp.

'Then you pay me today!' demanded the driver.

More seconds of the stand-off elapsed as Oscar assessed his situation.

Finally, he emitted what he somehow managed to verbally convey as his final unconditional offer.

'Do you a deal, then. I'll give you my last can of lager if you take me to town today. How's that sound?'

The driver was not convinced as he checked the road ahead and then the view behind in his mirrors.

'Sorry, Oscar. No can do. Its thirty pence or you walk it,'

'But I spent my last thirty pence on this can of lager!'

To their credit, the passengers, including Sandra, chuckled in unison as the engine of the bus eventually began to rev with its master's lack of sympathy. The driver now checked his own watch before indicating to pull out into the traffic.

'Then I'll see you tomorrow, Oscar. Bye!'

The doors hissed shut, forcing the persistent down-and-out back onto the pavement. The bus moved quickly on, accompanied by an unspoken three cheers of gratitude from all on board.

For all her instinctive dislike of the intolerant grump behind the wheel, Sandra suddenly felt that there was perhaps just the merest strand of humility behind his ever-ready image of disdain, after all.

The tiresome journey advanced on toward the town centre.

Sandra's disinterest in proceedings began to fester once more. Through the streaks of sunlight, a few drops of rain began to latch onto the grubby panes, severely distorting her already blurred reflection.

The lack of potency in the vista beyond the glass was beginning to encourage drowsiness. Sandra felt her eyelids suddenly becoming heavy. This was not a particularly good omen considering she had not even got to work yet.

Her attention was distracted by the sight of Mrs. Punch sitting two seats in front of her to the left across the aisle. Sandra had cruelly apportioned this nickname to the woman because of her curly short, back and sides haircut and hooked red nose that hung over a drooping mouth.

Never a smile; never a word. Mrs. Punch stared straight ahead as though she were the only bus passenger remaining on the planet. Zero acknowledgement from the woman of anything or anyone.

The next stop quickly beckoned, unveiling another character that upheld his own curious sense of style and mystique.

Primarily, Sandra had always been intrigued by his sense of dress.

The short middle-aged man with wispy strands of grey-blond hair - though more grey than blond - was a happy sort and always generous with his greetings as he weaved his merry way down the aisle every day.

Each passenger would be treated in turn as he passed them with a *Good Morning!* and they would usually endeavour to respond in kind.

Although for Sandra, the taxing rota of such false civility was now something of an effort as she had performed the act most weekdays for several years. Having said all that, at least the man seemed to carry an earnest and friendly disposition.

A rare attribute these days. Certainly, on *that* bus, anyway.

But it was the man's attire that continually perturbed her, giving cause for Sandra to wonder as to his place of work and occupation.

Adorned in a dark blue plastic rain jacket, zipped up to the chin, his trousers were black pinstripe, as though from the bottom half of a suit.

Large white running trainers protruded from the bottom of his bunching trouser hems. And this puzzling ensemble was completed by the fact that he carried with him a black leather briefcase.

The nagging search for a conclusive answer to his source of income left Sandra amused yet increasingly frustrated.

One day, she pledged to herself that she would eventually find out where he was going and what it was that he did when he got there.

If it was the one remaining question that still plagued her at the culmination of her time on God's Earth, Sandra Bancroft would refuse to vacate the mortal coil until her curiosity concerning this issue had been fully satisfied.

She often imagined herself lying on her death bed, the lights dimming and images blurring. Flashbacks from her history ticker-taping through her conscience as the grim reaper eagerly approached.

Yet she would always utter that final sentence and hang around just long enough for someone to answer her query.

What does the man with the briefcase and plimsolls do for a living?

When someone came forth with the solution to the riddle, she would then, and *only* then, allow the angels to take her.

With her distracted mind considering this and countless other futile conundrums offered by the morning's journey, she almost missed her own stop outside the town's main post office.

Luckily, most of the other passengers also alighted, jolting Sandra from her series of whimsical daydreams and allowing for a renewed if reluctant focus on the day ahead.

'Corrine! Sausage rolls need putting out! And put that fag out as well while you're at it! Rose! Have a word will ya? You're supposed to be supervisor, after all! We're due open at ten which is only two minutes from *now*! C'mon get yourselves sorted!'

Mick Turner placed a tray of freshly made steak pasties into the eye level oven whilst bellowing instructions across the shop. Initially a bakery when he opened nearly twenty years ago, Turner's had also developed into a very popular café which catered for the regular daily throng of shoppers and schoolchildren that waded through the precinct.

Rose Riley watched as Mick ventured back into the kitchen to prepare another tray of savoury delights. It was time to wield her wrath as acting under-manager of the establishment.

However, the subject of Mick's annoyance was seemingly not prepared to accept any chastisement at that moment, as she defiantly continued to puff away on her smoke.

'Bit of a monk on this morning, ain't he, Rose? What's up with him? Didn't he get a jump last night or something?'

Rose smirked at the crudity supplied by the junior serving assistant, but Corrine Smedley's blatant ignorance of the house rules ensured that Rose would willingly maintain her stance of partial authority.

'You know full well he prefers us to smoke out the back, don't you? So why insist on doing it out here where he can see you? And right near opening time as well! If a customer sees you, they'd be fully entitled to report us...'

The hiatus in mild castigation left Corrine with an opportunity to wriggle out of her wrongdoing.

'Yeah? Report us? Who to? Tell me, then?! You, see? You don't know what you're talking about, Rose! You're full of it! Just like *he* bloody is!'

It was hard work in the café at the best of times.

It was even harder work inducting a teenager in what might be termed as unacceptable catering practices.

'Look, Corrine. Just do as he asks. He's not had the best start to the day as it is, without you making things ten times worse. He does pay your wages, after all! Just remember that when you're cheeking him off!'

With the exaggerated reluctance of youth, Corrine finally stubbed out the cigarette in her empty tea mug and folded her arms in defiance.

'Huh! Call them wages? Not enough to get me pissed on a Friday and Saturday night they aren't! Slave labour! That's what we are, Rose! Bloody slave labour! I'll not be stopping around here as long as *you* have! I can guarantee that!'

Setting out the rest of the condiments on each table, Rose gestured toward the back of the counter with a nod of the head.

'Don't worry, Corrine. You'll soon get your wish if you keep this attitude up! And it would only be fair to call it slave labour if we could actually get you to do some labouring around here! Sausage rolls need putting out. He's told you once! Hurry up! Before he comes out again! I'm unlocking the front door now!'

With her customary huff and swagger, Corrine resorted to her last option of obedience and attended to her duties with a scowl on her face that would readily curdle cream.

Rose's frustration soon evolved into overwhelming relief as Sandra appeared at the shop doorway with her easy radiance and cheery greeting.

'Morning all! How are we today?'

Rose did not conceal her pleasure at the sight of her most trusted colleague of several years.

'Ayup, my love! Thank Christ you're here! Madam over there's having one of her idle days by the looks of things.'

Sandra glanced across to the angered features of the eighteen-year-old behind the counter and offered a wave. Having recently departed from one emotional teenager, she was in no mood to spend the rest of the day with another.

'Morning, Corrine love. Playing your elders up again, are you?'

39

The youngster deliberated on a reply as she arranged sausage rolls under the hot lights.

Corrine was rarely reserved in declaring the motives for any of her unpredictable sulks, and duly relayed the source of her frustration as the first customers entered the shop.

'Well…it's that frigging moan arse in the kitchen! He's done nothing but pick on me since eight o clock this morning! I'm sick of it! One of these days I'll…'

Suddenly, as was his habit, Mick appeared behind the counter unannounced with a platter of assorted cakes, which served to bring Corrine's tirade to a premature halt.

His wishes were conveyed in rather more considered tones to his second most senior member of staff.

'Morning, Sandra love! Can you do the till for me for an hour or so until it calms a bit? I've put the float in. Corrine, you're on service with Rose until table clean-up starts.'

Sandra waved and acknowledged her employer's request with a nod and a smile, but Mick had wasted little time in returning to the kitchen, rendering even the briefest of verbal exchanges impossible.

'He does look a bit flustered, Rose. I'd better get my backside behind that cash register, or I'll be the next in line for a telling off!'

Rose shook her head and placed a consoling hand on her friend's shoulder. Her tone was whispered, and unusually serious in nature.

'Don't whittle, pet, it's not you. It's not Corrine that's at fault either, but I'm not letting *her* know that!'

Sandra smirked and winked as Rose moved closer and unveiled the cause of Mick Turner's uncharacteristic despondency.

'He's had a letter this morning saying that the rent for the shop's going up for the third time in two years! I don't know the figures, but as you can see, he's definitely bothered about it!'

'Oh, right. We'll chat about it later, then.'

Sandra then gazed across to Corrine, who had now discarded her mask of annoyance and replaced it with her customer-friendly face, as two groups of senior citizens shuffling along to the counter with their empty trays.

Sandra called across the shop, causing not a little mirth among the elderly customers.

'Hang on, Corrine! Super San's on her way to take the money from all these wealthy pensioners!'

A ripple of laughter echoed from the incoming elders as they scanned the fresh delights under the hot glass.

Another day at Turner's was underway.

*****

The mid-morning business brought with it the typical mix of mothers with tots and a steady stream of grey-haired regulars. The natural cycle of work took Sandra's mind off the earlier discussion with her daughter, which had caused her some untypical concern.

She hoped that Laura and Craig would make things up. They were a lovely couple, if far too young to get too serious about one another.

Occasionally, when time allowed, Sandra would gaze beyond the shop window and onto the High Street, studying the various forms and figures that made their way through the precinct, evidently preoccupied with their own private business.

Rose had noticed Sandra's recent tendency to indulge in the odd daydream now and then, and with the customer demand for attention currently at a minimum, she ventured over to her friend to indulge in a bit of sensible female conversation.

'Penny for your thoughts, San?'

Sandra turned her head and sighed weakly.

'Oh…I'm alright Rose. I'm just looking at the people beyond the window, living their lives. Wondering who they are. Where they've been. Where they're going to. I feel trapped inside this bloody shop sometimes, you know. In fact, I feel trapped inside this *life* sometimes!'

Rose nodded and adopted a similar posture by resting her elbows on the counter.

There was a peace between them that endured for few seconds as Rose thought up something amusing to respond with.

'Be honest with me now, San. You're just eyeing up the blokes, aren't you? You know you are!'

Immediately, Sandra blushed at the very thought of the suggestion and gave Rose a playful slap on the arm, which resulted in mutual laughter.

'I am *not* looking at *men*, Rose Riley! I'm a bit old for leering at forty-two, don't you think?'

'Well…*I'm* not too old to lust after fellas And I'm ten years *older* than you are! I say, San. Look at the legs on that!'

Rose continued to giggle as from behind the glass she pointed to a bald, bespectacled gentleman, probably in his late fifties, whose length of stride carried his spindly frame at supreme speed past the shop.

Sandra shuddered in mock disgust.

'Ugh! No thanks! I have got *some* standards you know!'

Rose's urge to create some fun continued amid spluttered bouts of chuckling.

'Really? I thought he looked quite a lot like your Stuart!'

'Piss off if he did!' spluttered Sandra in astonished amusement, giving cause for one or two in the shop to glance upward from their cups of coffee and fruited tea cakes.

'Okay. What about him over there, then?'

Sandra squinted over to where Rose was gesturing but could not detect the latest source of her curiosity.

'I don't know where you mean. Describe him to me.'

Rose managed to stem her laughter just enough to convey the completely fabricated description.

'The eighty-year-old by the lamp post. He's hunched over. Like he's looking for dog muck on the pavement! Him there look! Him with his whippet on a lead! Now him I would not turn down if he offered himself on a plate!'

Finally, Sandra's vacant gaze rested on the target in question.

Both women buckled up with guffaws of explosive laughter just as Corrine came marching up behind them.

'Eh, you two! What's so funny?'

Rose and Sandra quickly adopted a feigned modicum of calm as Corrine attempted to explain a little problem.

'Nothing, love. We're just people watching.' smirked Rose.

The youngster evidently had an issue to explain to her more experienced colleagues.

'Can you sort that moaning git out over there in the corner? He reckons his Cornish pasty is cold. But he's been sat looking at the bloody thing for half an hour as I know of! Stupid old bugger!'

Rose and Sandra simply stared at one another for a few seconds until the smiles returned and quickly evolved into more laughter.

Corrine, as per usual, failed to see the joke and pleaded for some assistance in the matter.

'Look. What do I do with the old sod?'

Rose, as shop supervisor, retained her composure long enough to send Corrine back over to the elderly gentleman with a hot replacement.

She watched covertly with Sandra as the youngster offered the new pasty in front of the man without a word of apology, before returning with the more tepid article, which she duly replaced under the hot lights.

'Right, Rose. I've sorted out that old coot. I'm going around the back for a fag. Won't be long.'

Sandra watched as the teenager waddled to the back of the shop and placed a cigarette between her lips, before the staff room door closed behind her.

'You know what, Rose? That girl has no idea about customer service, has she? And she's become a right big-gob and all!'

Rose slowly shook her head in agreement, which preceded yet more chuckles.

'I know, Sandra, love. And to think…I taught her all she knows!'

*****

Five-thirty p.m. brought with it the end to trading. It had been comparatively busy, but then Thursdays always tended to be probably due to pensions, dole and wages being dished out.

Mick had gone home at his usual time of four o'clock. Corrine finished at her usual time of three o'clock. Rose and Sandra were left to sort out any leftovers that might be worth refrigerating for the following day.

They counted and double-checked the cash float before depositing the money bag in the shop safe. They cleaned. swept and mopped out the entire shop, leaving it looking like a new pin.

Despite enjoying the job and indeed working together, locking the premises at closing time was always their favourite aspect to any day.

'God my feet are killing me, Rose. I'll be glad to get on that bleeding' bus I know that much. It's been a laugh today, though.'

Sandra waited as Rose set the burglar alarm and secured the front door.

'Do you want a lift home, love? The car's just round the back.'

Sandra gratefully pondered the alternative offer but as always, decided to stick with her tried and tested routine.

'No thanks, Rose. I like the bus. It gives me fifteen minutes to relax before starting all over again at home.'

'I know what you mean. Well, I'm sorry to leave you to it tomorrow, San. I've got my hospital appointment, so I won't see you until Monday. Play nicely with young Corrine, won't you. Mick's staying with you tomorrow until closing.'

The friend's hugged their goodbyes.

'I hope all goes well, Rose. I'll be thinking about you.'

'Thanks, love. You're a good'un. Ayup…your bus is coming! You'd better hurry! I'll see you next week, San.'

Moving off in opposite directions, Rose disappeared into the early evening sunshine as Sandra tentatively trotted to the bus shelter.

The dreadful thought briefly entered her mind about the potential identity of the driver. She literally crossed her fingers in hope.

It was with immense gratitude that she saw her fears were to be allayed.

The offensive grump from earlier that morning was nowhere to be seen.

Once seated among the very recognisable collection of people on the bus, Sandra's thoughts soon wandered away from her woefully mundane surroundings.

Her mind travelled to a wondrous world far beyond her own reality.

A world she thought must exist somewhere.

Yet in truth, she never, ever suspected she would find it.

'No! It's no good, *Mum*! It doesn't look right. It doesn't *feel* right, either! I'll have to go back to Dorothy Perkins and try that black one again!'

Sandra was beginning to get a headache. Scanning the ever-swelling throng of shoppers, her eyes began to sting, and her mind began to wander to preferred quieter realms.

Whilst an initially pleasurable part of the week, it had now become habitual for her to accompany Laura into town each Saturday afternoon to assist her daughter's addiction to spending money on clothes.

But slowly and surely, the knowledge that she might be far better off sitting at home reading a book with her feet up had gradually tempered any maternal enthusiasm for the idea.

Particularly, today.

By Sandra's reckoning, her daughter's tenacious pursuit of the ideal summer dress had led them through twelve stores, seven fitting rooms and three and a half hours of battling for supremacy with ten thousand other members of the local public.

Forcing even an inane expression of enjoyment was becoming more difficult by the minute. Sandra had never been one for retail therapy. Come to that, neither had Stuart. So, where Laura inherited her passion for such a pastime, the Lord only knew.

'Okay, love. If you really want to, we'll go back to the first shop.'

Laura slouched and offered her mother a half-hearted vote of sympathy.

'But Mum. You look a bit bored. We can surrender if you want. We can try again next week.'

Sandra desperately wanted to accept the tempting invitation to race back to the bus terminus and immerse herself in the delights of the route homeward, but it would lead to the inevitable sulky tantrum from her daughter. Then no doubt she would encourage the subsequent argument with Daniel.

This will be unavoidable when he sees how disgruntled his sister is at failing to detect the exact item that she needs to sustain her existence and further impress boyfriend Craig.

Aside from these daunting considerations, it would take wild horses to drag Sandra back to repeat the entire charade in seven days' time.

'No love, I'm fine if you are. We'll carry on looking.' she grimaced.

Entering Dorothy Perkins for the second time that afternoon was an undeniably negative premise, but Laura's dogged determination to discover that elusive dream garment fuelled the search long beyond any logical constraint.

As they entered the throbbing clothes store, an assistant recognised the pair from earlier that day and displayed what Sandra interpreted to be a genuine expression of pity.

Or of course, it could have been a mocking sneer.

'What's so important that you get this dress today anyway, love?'

A mother's ignorance in matters of fashion seemingly knew no bounds. Laura wasted no time in clarifying the situation.

'I'm staying at Craig's tonight, silly! So, I need a new dress to go out in, don't I? We're going to his brother's birthday party. So, I've got to look good, haven't I, Mum?'

'Yes, love. Course you have.' Sandra yawned, discreetly scanning the frayed cuffs of her own denim jacket.

Expectancy rarely delivers one's desires.

Likewise, hopelessness allays the prospect of any disappointment.

Sandra did not think that Laura would ever find the holy article she was looking for. She stared vacantly at her own forlorn reflection in a full-length mirror as her daughter ventured enthusiastically to the changing rooms with three different designs hanging over her forearm.

'What are you going in there for, Laura? Why don't you just lay them on yourself out here just to get an idea?' Sandra enquired, naively.

'Because it's something I need to do! I must be privately happy with the look before I show you. Trust me on this, Mum.'

Sandra intermittently studied the image of herself in the mirror-clad pillar.

Not at all bad, today.

Mildly modern-looking; positively slim in boots and jeans. Relatively attractive for forty-odd. Figure levelling out at a ten to twelve at a short distance. Hair mid-length. Needed a trim but the style would pass as contemporary.

She smiled to herself as thoughts of Laura's constant self-image predicament washed over her mind. Thank goodness her daughter was only a size eight! Skinny like her father and brother. Perish the thought that she should ever acquire any meat on her bones!

She would never be able to buy clothes if she were any bigger than an eight! Heaven, please forbid such a nightmare. But all teenagers take their physical shape for granted, she supposed.

Sandra had done so for most of her life, although felt fortunate that she had been blessed by Mother Nature to a certain degree.

These and other illuminating thoughts paraded themselves through her conscience, soon to be interrupted by Laura's unexpected emergence from the fitting area which was announced with an animated squeal of victory.

'Got it, Mum! Look at this! What do you think?'

Sandra scrutinised Laura's slender form as she pirouetted across the shop's carpeted floor in a short, black number that hung just below the knee.

A mother's verdict was profoundly positive.

'Erm…yes…very…sexy. And very functional. Do you like it then, love?'

A mistake.

She swore to herself never to ask such a question once Laura had made her final selection. By default, the nature of the query would throw a shroud of doubt on a daughter's fragile contentment regarding the chosen item. No sooner had she spoke Sandra then cursed her albeit feigned over-interest in the tedious debate.

Yet luckily, she was fortunate that destiny had already ordained the garment to be purchased.

Laura Bancroft, materialist in the making, even at seventeen-years-old, was finally *happy*.

'Yes, Mum! I *love* it! I've *got* to have it! Yes! I'm having it!'

Thank the maker for his mercy on my soul! Sandra thought to herself, before offering two twenty-pound notes to her brimming, beautiful offspring.

'What's this, Mum?'

'That is forty quid, love. For the dress. I'm buying it for you.'

Laura seemed genuinely astonished by her mother's unwarranted generosity.

'But why? I've got some money. That's why I did the overtime at the supermarket last month.'

'It's not a problem, Laura. Honestly.'

'Can you afford it?'

'You're holding the money in your hand, aren't you? Let me treat you. To show how glad I am that you and Craig are happy again. You've had a tough week. I want to cheer you up. Because that's what Mum's are for, isn't it?'

Laura again studied the cash in disbelief. Her mouth hung open as her wide blue eyes began to moisten.

'But Mum…that's…brilliant…thanks!'

Mother and daughter embraced tightly in the middle of the store. It was a loving and tender union, but also humorous and light-headed, with every potential for emotional outpouring from both protagonists.

Luckily, Sandra rescued the impetus and retained the jollity of the moment.

'On one condition, though!'

Laura looked deep into her mother's brown eyes and nodded eagerly.

'What, Mum? Anything! Just say it!'

Sandra gestured to the front of the store with a jerking thumb.

'That once you've bought the damn thing, we can get out of here and get the bus home!'

'Can we just nip to Miss Teens first? There was a lovely belt in there that would go really well with the dress…'

Sandra looked up to the heavens.

It *was* too good to be true after all.

*****

Number Twelve, Orchard Road shone like a distant welcoming beacon in the warm sunshine of late afternoon. Sandra's subconscious dejection began to surface as she and Laura approached the front gate.

As did her aching feet.

'Well…here we are again. Back at the palace of variety!'

Laura chuckled at her mother's humorous philosophising but could offer little in the way of an appeasing answer as they entered the hallway.

Daniel was sprawled comfortably across all three seats of the three-seater settee. The last minutes of the Cup Final blared loudly from the TV screen, almost causing the lounge windows to buckle.

Sandra's initial attempts at communication proved futile.

'Dan! Turn that telly down! Are you deaf?'

Her son's reply was barely audible above the television volume.

'Coventry are beating Spurs, Mum! In extra time! Cracking game!'

Daniel was evidently consumed by the match. His next move was to lift a leg, stretch it, break wind, and replace it back where it came from.

However, once he had spotted his sister parading herself in the new attire some minutes later, it did not take him long to rouse his concentration from the action on the screen, to the action in the kitchen.

The TV speakers were suddenly eclipsed.

To be replaced by the enquiring voice of a curious fifteen-year-old.

'Ayup, you two! Did you buy me anything, then?'

Mother and daughter smiled at one another before resting their gazes on the cherubic, lanky teenager that stood expectantly before them.

Sandra hoped to avoid a scene of sibling conflict, but Laura was not about to pass up the chance to frustrate her baby brother.

'Well…Mum bought this for me. I don't think we got anything for you, though. No…I'm pretty sure you've got absolutely *zilch*! *Sorry!*'

Daniel's lower jaw dropped open as he eyed the summer dress with disgust.

'What? How come? You've got a part-time job! You're *loaded*! I've got no job! I'm bloody skint!'

Sensing the imminent likelihood of World War Three, Sandra jumped in to defend the purchase.

'It was just a treat, Daniel. Your sister did not have a good week. I just wanted to cheer her up. That's all.'

'Yeah, but Mum! How come I didn't get nowt? Can I have the money instead, then?'

Filling the kettle and switching on the portable stereo, Sandra produced some justification for leaving her son empty handed.

'If I remember correctly, you had new football boots at Easter. Remember?'

Temporarily stunted by the damning recollection, Daniel found himself to be confronted by a worrying loss for words. He glared at Laura as she continued to adorn an expression of untouchable supremacy.

Kissing her mother on the cheek, she then poked her tongue out at Daniel's frothing features.

'I'm off to run a shower and get ready. Craig's coming round for me at half-six.'

Daniel waved sarcastically at his sister as she danced into the hallway and up the stairs.

'Oh…I get it now…to cheer her up. Because she has a plank for a boyfriend, and they can't go for half an hour without a crisis. Pair of idiots.'

Sandra was tired and did not wish to embroil herself in a domestic debate about an issue which was effectively, nobody else's business but Laura's.

'Yes, they are a pair of idiots. But you'll be in love one day, Daniel. Then you'll understand all about the heartache and strife involved.'

'Huh! No thanks! I don't want to end up loopy like Laura or nutty old fossils like you and Dad. No way! Fifteen 'til I die, me!'

Sandra laughed at the flippant misconceptions of her wonderfully buoyant son.

And then the thought settled in her head that Daniel wasn't that wide of the mark with his statement.

'Oy! We're *not* nutty old fossils! Where is your father anyway? Is he back home from his meeting yet?'

By now, Daniel had resumed his former position in front of the football, giving cause for Sandra to repeat herself in an increased volume.

'Dan! Did you hear me? I said where's your nutty Dad?'

The answer she sought was rapid in its arrival.

'Hello, darling! Good day shopping, I take it? What's this about me being nutty?'

She offered a glare of mild scorn to Daniel, who had witnessed the approach of his father through the back door, but naturally declined the opportunity to forewarn his mother.

Giggling on the settee, he offered her a cheeky wink as she wriggled with her feeble excuse.

'Oh…nothing, dear. I didn't mean *you* were nutty. I meant that specimen of a son over there! What have you been doing?'

Stuart removed his gardening gloves before re-boiling the kettle and reducing the raucous output of the radio.

'Oh…just priming my marrows down the garden. As I suspected, there is another grower's meeting tomorrow. Sorry dear. I'll have to eat out again. I've got to take along some of my prize tomatoes as well. So, I'm just prepping them now!'

There was very little Sandra could offer in reply to such a passionate declaration of commitment to greenhousery.

So, her completely sane husband had been polishing his vegetables Well, there were an infinite number of worse things he could have been doing, she supposed.

Her communication with Stuart lasted approximately forty-seven seconds.

Retreating down the garden path with his mug of tea, her devoted spouse announced that he would be ready for supper at about seven o'clock aa he offered a parting shot.

'I should have my cucumbers done by then, as well!'

Having kept one ear on proceedings in the kitchen, Daniel now found himself in an unassailable grip of mirth as his mother stood bemused with her arms folded in the lounge doorway.

Her son's undiluted amusement served to induce a chuckle of her own.

Family life at Number Twelve was farcical at times.

Yet underneath the moments of humour, there was a disaffecting sensation that Daniel's casual diagnosis of his father's mental state, might well be more accurate than Sandra first suspected.

*****

Sunday mornings were generally reserved for housework and preparing the family's traditional roast dinner. Having vacuumed and polished as soon as Daniel had gone to play football and Stuart had gone to play with his vegetables, Sandra found herself suddenly confronted by an alarming situation.

There was a prime, large, fresh chicken in the fridge waiting to be cooked. And nobody around to eat it.

Laura had stayed at Craig's parents last night and had been invited to stay on for Sunday dinner. Stuart had taken a packed lunch to his meeting as the pressure of horticultural comparison with other club members would mean he wouldn't be home until teatime.

And Daniel's usual Sunday routine had developed a liking for going to a mate's house after the kickabout, to crash out for the afternoon.

It was certainly not viable to prepare a full Sunday lunch for one.

Well, Sandra was not strictly alone.

Miss Jones had been circling the kitchen since the crack of dawn to assert her claim to a portion or two of succulent breast.

53

Sadly, a feline's ambitions would be in vain.

Her appetite would not be sated by chicken today.

In pondering this most serious of domestic problems, Sandra slumped into her favourite armchair with a mug of tea and let her gaze wander over the two magazines on the coffee table.

'Homes & Gardens' or 'Smash Hits'; a mind-blowing pair of options.

Despite the mildly diverting backdrop of the radio, she listened carefully to the silence of the house and another worrying thought encroached.

She did not like the tranquillity.

Not one little bit.

The lack of family atmosphere.

The absence of warfare between her offspring.

She even missed the sometime confounding presence of Stuart, intermittently stomping a dirt-encrusted path across the kitchen tiles.

Miss Jones conceded defeat regarding the likelihood of sampling any roast dinner and curled up at her mistresses' feet. Not a sound was to be heard, bar the alluring tones of Simply Red.

Sandra's focus ventured beyond the room and through the bay window. Up beyond the skyline and above the clouds riding on their azure canvas. What it was that she sought, she knew not.

But nevertheless, her search was compelled by some unspoken force or other.

In desperation to introduce some positive element to her Sunday experience, the omnibus edition of Eastenders was considered with constrained vigour. However, the stark reality was that it only served to induce a state of dormancy after fifteen minutes.

This in turn evolved into a gentle doze, which was only interrupted two hours later by the first in a procession of returning relatives.

Vaguely interested in the days that each of her loved ones had enjoyed, Sandra made bacon sandwiches as she received a vibrant run-down of events from the returning clan.

Laura had suffered with a hangover all day after an early morning finish to last night's party.

Stuart's club members had been alarmed by the unusually large dimensions of his gherkins and the congratulations for his onions were overwhelming.

Oh, and Daniel twisted his ankle on the park.

Not surprisingly, there was united frustration at the sight of bacon sandwiches instead of a chicken dinner. The fact that nobody had been at home to eat a chicken dinner seemed to be an irrelevancy.

In truth, Sandra's lazy Sunday had flashed by in a sleepy blink of an eye.

Having fed her family with the substitute snacks, she managed to stay awake until the last twenty minutes of Inspector Morse.

But fatigue crept back slowly but surely into her head.

Unfortunately, Monday morning's kick start needed Sunday night preparation time these days. Having finally kissed her loved ones as they trooped upstairs to bed, Sandra pledged to join them after tidying up yet again.

She stood in the kitchen as reminders of the weekend displayed themselves around the room.

Laura's new black summer dress hung off the back of a stool begging to be laundered. Sandra could smell the spilled beer and cigarette smoke on it from five yards away.

Likewise, Daniel's collection of used football kit lay rolled up in a stinking bundle at the foot of the washing machine.

And two golden rosettes for prize-winning leeks rested proudly on the work surface.

Adorned in her pink flannelette nightgown and white fluffy slippers, Sandra filled Miss Jones' bowl with a midnight snack before glancing at the clock on the kitchen wall.

In seven hours, Mick would be lighting the ovens at Turner's.

In ten hours, she would be there once again, ready to serve her ever-eager public.

The adrenaline-fuelled schedule of a loving wife and mother really was a non-stop rollercoaster ride of thrills and spills.

Yet unbeknown to Sandra Bancroft as she eventually traipsed her weary ascent to bed, Monday would provide an unexpectedly diverting change to the usual timetable.

5

ALONG CAME A STRANGER

'Cheese pasties! We're all out!'

'Okay, Rose. Thanks, love.'

In compliance with the under-manager's request, Mick returned to the kitchen as Rose tallied the half-day takings.

Sandra wiped down a couple of tables before clearing and re-filling the pot-washer. Whilst only just after one p.m., it had been a busy morning for Turner's. Her feet felt like she had already done a week's work in three hours.

Finally, with a lull in service creating time for a well-earned chat, Sandra managed to approach Rose regarding her hospital appointment.

'How did you get on last Friday, love?'

Visually confirming that Corrine was out of earshot in the kitchen, Rose beckoned Sandra behind the counter to the front window and relayed the outcome of her visit in a purposely lowered tone.

'Well, I need a couple more blood tests for them to be sure, but it looks like I'll need a hysterectomy. This will ensure that I'm in the clear. That's to be absolutely certain. The consultant said there's little other proven alternative. So, I don't know what's happening for sure yet. Possible another biopsy. Time will tell.'

Sandra's heart sank at hearing the news.

'Oh, I'm so sorry, love. Are you bothered about it?'

Rose again glanced along the counter to affirm the secrecy of their conversation before replying.

'Well, I'm just glad they haven't got to do that bloody scraping procedure again. I couldn't sit or stand afterwards! Bloody horrible, it was! But it sounds like it's given them the answers they needed for now, so I suppose it was worth the pain.'

The expression of sympathy on Sandra's face forced Rose to offer some reassurance.

'Sandra…I'll be okay. Don't whittle yourself.'

'Fingers crossed you don't need the surgery, eh?'

'It's all quite common apparently. Any road, that's enough about boring old me. How was your weekend?'

Sandra struggled to relate any positive developments on a personal level.

Probably because there were none.

'Fairly uneventful…aside from the usual. Clothes shopping on Saturday with Laura. Nothing earth-shattering to report. Stuart had two days of garden meetings. Bacon sarnies for Sunday dinner. Really riveting stuff. What about you?'

'No, me neither. Been resting up. Doctor's orders. So, I've had to knock the jogging on the head for a bit!'

The two friends laughed together.

It was such a pleasant feeling for Sandra to listen to humour. It bothered her from time to time that her life seemed so lacking in laughs when she was not at work.

As her thoughts dwelled on the next task she was interrupted by a sharp tugging on her tunic. Rose had grabbed Sandra's sleeve with one hand, whilst pointing excitedly through the shop window with the other.

'Ayup, San. Look at him out there! Wouldn't mind inspecting his vegetables, would you? Bloody gorgeous, or what?'

Sandra strained to see where Rose was looking.

The High Street seemed to be teeming with people, which was fairly irregular for a Monday lunchtime. She scanned along the moving parade of shoppers but to no avail.

'Where are you looking, Rose? Who do you mean? Not the bent up old man joke again, is it?'

Again, there was a sudden wrench on Sandra's apron.

'There! *Look*! Just about to cross the crossing. The guy in the long black coat. Tall, tanned, and tasty…just how I like 'em! He was in here the other week when you were off. Drop-dead scrummy, or what?'

Still Sandra continued to scrutinize the myriad of figures beyond the glass.

Tall? Tanned? *And* good looking?

In *this* town?

Then Sandra saw him.

Six feet of pure, muscled masculinity postured teasingly just twenty-five yards away, coolly waiting for the little green man to appear.

Sandra glanced at Rose, who now adorned a smile as wide as the High Street itself, as the current subject of her semi-mocking lecherous desire began to make his way across the road…and directly toward Turner's.

Rose called across the shop to attract the attentions of the youngest member of the team.

'Hey! Corrine! Mister Denims is back! Hey! Corrine!'

The teenager bounded from beyond the trolley full of dirty pots.

Within three seconds she was behind the counter and clattered into her two colleagues.

All three were now transfixed by the sex god that hovered outside.

'Can you remember him, Corrine? Sandra wasn't here. He came in a week or two back.'

Corrine was practically shaking with anticipation as her focus followed the man's movements.

'Yeah, Rose! I remember alright! He had tea and toast. Flipping lovely, aint he!'

'Who did you say he looked like, Corrine? It was Nigel somebody or other, wasn't it?'

The youngster chuckled at her elder colleague's playful ignorance.

'Not *Nigel*! *Nick*! Nick *Kamen*! The pop singer and model! The guy on the advert that took his jeans off at the launderette to wash 'em. He's the spitting image of him!'

Sandra continued to observe the unfamiliar figure through the glass as he now loitered on the nearside pavement and checked his watch. How he hadn't seen the three drooling bakery assistants with their noses glued to the windowpane behind him, she could not fathom.

Sometimes, Rose and Corrine were as subtle as a hippo sitting in a bathtub.

In their state of lustful exhilaration, none of the three had noticed Mick Turner standing behind them with his hands on his hips, partly confused and partly ready to breathe fire.

'Any chance of some work being done, girls? I'm sorry to interrupt the show and all that, but one or two people have been rude enough to walk into the shop and I think they might want some service!'

Immediately, Rose and Corrine jumped to attention and returned to their duties, leaving Sandra to deal with the latest customers.

Mid-way through handing over plates of sausage rolls, teacakes and cans of pop, Sandra observed Rose at the back of the shop waving frantically in her direction.

Sandra mouthed her dumbfounded curiosity in response, not being aware of the reasons for her friend's strange behaviour.

But all soon became very clear.

Nick Kamen's doppelganger had just walked in.

And yes, Corrine was spot on.

The closer he came, the more she played through the Levi's advert in her head. Indeed, he was tall, tanned, and scrumptious, just as Rose had dictated.

The instant physical reaction to what her mind had absorbed was uncanny. Sandra's heart began to beat a little quicker and her stance became ever so slightly unstable as the handsome beast scanned the interior of the dining section. He seemed to be a little lost.

Seemingly unsure as to where he was or where he needed to be. Sandra felt her cheeks flushing as he suddenly advanced toward the counter and finally connected his enticing gaze with hers.

She suddenly lost control of her own facial expression, guessing it might have fallen somewhere on the grid between gormless romantic and infatuated schoolgirl.

'C-can I help you, sir?' Sandra squirmed, in complete, unashamed, childish embarrassment.

The response was a smile to melt the heart of any woman. His blue eyes shone like sapphires. Yet he still appeared to be a little confused.

On closer scrutiny, his skin wasn't strictly tanned. But it certainly held an olive, almost continental hue.

His voice was soft, clear, and direct.

'Oh! Hi, there. I was supposed to meet my daughter in here at one-thirty, but it seems she hasn't arrived just yet. I'm a little early, though.'

Sandra could see Rose and Corrine bobbing in the background, vying for a front row seat on proceedings. Yet somehow, she could not fully avert her eyes from the incredible specimen of manliness standing before her.

'Can I get you something…while you wait for her?'

The man checked his watch once more and scanned avidly through the front window before responding.

'Erm…okay…I'll have…erm…'

Sandra could not resist the opportunity to interrupt him.

'Tea and toast! Am I right?'

He was inevitably taken aback by Sandra's assumption, but his mask of initial surprise swiftly reverted to an intergalactic smile of legendary prominence.

But this time it was a far more endearing, relaxed expression of comfort.

'Yes! Tea for one and…two rounds of toast. Perfect. Yes, please.'

'White or brown, sir?'

'Granary please, madam.' he added cheekily.

Sandra smiled inside as she confirmed the till.

'That will be one pound ninety, please. Take a seat and I'll bring it right over to you.'

Having dealt with the transaction, she watched as the stranger eyed a table by the window and veritably floated toward it. She studied his movements, immediately struck by the fact that they perhaps seemed overly hesitant and precise. It was almost as if he were walking in slow motion, as though deliberately parading his male wares.

Sandra also realised as she popped two slices of wholemeal bread under the grill, that her chest was now inexplicably pounding like a bass drum.

Overwhelmed by the improbable good fortune of Sandra's close encounter, both Rose and Corrine scampered to her side to get a full review of the exchange.

The teenager purred as she stared longingly at the hunk in the corner.

'Perfect, isn't he? Absolutely bloody *flawless*!'

Rose nudged Sandra as the opportunity to make fun of the youngster was too good to turn down.

She leaned toward Corrine and whispered in her ear.

'You fancy him, don't you, Corrine! Go on! Admit it!'

The one thing that Sandra knew about teenagers in modern times is their total lack of inhibition and brimming bravado.

Corrine Smedley was no exception to the trend.

'Not half! In fact, I think I'll go over now and chat him up!'

Leaving her colleagues in astounded silence and mouths agape, Corrine ventured over toward the partial newcomer.

However, her ambitions were quickly thwarted as a young woman entered the shop and reached his table first, before nonchalantly crouching and planting a kiss on his cheek.

Now with tail firmly between her legs, Corrine returned to her rightful position behind the counter.

Rose again could not resist the chance to mock the young apprentice.

'Looks like he's well and truly spoken for! Bad luck, Corrine. Stick to chatting up the pensioners. You might have better luck with one of them!'

Sandra had maintained her peace throughout the show whilst preparing his order, only seeing it fit to enlighten them both as to the identity of the attractive blonde who now sat with Nick Kamen at his table engaging in conversation.

'That's his daughter. He arranged to meet her here. You were right about the tea and toast, though. That's what he's just ordered. You can take it over to him if you like. Here.'

Like a new-born lamb on the first day of spring, Corrine veritably skipped across the shop with the tray containing the demigod's request.

Rose and Sandra looked at one another in unbridled amusement.

'I say, Rose. Aint it grand when you're young? Anything in trousers, isn't it?'

Rose eyed her friend with a certain, undefined pang of suspicion as Corrine danced around his table like a doe flirting with a buck.

'I noticed that *you* didn't hang about in finding out about some details on him either, did you Sandra Bancroft? I'm going to have to keep my eye on *you* as well I reckon.'

'Don't be *daft*!' Sandra blushed, guiltily.

Rose would not stop staring at her.

Which only served to compound her coy reaction.

Sandra was not a very convincing actor.

'Daft, am I? Your cheeks are the colour of them plastic chairs! I don't think I'm being daft, Sandra love. Look! He's even looking right over at you as we speak!'

Sure enough, Nick Kamen's eyes were fixed in Sandra's direction, accompanied by that incredible smile. She squirmed inwardly, whilst responding with a delicate wave in a feeble attempt to mask her unease.

Corrine returned to the counter, beaming like a cat that mistakenly supposed she had got the cream.

'He wants the same order for his daughter! Another tea and two toast! I'll do it. And I'll take it over as well!'

Paying the matter little more thought, Sandra and Rose resumed their tasks around the shop. Time seemed to be ticking by much slower since the dinner-time rush. Sandra looked at the clock. Three hours to go until she could leave for home. The stream of customers had now dwindled, leaving opportunity to clear up some areas a little earlier than normal.

Sandra centred her concentration on scouring some oven trays ready for the following morning. She said her goodbyes to Corrine, who, habitually of late, had managed to cajole an early finish time out of Mick.

Of course, it would incur a loss of pay, but young Corrine always seemed desperate to leave the shop after dinner time to dash off and meet somebody.

She bid her farewells to her colleagues, which included an exaggerated wave to her latest favourite customer through the window as she departed. And to his mild-mannered credit, Nick Kamen jovially waved back in response.

Sandra continued to tick off the cleaning chores as a rivulet of perspiration trickled down her nose.

She wasn't a major fan of Mondays.

The boredom of sterilising kitchen utensils was the one singular bind of the job. Her imagination always wandered elsewhere when undertaking the mind-numbing yet very necessary mission.

Back to that world so far away.

Where dreams were born and lived out.

Where the unknown was a constant temptation.

Then bouncing back again to Earth, she found herself pondering such vital issues such as the likely prospect of what she might cook for the family's evening meal.

Then without warning, workplace responsibility and prospective domestic tedium were suddenly banished from her thoughts by a voice from paradise.

'Hello? Can I pay my dues, please? I still owe you for my daughter's order. One-ninety, I think you said.'

Spinning around in delighted shock, Sandra turned to see him standing beside the till. Once more, she felt her cheeks evolve to crimson and her pulse incredulously increased its rhythm as she tended to his needs.

She felt his eyes resting on her as she wiped her clammy palms on her apron, counted his change and thanked him for his custom. Her transfixed gaze stayed with him as he fingered the contents of his wallet.

It seemed the right time to venture back to the great beyond with some polite conversation.

'I'm sorry for Corrine flapping around you earlier. She gets a little over-excited. Might I say you have a very beautiful daughter. She reminds me very much of my own in her looks.'

The man seemed very flattered by the comment.

'Thank you, so much. By the way, don't worry about the waitress. I don't mind young ladies flirting with me. I've gotten used to it after all these years!' he winked, oh so casually.

Sandra chuckled to herself, completely bowled over by the confidence of the smirking specimen of masculine perfection standing before her.

Her own desire to extend the banter with him was also growing by the second.

He obviously had a sense of humour to match his appearance.

'My oh my! Big-headed as *well* as good-looking! What a very dangerous combination!' she chirped, helplessly.

The hunk leaned closer across the counter and lowered his tone.

Sandra inexplicably wilted into him as she detected the delectable aroma of his aftershave.

'Thank you for looking after me, today. I'll be seeing you again, I hope.'

As though it was the most natural thing in the world to do, Sandra beamed her most seductive if completely unrehearsed expression of feminine appreciation.

Albeit an expression only ever practiced very occasionally in the bedroom mirror. And absolutely, *never* previously deployed in public.

She swallowed an untimely lump of glorious trepidation.

'Nice to meet you…I'm…I'm sure we'll see you again then… perhaps.'

With a final, intoxicating, mind-blowing, double-pronged grin and wink, the man left the shop to join his waiting daughter.

From her position behind the till, Sandra covertly observed the pair as they linked arms and walked slowly away from the premises, until finally merging with the throng of pedestrians outside.

Hidden from view at the back of the shop, Rose watched her friend's whimsical posture and glazed visage, but opted to say nothing.

Sandra continued vainly in her attempt to scan the father and daughter through the crowds.

Then, suddenly, they were gone.

He…was gone.

Completely, yet somehow regrettably, totally vanished from sight.

And just at that moment of unfathomable, unidentifiable sense of loss, something primeval and completely instinctive within her subconscious, willed for his return to be sooner rather than later.

6

MEET THE BATTLE-AXE

Sandra woke from a deep sleep on the Wednesday morning with a decidedly acute hangover. The previous day's uneventful life schedule had been concluded with the weekly evening trip to the local bingo hall.

Together with Rose and Corrine, the trio habitually met up every Tuesday night with two other regular bingo fanatics that they had become steadily acquainted with during the previous months.

If she were being honest with herself, Sandra could happily take bingo, or leave it well and truly alone.

Strangely, Rose and Corrine now deemed it to be a sacrosanct aspect to their social calendar. However, the gnawing drone of the number caller in his golden glittery jacket and the list of humourless quips he felt obliged to relay each time a ball popped up, had quietly eroded Sandra's will to participate over time.

Especially when suffering the ill effect of seven halves of lager as the alarm clock chimed in her ear at the stroke of seven a.m. the next morning.

Dragging herself from the bedclothes to begin preparing for the imminent awakening of her family was achieved purely by a poorly executed combination of guesswork and very careful manoeuvring from the landing, down the stairway and around the kitchen.

Thankfully, Miss Jones made herself the priority figure and was fed and watered before the other inhabitants of Number Twelve rose from slumber. So at least the cat wouldn't be getting under anybody's feet if she were back in bed before the others dragged themselves out of theirs.

How Sandra wished she was afforded the same luxury.

When oxygen did finally begin to steadily inject itself into Sandra's spouse and offspring, it was a pleasant change to see that all seemed sociable and positive with the Bancroft clan that particular morning.

Stuart seemed appeased by the current state of the share markets and didn't even moan about his broken egg yolk.

Laura hadn't fallen out with her boyfriend for over twenty-four hours and therefore Daniel had no viable angle to poke fun at his sister at the table.

Even further toward the plus side, he needed nothing laundering at the last minute. But he did bemoan the fact that the batteries in his Walkman had died and that there were none spare in the kitchen drawer.

Unsurprisingly, nobody noticed that Sandra was in a mild state of dysfunction due to her dalliance with alcohol the previous night. Nobody even asked if she had a good night! There was nobody awake when Rose dropped her outside the door at half-past midnight. Apart from Miss Jones of course, patiently awaiting her late-night titbit.

So it was that Sandra played the act of martyr to perfection whilst cooking three full English breakfasts, and it was with a persistently throbbing skull that she kissed them all out of the front door in a staggered if punctual procession.

The only partial reference to her sufferance came from Stuart as he pulled open the car door and hung his suit jacket in the rear seat.

'You alright, love? You're a funny colour!'

The coffee tasted heavenly as Sandra finally sank herself into the armchair. Miss Jones curled herself up under her mistress' legs and the two shared an intimate moment of blissful, silent recovery.

Fortunately, today was Sandra's day off from working at Turner's.

Her mental celebration of the fact was however tempered greatly by the impending ritual of the weekly visit to her mother's.

Sandra was a glutton for such punishment.

There was no other rightful explanation for the voluntary trek to the supermarket to do her mother's shopping and then take it to her bungalow for a reluctant yet always negative appraisal of her efforts.

There were some justifiable sticking points regarding the notion of helping one's elderly mother. Point one; Phyllis Baxter was more than capable of going shopping for herself.

Point two; the act of incapability that her mother displayed on a regular basis was sometimes convincing but always conveniently temporary.

Point three; Sandra supposed that fetching groceries for one's mother was the dutiful thing for a daughter to do.

Having first attended to priorities in her own little nest, Sandra dressed herself as the consequential pain of wilful inebriation began to slowly subside. No time or indeed desire for a physical inspection today.

Sandra felt rough and had no wish to visually confirm the fact.

But things were certainly looking up as she left the house.

Thankfully, the bus shelter was vacant. No need to feign interest in a conversation with any locals, then. The journey to town was rather more sedentary due to the later time of day. The customary collection of odd characters was absent.

Even better, the grumpy bus driver was not driving today.

Even more promising than that, the jaunt around the aisles of the local Sainsbury's proved to be far less taxing than usual.

Indeed, once outside the supermarket and laden with two bags of shopping, the fifteen-minute walk to her mother's house held little in the way of its usual shroud of foreboding.

In fact, Sandra's mood was becoming particularly upbeat as the day progressed. Most odd.

Indeed, she now felt unusually sprightly for the time of week. It would have been no exaggeration for Sandra Bancroft to claim that she was even slightly happy with life, as she pounded the pavements in her court heels with the carrier bags weighing down on her shoulder joints.

On she went toward the unpredictable list of moans and groans that her mother traditionally offered by way of thanks for her daughter's love and consideration.

Normally a premise that filled her with angst.

But today, strangely, nothing would deter her from the need to feel positive. Not even the increasingly likely prospect that her mother may need her incontinence pants changing at some point during the visit.

Thankfully, accidental self-urination was not a frequent occurrence for Phyllis. Coincidentally when it did take place, Sandra would always be on hand to tend to the resultant mess.

As she bounced along, Sandra could not source the cause of her unwarranted cheerful disposition, nor could she detect the reasons for the absence of her typically disdainful approach to this episode of the weekly routine.

She felt injected by some inexplicable power of goodness. From whence it came, she knew not. But its grip was tangible and resolute. Even if initially accompanied by the thumping lager headache.

As was the custom, her mother would wait by the front window with arms folded and scan the street beyond for her daughter's approach, as if awaiting an unwanted visit from the tax man.

When Sandra eventually passed the lounge window and smiled eagerly at her mother, the scowling expression on the elder woman's face could ably be described as comparable to a gargoyle in a thunderstorm.

But Sandra's mood would not be darkened today. She was adamant about that. Making her way to the rear of the bungalow, she stood outside and waited for the back door to be opened.

And she waited.

And she waited longer.

And the shopping bags became gradually weightier.

She lowered them to the floor and knocked repeatedly to confirm her arrival.

Until finally, her mother's suspicious tones carried through the locked wooden door.

'Who is it?'

It was a game that Phyllis had an affinity for.

Acting totally senile, whilst being in total possession of all her faculties.

'You *know* who it is, Mum! You've just watched me walk down the entry! Open this blessed door!'

Again, a silent few seconds ticked past.

Sandra's resolve in trying to maintain a policy of light-heartedness had started to become slightly unbalanced by the mischievous antics of the grey-haired octogenarian that hovered on the other side of the frosted glass portal.

Phyllis's muffled tones were rapidly beginning to erode Sandra's upbeat mood.

'You must *prove* who you are. You got any ID? You can't be too careful these days, you know!'

So much for retaining her patience.

'*What*? Mother! Open this bloody door! NOW!'

Another hiatus occurred as Sandra silently fumed.

'Give me your secret knock. Then I'll know who it is!'

Now the daughter felt herself becoming decidedly aggravated by the mother. She retrieved the two bags from the floor.

'Right! I'm taking this shopping back! You obviously don't want it!'

Sandra feigned her dramatic departure from the scene and hid around the corner of the bungalow, out of sight.

There she waited.

And waited further.

And the shopping seemed suddenly weightless as the click of the back door latch confirmed her mother's reluctant submission in the game.

And then Sandra heard that soft little voice that suggested butter night not melt.

The same affectionate tone that was sometimes capable of taming dragons in caves and warding off vampires from shadowed rooms.

'Sandra? *Sandra*? You haven't *really* gone…have you? Hey, our San?'

Sandra wanted to burst out laughing at the silliness of the whole charade.

Just to hold out for a few more telling seconds. It was wonderful to have the upper hand, however short-lived the taste of triumph might be.

'Sandra? If you're round that corner! I swear! I'll tan your hide!'

With the declaration of war imminent, Sandra re-appeared in front of her mother consumed by a fit of the giggles.

'You shouldn't do that to an old woman! I could report you to the authorities for cruelty!'

'That would be a waste of time as they'd end up feeling sorry for *me* for having to put up with *you*!'

The expression of begrudging disapproval in her mother's features only served to induce further mirth.

'It's alright you taking the mickey! Us pensioners must be very careful who we let into our homes these days!'

'Oh, shut up mother, and get yourself inside!'

Once both were in the kitchen, the scripted rigmarole could begin in earnest. Phyllis hovered behind her daughter as the two bags were placed on the kitchen table and an air of disapproval descended.

'I hope you haven't spent too much! Let's have a look then!'

Sandra would have to carefully display all purchases on the worktop surface. Then, one by one, Phyllis would scrutinise the price, brand and sell-by dates before giving her daughter either a nod of acceptance or a grimace of distaste.

Then, only when her mother was appropriately satisfied, Sandra could place each item in its appropriated storage space.

On average, Sandra bought twenty items a week to keep her mother from meeting starvation. The vital examination process should realistically only take five minutes maximum. Yet some weeks, the two could be found debating on the chosen comestibles for over an hour or more.

But today, Sandra did not mind.

Not one single bit.

And she had no idea why.

Especially when considering that the running commentary from her mother was more ungrateful in tone than ever.

The list of gripes was endless.

'These cobs feel hard!'

'Turn them tins around in the cupboard! I can't see the labels!'

'That banana's bruised!'

'There's a crack in that egg!'

'This pie is out of date tomorrow!'

'You forgot toilet roll!'

Eventually, the groceries were apportioned to their correct homes and the kettle could finally be switched on. The next part of the itinerary would see Sandra make her mother's favourite sandwich.

Cheese and beetroot.

Two slices.

Cut into triangles.

With a nice cup of sugar-less tea.

For ease and convenience, she would make herself the same sandwich, if only for the chance to sit down and take the burden off her feet for half an hour.

The negative aspect to this arrangement was that it gave Phyllis a static audience on which to vent her spleen regarding all and sundry.

It was a true test of endurance for any forty-two-year-old woman.

What was worse, the usual reams of questions encouraged the usual weekly answers.

And the same, bigoted, prejudiced declarations in her mother's summings-up.

'How's that boring husband of yours? Still a banker? Well, he always was…wasn't he?'

'Still playing with his carrots every night? About all he's good for!'

'Has he spent any money on you this year? Tight as a duck's arse, that one! Always said so! Second hand wedding ring, indeed!'

'You want to tell that beautiful granddaughter of mine to dump the cry-baby! Still, I suppose it could have been worse! She could be courting one of them foreigner types!'

'Get that young lout of a grandson to come around here now and again! I haven't seen him for bloody ages! I've got loads of jobs lined up for him!'

'You still making cups of tea for old men in that cafe? I don't know. I thought a daughter of mine would amount to a lot more than that!'

And so on.

And so on.

For over an hour, Sandra listened obligingly, as Phyllis talked at her. There was little need to inject any sense of originality or logic to the conversation. It was a well-trodden, one-way dialogue that exemplified the total misery of a lonely and bitter old woman.

But Sandra loved her mum dearly.

She also pitied her to a large degree.

Losing a husband and father when the only child is barely ten years of age must have been horrendous for her.

Even though Clive Baxter succumbed to his heart attack over thirty years ago, his doting widow had never truthfully come to terms with the fact.

Evidently late starters in the rearing of their own family, it was surely not expected that Sandra's father would never see his daughter grow up. And so, it seemed only correct that the mother should off-load some of her frustration onto the one solitary person left in the world that now gave Phyllis the time of day.

But Sandra felt the loss of her father with equal pain.

A subject that Phyllis had never broached with her in earnest.

Eventually, with duty done and insults cast without reproach from blissfully ignorant and innocent targets, it was time for Sandra to leave her mother for another seven days of an unrequited life in the doldrums.

But a daughter's inner solace was not to be tarnished.

She stepped out of the back door as she had entered it. Smiling and hopeful for her future. She kissed her mother on each of her leathery, wizened cheeks and engaged in a close, if lukewarm embrace.

The bones of the eighty-one-year-old poked through her cardigan as though acting as sharp reminders of her life of strife.

Yes. Sandra loved her mother.

Not everything *about* her, mind.

But most of what was left after the nasty stuff was said was more than acceptable.

On reaching the end of the front path to make for home, such consoling thoughts were disturbed by the feint calling of a supposedly kindly old lady.

74

The delicate tones followed Sandra along the pavement, drawing her attention from a beautiful, fictional place and back to the realms of impending maternal distress.

'Sandra! Hang on a mo! I think I've wet myself! Can you run us a bath before you go, love?'

7

THE RETURN OF NICK KAMEN

A fortnight could easily seem like two years for Sandra these days.

There was little distraction in her typical schedule that would effectively make the time pass quicker. Similarly, her familiarity with predictable minor events caused the days to chug along without any fulfilling incentive or apparent purpose.

Turner's provided suitable minor spasms of entertainment to allow the working shift to expel itself amiably, but in truth, serving up portions of Victoria sponge and ham salad baguettes contributed little toward serving the soul.

Especially when surrounded by so many apparently miserable customers for seven hours a day. Many of them carried expressions that would stop clocks.

Rarely was there to be heard a *please* or a *thank you* for the efficient service with a smile. In fact, there was little sense of gratitude, whatsoever. The older generation generally emitted a presence that gnawed readily at Sandra's typically upbeat temperament.

Some days it felt akin to catering for a room full of Phyllis Baxters.

Then one particularly predictable Thursday morning in mid-June, a light switched itself back on in her murky itinerary.

Wiping down the sandwich trays with a damp cloth, she glanced beyond the front window as per normal, just to ascertain once more that there truly was life beyond the bakery.

The vision that suddenly illuminated that shadowed corner of her mind caused her heart to involuntarily twitch.

He…was in position again.

Waiting at the pedestrian crossing. Again.

Sandra dragged the cloth slowly and continued to scan the incredible stranger, who was now making his way steadily towards Turner's. Again.

It was no longer a twitch.

Her chest had now begun to thump.

He…had now entered the shop. Again.

And Sandra consequently vanished into the kitchen amid pangs of unrelenting, feminine queasiness. She pulled the door shut and peered through the port hole, oblivious to the activity behind her.

'Ayup, Sandra. You alright? You look a bit red in the face, my love. Do you need to sit down a minute?'

Mick's concern as he kneaded a large ball of fresh dough was understandable and appreciated.

Yes, she *could* do with sit down thank you very much.

Rose turned from making pies at the adjacent table and offered her friend an inquisitive glare over the rim of her spectacles.

Sandra tried to gather her wits and offered a swiftly fabricated reason for the unannounced retreat from front of house.

'Er…yes…sorry…just wondered if…erm…the…mini quiches are done… yet.'

Mick checked through the window of the oven door as Sandra stole a glance back through the hatch to the serving counter.

Rose did not offer opinion as she observed her friend's uncharacteristic behaviour.

Mick's declaration seemed to fall on deaf ears.

'I'm not even cooking mini quiches today, Sandra. But can you check the pasties out front for me, though? Might need to chuck some more in for the school rush.'

Sandra did not respond as she avidly scrutinised the exchanges that were now transpiring in the dining area.

Rose finally opted to speak, now curious as to Sandra's nervous demeanour.

'Sandra? What's wrong, love?'

Suddenly her hearing began to work once again.

'Yes…fine, Rose…sorry, Mick. Yes! Pasties!'

Tentatively emerging from the kitchen, Sandra observed the scene.

Her heart still pounding, she tried to calm herself.

Whilst wondering what it was that should have suddenly made her feel so vulnerable.

Rose continued to watch the surprisingly furtive display from her supposedly mature, responsible, level-headed colleague.

At that precise moment, from around the back of the crockery trolley, Corrine blazed into view adorning an enormous smirk of satisfaction.

'Sorry, San! I got to him first! You missed out there!'

Striving desperately to feign ignorance on the issue, Sandra asked for an explanation to Corrine's excitement.

'What you on about?'

Corrine drew closer and muttered in Sandra's ear whilst gesturing to the corner of the dining area with a jabbing thumb.

'Mister Denims is back in town! And I've taken his order. So, leave him to me if you don't mind! Bad luck, darling!'

Sandra giggled nervously whilst secretly wanting Corrine to explode on the spot.

A mild sense of anger started to fester within her.

Yet the perspective on events was wildly distorted.

She fought to ascertain some sense of rationale.

God, what was happening? She was in her early forties, yet unwarranted juvenile coyness was rapidly evolving into pubescent jealousy.

Sandra glanced quickly across the room to where the subject of her attention was sitting, studiously reading his newspaper.

Then a thought struck her.

It was surely time for an emergency make-up check.

As if possessed by some addictive craving, she ignored the pair of elderly customers that had only just approached the serving counter and walked quickly to the back of the shop to the staff changing room.

Grabbing her handbag from under the table she then made for the toilet. In front of the tiny, cracked mirror, Sandra frantically prodded her features for blemishes before hastily topping up the application of some eyeliner.

A dab of, foundation and just a touch of lip stick would have to do. She then ran both sets of fingers through her brown hair, checking for damning strands of grey and split ends.

Now, wearing make-up for kitchen work is renowned as bad practice. Terrible for the complexion. But she wasn't going to be outdone by a silly teenager.

No way, Jose!

Even at forty-two, Sandra Bancroft could still kick it with the best of them.

Then an unsolicited emergence of feminine honesty suddenly zapped her bewildered conscience.

She stopped and stared once again at the scarlet-hued, tormented face in the broken reflection and rapidly analysed the crazy thoughts that had just cursed her baffled mind.

Thoughts such as: *what on Earth was she bloody doing*?

And furthermore: *why on Earth was she bloody doing it*?

Attempting to settle herself down and feel something like the relatively normal human female from five minutes ago, she gave final approval to the passable if refracted image in the mirror.

Sandra then returned to the dining section, just in time for destiny to take a firm hand in events. Corrine was serving the elderly couple that Sandra had deserted earlier. Then Mick's disgruntled boom resonated through the kitchen doorway toward the youngster.

'Corrine! Check the pastie tray, will you? And fetch these bloody pies for me, love? I don't know where Sandra's vanished to.'

The youngster instantly glared at the returning figure in question, who now quietly resumed her position behind the till, desperately trying to avoid looking in the direction of a certain gentleman's table.

Yet more ridiculous images flashed though her brain.

What was making her act so strangely?

Was she finally losing her mind?

Was Sandra Bancroft finally succumbing to the inherent barbed mental state of her mother?

Or was it something more real?

Something more sensitive?

Should she try and embrace these waves of anxiety, rather than shun them?

Could it truly be the gorgeous stranger that had unwittingly initiated such adolescent and involuntary responses?

Then the smiling vision of Rose appeared from the corner of the room to erase the all too brief visions implanted in Sandra's head.

'I've taken your latest heartthrob's order over, Corrine. He says thank you very much.'

Rose winked at Sandra, which usually preceded a bout of gentle teasing. The teenager scowled with disgruntlement as she rattled cups and saucers for the now impatient pensioners.

'Oh…and by the way. I've told him that you think he looks like Nigel Whatsizface. The model bloke. You know who I mean. Well, I don't think he knew who I was on about, anyway. But said he was very flattered by the comparison whoever it was we were comparing him to.'

Now Corrine's mild anger was eclipsed by unbridled shame as she placed both hands over her mouth.

'You didn't say *Nigel*? Rose! Tell me you didn't tell him I thought he looked like a *Nigel*!'

Both Corrine's tormentors laughed loudly as the youngster's cheeks turned bright pink with anger.

'Jesus, Rose! You're a bloody nuisance!' Corrine sneered.

The supervisor held her stomach as she responded.

'I know I am…but it's worth it cos the look on your face is a picture! Anyway, I shouldn't get your knickers in a twist, love. He doesn't fancy you. He wanted to know if the beautiful brunette was working. So, I suppose that means he's got his eye on this one here next to me, doesn't it!'

Now it was Sandra's turn to feel the heat of the spotlight as Rose's words registered like a lead weight in the forefront of her mind. Her stomach churned instantaneously, and she felt the tiny hairs on the back of her neck stand on end.

Her legs started trembling. What the Hell…

Leaving her colleagues to chuckle to themselves whilst being blissfully unaware of her response, Sandra ventured back to the kitchen with the result of the pastie check and finally retrieved the fresh tray of pies that Mick had declared ready for serving moments earlier.

Any task that kept her away from the scrutiny would suffice at that precise moment.

*****

The lunchtime rush came and went with the boisterous array of uniformed pupils evidently avoiding the meagre offerings in the secondary school dining hall.

As usual, Corrine wormed her way out of work early. Unusually early today however, after bidding a sorrowful, somewhat deflated farewell to the olive-skinned hunk she was evidently consumed by.

Sandra had now returned to Earth and resumed with various missions out front, as Rose continued to assist Mick with preparation in the kitchen.

The delectable stranger continued to scan his newspaper, occasionally lifting his head to observe incoming customers. Sandra had made a point of staying out of his way since learning of the supposed interest.

This could have been a fabrication by Rose of course. Sandra might well have been reacting to a comment that was never even uttered.

Yet the intrigue that it had created within her was intensely overpowering.

The merest thought of being noticed by another man did incredibly strange yet exciting things to Sandra's state of being. But she was determined to blank out all such other-worldly thoughts.

Yet it was proving extremely difficult to focus, knowing that someone other than her husband might find her attractive. It had been so many years since she had received any compliments in earnest.

Of course, Rose Riley was well known for her sense of imagination, but it had never been directed at Sandra. Not for the sake of workplace mockery, anyhow.

Desperately trying to keep her mind on the tasks at hand, her concentration and sense of proportion eventually faltered as she replenished the stack of trays near the front door and began to clear a recently vacated table.

From nowhere, he appeared behind her.

She was cornered.

Not a word was spoken, yet she felt his soothing, irresistible presence close by.

Again, the scent of aftershave lingered in the air. Not too heavy, but more than enough to allure the senses.

After deliberating the wisdom or indeed the weakness of turning to meet his spellbinding gaze, bravado won the day. She spun on her heels with a teapot in one hand and a dish cloth in the other.

Melting helplessly under his silent stare, she struggled to conjure the first line of the conversation that she anticipated he wanted to indulge her with.

Despite her mountainous reservations, Sandra wilfully succeeded with untamed yet ably convincing flair.

'Well, hello again, Mister. How are you, today?'

He nodded and smiled the smile that could simultaneously break a thousand hearts and seduce a thousand more.

'I'm good thank you, Missus. How are you, today?'

Sandra nodded eagerly, carefully pouting her lips as she had practised a thousand times for the past fortnight.

'You look busy.' he beamed.

'Well...yes, it has been...I suppose so. Your daughter not with you today, then?'

He glanced beyond the window to the High Street.

'Oh...Annette? No. Not today. She's studying at the university. Morning lectures and all that.'

Sandra suddenly felt discomforted by the exchange, as if expecting to be detected by an unwanted intruder.

But the novelty was all-consuming.

'Oh...a clever girl, then. My daughter's doing A-levels. She wants to go to university, too. If we can afford it, that is.'

The man shuffled uneasily from foot to foot and reached down to rub the tops of his thighs. He noticed Sandra's expression of bemusement as she observed the gesture.

'Oh...just a bit of cramp. I get it a lot these days. By the way...forgive me for asking, but what is your name, again? I feel a bit rude coming in here knowing all the staff. But your name escapes me for the moment.'

Sandra chuckled at the thought of Corrine and her buoyant mood of earlier.

'Oh, so the other two have introduced themselves to you already, have they?' she chuckled.

With a knowing glint in the eye the stranger nodded slowly, fully expectant of her forthcoming reply.

'Well, my name is Sandra. And if you were wondering, I'm forty-two...and...and I'm not at all sure why I just told you that second bit!'

Now both laughed heartily as the harmless flirtation continued.

'Well, I never ask a lady her age. But I guessed about right. Only a couple of years older than me. That's good.'

She listened, slightly puzzled as to why the proximity of their ages should be relevant. Aside from it obviously being *good*.

A pause ensued, possibly signifying the end of the discussion.

'Oh well, Sandra. I'd better be going, I suppose.'

Watching as he slowly made his way to the front door of the shop, she waited...and waited...and still the stranger seemed intent on keeping his identity a secret.

Almost frustrated by the one-sided game, though careful not to show it, she finally relented to her will and interrupted his departure.

'Is Nigel your real name...or are you called something else by any chance?'

The handsome visitor chuckled, knowing full well that Sandra was hovering with a need to sate her curiosity.

'Well…' he smiled. '…I thought you'd never ask.'

Sandra bobbed in the doorway as he stepped out onto the pavement, which was being bathed by warm sunshine. Folding his newspaper under his arm, he finally faced her and engaged his deep blue eyes to her.

Involuntarily, she watched his lips move as he spoke.

'It's Andy. I've no idea who this Nigel fella is, though. No doubt I'll see you again soon, Sandra. Bye-bye for now.'

Her responses were muted, as though his farewell felt oddly mis-timed. Something told her that she did not want him to walk away just yet.

Observing him wander off toward town, she did not suspect that anyone else had witnessed the encounter.

Yet perversely, Sandra did not care, for at that moment she was on a different planet, with different people, with different feelings.

Fortunately, Rose Riley was not one to gossip.

Especially about close friends.

Opting to forego any discussion on the brief dalliance that she had just seen occurring in the shop doorway, she returned to the kitchen, keeping initial thoughts on the matter well and truly to herself.

*****

At closing time, Rose and Sandra locked up as usual before going their separate ways. As she punched the code to set the alarm, Rose glanced to her friend and colleague.

She had detected a tangible change of mood in Sandra during the day.

Ever since *he* had visited and spoken to her.

Sandra was outwardly coy yet radiant inside. Being a woman of experience also, Rose easily recognised the signs of someone who had been flattered and was feeling duly inflated by the fact.

84

Rose understood fully that it was an enticing sensation, to be sure.

And she could see that Sandra had been inwardly rocked by the brief attentions of the chiselled Adonis that had called in earlier.

As they joined in their customary embrace on the pavement, Rose smiled as they parted and began to walk in the opposite direction.

Finally, the temptation was too great to resist.

'So?'

Sandra stopped a few paces away and turned to look at Rose, trying desperately not to reveal her inner smile.

'So? What do you mean…*so*? So…*what*?'

Now grinning from ear to ear, Rose continued to gently probe her friend and colleague.

'So…what's his bloody name then?'

Sandra's now barely concealed mirth encouraged a childish giggle before she shook her head and continued to make for the bus stop. In turn, her own bubbling excitement breached a frail wall of resistance.

She spun on her heels once again to find Rose exactly where she had left her, only now Rose was laughing heartily too.

Oh well. What the hell.

'It's Andy. Okay? But I thought you knew that? He said you and Corrine had told him your names?'

'No, Sandra. I think he used that line to get *your* name out of *you*.'

Rose's continued chuckles echoed after Sandra as she walked to the bus stop. In her own little dream-world, the bus pulled up, yet it occurred to her minutes later as it trundled along, that she could not even recall getting on board.

The journey home seemed to take mere seconds as a myriad of thoughts rushed through her mind.

Nothing seemed typical at that moment.

She seemed detached form the usual tedious daily palaver.

She noticed nobody else that got on or off the bus.

Indeed, she very nearly missed her own stop due to being on that other planet somewhere.

In a different time, somehow.

Feeling like somebody else.

A different version of herself

On current evidence, a version of herself that she didn't yet know about.

8

DOMESTIC DISTRACTIONS

The weekend brought with it the gruelling agenda of wearisome household demands.

Namely, washing, cleaning and a week's worth of ironing. A timetable intercepted only by sporadic bouts of cooking.

Then followed again by more cleaning, washing, and ironing.

However, it was most pleasant not to have to rise with the alarm clock. But the opportunity to lie in bed and simply muse on the list of missions that lay in wait, only offered contemplation time for actively evading performing such miracles.

Stuart had woken early on Sunday and was downstairs watching television with a bowl of cereal on his lap. In her husband's lukewarm place under the bedclothes, Miss Jones had quickly taken root and was purring to her heart's content.

Sandra confirmed the time on the digital clock radio to be eight-thirty-eight and let her head fall contentedly back into the soft pillow. Listening to the cat's engine billowing beneath the sheets was comforting, and she temporarily interrupted the feline vocal flow by reaching across and stroking Miss Jones' tummy.

The customary morning crescendo of family movement did not generally occur at weekends of late.

Daniel was undoubtedly still in bed. And would undoubtedly stay there until noon at the earliest unless he was meeting friends for football or some such outdoor pursuit.

Laura had again stayed over at Craig's, so no doubt fireworks were imminent on that front.

This was a recently formed habit over which Stuart had expressed some paternal disapproval. He believed that seventeen-year-old girls shouldn't be allowed to spend such nocturnal time together with their boyfriends. Of course, he was primarily concerned about the chances of his daughter being tempted to indulge in activity of the physical kind.

He was an old-fashioned type and very set in his ways with his approach to certain aspects of life.

When invited to offer an opinion on the matter, Sandra had claimed in jest that Laura and Craig wouldn't be able to avoid arguing for long enough for the possibility of sex to rear its ugly head.

Stuart's fears had not been overly allayed by the light-hearted standpoint of his wife, whose humorous overview secretly masked the wish that her husband would take the same avid interest in his *own* sex life as much as he did his daughter's.

But of course, Sandra did behold a certain sympathy with Stuart's concerns.

Seventeen was still relatively young, after all.

She looked and acted like a woman of twenty-five, but Laura was still their first-born.

But by the same token, kids were kids these days.

Aside from locking them in their bedrooms at night to keep them from straying into dangerous territory, what should a mother and father do? Sandra believed that modern parents had to allow their offspring some natural freedom. Show them due trust. Stuart believed that such theories only worked in the world of Mills and Boon.

But then again, Rose once locked her twenty-one-year-old son in his room as a supposed punishment which then led to him breaking his bedroom window, snapping a drainpipe, then jumping onto the front lawn and breaking an ankle in an exhaustive effort to meet his girlfriend for a romantic liaison.

No. Imprisonment wouldn't work. Far too much hassle for all concerned. Such restrictive measures seemed extreme and futile.

And so unnecessary.

And regular teenage breakouts could be potentially expensive.

Stuart would have to learn the art of hoping his children make sound decisions by utilising their own intelligence and initiative.

It may well be one of the hardest things a parent has to endure, but adolescence is a very tricky period for parents and children alike.

It would be very easy for a worried father to do or say the wrong thing at such a sensitive time.

But in truth, it wasn't an issue that reared its head all that often.

Anyhow, Stuart's own head was usually full of cricket, shares and vegetables these days.

Maybe once growing season is over it would be a good chance to reacquaint himself with the absent bedroom activity that he once shared with his spouse, instead of fretting about the ripeness of his chillis or the state of the FTSE index.

As far as Sandra was concerned, she had no need to feel any trepidation regarding Laura's sense of responsibility.

In truth, Sandra was slightly *envious* of her daughter. Lucky girl.

There was one issue in particular which suddenly eclipsed Sandra's thoughts at that moment as she lay smothered in the warmth of the bed.

Whether or not she should present her unclothed self to the dress mirror and undergo the rigours of her personal physical inspection, or whether she should resist such mental trauma until Monday morning at nine o'clock when the house would be hers and hers alone.

No. Sod it.

The tummy was rumbling.

Time for some breakfast.

Wrapping herself in her pink flannelette nightgown, she inserted her feet into the ever-ready white fluffy slippers and wearily descended the stairs.

The financial bulletin blared from the TV screen, fully holding Stuart's attention as his wife entered the lounge doorway.

'Morning, dear. Coffee?'

A nod of the head and a chomping of cornflakes was the response akin to a 'yes'. Sandra shuffled into the kitchen and duly switched on the radio, kettle, and grill. The scene beyond the window was grim.

Unseasonal grey clouds sat upon greyer skies.

Madonna endeavoured to lighten the dour vista outside with upbeat words of feminine optimism as Sandra inspected the date on the sausages.

Best before the day before yesterday. They would do.

Despite her apparent depth of sleep, Miss Jones was suddenly alerted to activity in the kitchen and had instinctively followed Sandra downstairs to be greeted by a full bowl of food.

Dragging his yawning form from the armchair, Stuart plonked himself at the kitchen table to begin his ritualistic examination of the Sunday Times which had just dropped through the letterbox.

He glanced casually at his wife and muttered an opening to a conversation.

'Any plans today, dear?'

Sandra scratched her head, overwhelmed by the potential excitement of a mountain of ironing and then an afternoon's hoovering and dusting.

'Nothing thrilling. Have you got a growers' meeting?'

'Not today, love. I feel like I've hardly seen you all week. It will be nice to spend a bit of time together.'

Despite his honourable intentions, the prospect threatened to encourage sheer, undiluted boredom in her.

Quality time together?

Oh…joy of joys. Contain yourself, Sandra.

Daniel had evidently been roused by the alluring scent of fried offal and resembling an image of death warmed up, he entered the fray before slumping his wiry frame at the table opposite his father.

Sandra conveyed her sympathies at the sight of the forlorn-looking teenager with a throbbing head.

'You look rough. Good night last night on the cheap cider, was it?'

Daniel simply nodded and uttered a grunt. Stuart's personal concerns regarding his offspring also centred on another issue.

'I'm not sure it's a good idea for someone of your age to drink so much. It can develop into a habit if you let it. Then you really have got a problem.'

Daniel looked across at his father as though he had just ridden into the room on the back of a T-rex with a bone in his mouth.

'Get with the times, Dad. *Everybody* drinks. It's not a sin anymore! Anyway, I bet you had a few hangovers at my age, didn't you?'

Sandra smirked as she turned the sausages. She was fully aware of her husband's strict upbringing and strait-laced principles.

She also believed that Stuart wouldn't do his credibility within the family any favours by confessing to them, either. Oh well. Too late.

'Certainly *not*! I didn't touch alcohol until I was twenty. And even then, it was only a bitter shandy! I've never gotten a taste for the disgusting stuff. And I hope you don't, either! You just have to look in the mirror to see what it does to you!'

There was a hiatus in the conversation as Daniel rose to his feet.

'Yeah…well…brilliant party, though! Loads of girls there! It was worth the bad head just to get the chicks!'

Sandra was careful to avoid engaging with Stuart's alarmed grimace as she struggled to conceal her giggles.

'Mum…we got any aspirin?' squirmed her son.

'Bathroom cabinet, love.'

Again, his father was quick to jump in with a staid viewpoint.

'And tablets aren't a cure, either! You're far too young to be swallowing pills! You youngsters are so weak-minded!'

Daniel stopped in the doorway and called to his mother.

'Can you shout me when breakfast's ready, Mum? I'm just going to hang myself due to severe depression brought on by parental concern!'

Sandra could not help but laugh as she waved a fork in his direction.

'Okay, love. But bring all your dirty washing back down with you before you depart the universe. And I mean from *under* the bed as well around it!'

*****

Every Sunday morning, Sandra would speak to her mother on the telephone after breakfast. This religious charade could take up to an hour, with Phyllis invariably doing most of the talking.

Stuart flinched inside as battle loomed on the horizon.

Having washed the pots and embarked on the first load of laundry, she sat herself down next to him on the sofa and dialled the number.

It was all he could do to endure Sandra's minimal replies to the inane raving and complaining of Phyllis Baxter. He writhed, grimaced, and shifted his weight from buttock to buttock as he fought to concentrate on the sport pages.

The side of the dialogue that he heard seemingly served no purpose, other than to cause grave annoyance to those in proximity.

'Hello, Mum?'

'It's me.'

'Sandra.'

'Your daughter.'

'Yes.'

'Why didn't you pick up first time?'

'So why did you pick up second time, then?'

'Are you okay?'

'Yes. We are too.'

'Do you need anything bringing. later?'

'Well, have you run out of anything?'

'Well, think!'

'No. You've not got toilet roll?'

'Okay.'

'How have you coped, then?'

'Oh…you've got a bit left.'

'Are you desperate or can it wait until Wednesday?'

'Okay.'

'Wednesday, then.'

'Are you alright for basics?'

'I don't know. Bread? Milk? Soup?'

'What about something for dinner?'

'Are you going out with your club friends?'

'Or do you want to come here?'

'For dinner?'

At this juncture, Stuart offered his wife an expression of wilful denial by furiously shaking his head.

Sandra smiled into the mouthpiece.

'No…okay, then.'

'Yes. We're all fine.'

'So, you don't need anything?'

'Okay. Are you going out today?'

'I don't know. Are you seeing friends?'

'You don't need me to visit, then?'

'Oh, don't start all that mother!'

'You've got loads of friends.'

'Yes, I did.'

'I came on Wednesday last week.'

Stuart lowered his newspaper and pretended to play the violins to accompany Phyllis' predictable pleas of loneliness.

Sandra responded with a playful slap on the shoulder and attempted to conclude the exchange with her dear mother.

'Listen, Mum. I'll see you in the week as normal, then.'

'Yes. I'll bring shopping with me.'

'No don't worry I'll ring you Tuesday night to check.'

'No, Stuart won't be coming with me!'

It was Sandra's turn to stifle her giggles as her husband furrowed his brow in a gesture of feigned offence.

'No. I promise.'

'See you soon.'

'Yes. Bye!'

Disconnecting the call, Sandra could not help but laugh at the ongoing animosity that festered between her mother and her husband.

Stuart tried to smile, but secretly felt like arranging an assassination attempt.

'Do I take it that the beast from the east is in fine fettle, then?'

'She is indeed! And she sends her best wishes to you too!'

93

He simply rustled the pages of his read in frustration.

At that moment, Daniel ambled back through the lounge doorway with an armful of dirty washing. His expression conveyed displeasure at the unannounced entrance of his sister into the house, who had stormed upstairs in the usual flood of emotion.

'Jesus, Mum! She needs certifying! Can't we get her sent away for therapy?'

Sandra's attentions focused on her scowling son.

'What's up? She had a row with Craig again?'

Daniel dropped the clothes in front of the washing machine and scratched his behind.

'What do you think? Why can't she go down the garden and cry about her love life? Why do we have to suffer every day?'

Sandra chuckled and resumed the mind-blowing task of separating coloured linen from whites.

'Like I keep telling you, love. It'll be you one day. Some girl will sweep you off your feet and your head will be all screwed up. Just like your sister's! Try and be a little more sympathetic, eh?'

Daniel was not convinced by his mother's appraisal of the situation.

'She nearly sent me flying downstairs! And she swore at me! I could have broken my neck carrying my own dirty pants!'

Stuart glanced up from the back page of the newspaper and examined the mocking sense of exasperation in his son.

'I don't suppose you upset her further by offering an unwelcome and hurtful comment as she walked through the door, did you?'

Daniel glanced at his mother before grinning inanely.

'No! Well...maybe I...'

Sandra shook her head in disapproval.

'Yes, then! You *did*, then! Maybe you should leave well alone. Are you going out today?' sniggered Sandra.

'Maybe. Perhaps back to Taylor's house. He's rented a couple of videos that must be taken back to the shop tomorrow, apparently.'

'Well, when did you last have a shower?'

The youngster pretended to think.

An act which did not convince either parent of its authenticity.

'Go on! Up the stairs you mucky urchin! Now! And don't put the same boxer shorts on afterwards! There are loads of clean pairs in your drawer!'

Mother and father watched as their son disconsolately exited the room. Sandra felt compelled to shout after him as he trudged up the stairs.

'And don't just run the water and stand outside the cubicle! Get yourself wet. And use some *soap*! Or I'm coming to do it for you just like when you were five-years-old!'

A distant murmur travelled through the hallway which passed for a reluctant affirmative. But Sandra wasn't quite finished with the instructions as she bellowed from the lounge doorway.

'And leave your poor sister alone!'

Typically, there was no response to this additional request.

Stuart rose to his feet and checked his watch.

'Right then I might have an hour in the greenhouse. There's the rugby on TV this afternoon.'

Embracing the prospect of another dynamic and electrifying Sunday, Sandra sighed and began to think about dressing herself.

The emptiness of reliability began to haunt her.

Bound by the rigours of uninspiring duty.

Immersed in a busy void of the empty and the foreseeable.

Wishing she was entrenched in that elusive, exciting, faraway place that occasionally tormented her in dreams.

9

BEDS ARE FOR SLEEPING IN

Sunday evening always brought with it a sense of undiluted anticipation for Sandra. Perversely, the return to work on a Monday generally made her feel upbeat after two full days of playing housewife.

The forty-eight hours just experienced had passed by so slowly for some reason. Sandra could not apply herself to the agenda of household renovation that she usually attacked with such vigour.

To sum it up, she simply could not be bothered.

And this bothered her to a degree.

Normally she would make a hygienic assault first thing on a Saturday, then everything would be ship-shape by Sunday afternoon in readiness for the family to replay their trail of destruction over the next few days.

But this particular weekend, every pending task seemed like an insurmountable obstacle. There was washing that still needed washing; dust that still needed dusting. And ironing galore. Suffice to say that the iron had remained in the cupboard under the sink.

The worrying aspect to the sudden reduction in her matriarchal enthusiasm was that nobody else in the house had even noticed the decrease in her output.

They just went about their business. Oblivious as usual.

Adeptly weaving their way around the piles of smelly clothes on the kitchen floor. Ignoring the unkempt state of the bathroom. Happy for Sunday roast to be on the table at three o'clock instead of the ritualistic time of one p.m. sharp.

Giving Sandra even more cause for concern was the fact that she was suddenly inclined to be least concerned with attending to the family's needs than the rest of the family put together.

Her mind was centred elsewhere for some reason.

And she had no idea as to why its location had shifted.

Constructive thoughts were deemed simply impossible.

She wasn't even pushed to enquire as to the reason for Laura's daily bout of upset. This was mainly because twelve hours later, as it typically proved, everything would be rosy in her daughter's world again.

The drama was always temporary.

And so came the aforementioned Sunday night.

The pots cleansed and put away.

The late-night schedule panned out thus.

A mind-numbing episode of Bread was followed by an even more mind-numbing episode of That's Life. This double delight was then succeeded by a body-numbing soak in the bath.

Drinking chocolate was scheduled to accompany eventual bedtime.

Lying immersed in the scented bubbles, Sandra's train of thought took her somewhere she had not visited for many months.

Perhaps even years.

Back to the days when she and Stuart would engage in the act of taking a bath together. With Laura asleep in the carrycot beside the tub, they would enjoy the time with each other as young and happy couples should have the right to do.

And yet now, here, nearly twenty years later, Sandra bathed alone whilst Stuart sat upright in bed. Donned in his striped pyjamas indulging in the latest novel from Jeffrey Archer or attempting the Sunday Times crossword.

Whilst a few short feet away on the other side of the landing, Sandra lay in solitary confinement with her nakedness. With only her reflective diversions to keep her company regarding what had passed her by.

And what perhaps would never return.

Passionate clinches that would lead to more explosive physical bonding. Spontaneous displays of love and unrestrained desire for one another were commonplace daily occurrences.

Was the downturn in intimacy a natural evolution for every husband and wife?

More potently, was such a sultry scenario ever truly present in their marriage to begin with?

She strived to recall, and often failed to address an accurate picture of their history together.

The thoughts of such supposed loss had rankled with her for a year or two now. But during the past few weeks the sorrowful sensation was far more provocative in her mind. Along with other connected side issues.

The kids had all but grown up. They were practically independent. Yet she and Stuart now lived their lives almost as brother and sister, as opposed to loving, energetic spouses.

Actually, it wasn't quite as exciting as being brother and sister anymore as they never even squabbled about anything anymore!

In fact, communication was ordinary and perfunctory at best.

Not one iota of spontaneity or randomness arose between them.

Every arising household subject was dealt with in perfect, blissful, sensible, boring, logical, diplomacy.

No truly emotional peaks or troughs.

Just plain, untroubled, sailing.

Yet the need for such analysis of her marriage status had never arisen before. It was only a recent urge. A creeping wilful necessity for self-examination regarding all aspects of her existence.

But why she should unexpectedly feel such an urgent desire to deconstruct, criticise and scrutinise her life, she had no comprehension.

After all, nothing was *amiss* in her cosy domain.

Stuart was a loyal and loving husband and father.

The kids were healthy and happy.

There were no money worries.

So, what could that elusive thing be that she might be searching for?

Why were grey clouds of discontentment forming above her?

What motive did Sandra Bancroft have for feeling so disenchanted with her little lot?

She was mentally stable. So far. As far as she knew.

Nor did Sandra believe in the midlife crisis or the early menopause.

So, she must have been subjected to a spiritual malfunction?

Maybe Stuart simply didn't find her attractive anymore?

Yet she didn't feel ugly. Far from it. Her naked reflection didn't look too offensive. In fact, she was secretly proud of what genetics had bestowed upon her.

Maybe it was necessary for her to initiate replacement of that which appeared to be currently missing? Perhaps she should take personal responsibility for the absence of closeness between her and the man she married?

Hauling herself from the cooling bathtub, she reached a decision.

She would try and seduce her husband all over again.

That very night.

As he lay in bed. Reading. Unsuspecting. In his pyjamas.

She would be the one to initiate rediscovery of the fire that once burned between them and fuelled their mutual desire.

She would be the one to reignite the forgotten throes of passion.

'*Jesus Christ*!'

Stepping onto the bathroom floor, the cold air caused goosebumps to form on her breasts, limbs, and buttocks. She immediately reconsidered the strategy about to be implemented in the bedroom.

So much for naked abandon.

It was perhaps a little too chilly for such a prospect.

Even in July.

But her subconscious swayed her once more.

This was no time for cowardice.

She would persevere with her aims.

The objective needed to be confronted and accomplished.

Sandra dried herself, rapidly trying to inject some warmth into her bones. Hardly a build-up to the advent of sexual adventure, but the damp air was taking a frigid grip on proceedings.

Wiping the steam from the bathroom mirror, she inspected her reflected form before applying deodorant, perfume and body spray and tied her wet hair in a bun. There was no time for drying it properly.

Finally comfortable with the image in the glass, she unhooked everything from behind the bathroom door in an effort to locate her short, flimsy, silken thigh-length nightie which she felt sure had been hanging there since she last utilised it on their wedding anniversary a few months before.

Not that the garment had the desired effect then, either.

Sandra frantically searched through the selection of dressing gowns and bath robes. It soon became evident that her exploration was in vain.

'*Shit, man*!' she commented under her breath, as a sudden draught induced an instant reacquaintance with the shivers.

Oh well. A clean towel would suffice. She would be naked, vulnerable and at her husband's brutal mercy in a few seconds' time anyhow. The presumed necessity for some exotic attire seemed rather unnecessary.

Bare-footed and ninety percent moisture-free, Sandra padded her way from the bathroom closely followed by Miss Jones who had become both confused and intrigued by the odd display of Sunday evening stealth.

With the time nearing midnight, Sandra reached the landing to hear the barely audible volume of Daniel's portable television.

Switching off the landing light, she then listened with her ear against Laura's bedroom door. Not a sound to be heard. She must be exhausted after all the romantic torment she had suffered over the past two days.

So, just one bedroom left.

Yet, no sooner as she poked her head around the door, it was clear that the game was already up. She observed Stuart through the semi-darkness. Pen still in hand, newspaper on stomach, glasses perched on nose, upright in bed.

Fast asleep.

Snoring like a recumbent buffalo.

Totally oblivious to his wife's good-natured intentions of having him ravish her until the sun came up the next day.

So much for spontaneous planning.

Furiously accepting defeat, Sandra shuffled quietly to her bedside drawer and retrieved a large Winnie the Pooh t-shirt, slipped it over her un-sated naked form and then slipped into bed beside the rumbling sinuses of her loved one.

Reaching across to send the bedroom into darkness, Sandra was mildly put out by the dormant figure taking up some of her side of the bed.

As she wriggled into position, ironically being careful not to disturb him, her thoughts unexpectedly veered into a sense of inner gratitude.

It seemed that reawakening one another's sexual needs were now secondary to a good night's sleep.

At least, it was apparent that what Stuart's viewpoint was.

But then again, how was he to know his wife was about to set about him with all her old magic?

Yes. Sandra was now relaxed about the whole scenario.

Succumbing to the terminally infertile desert that was her boudoir, she assumed the foetal position and dreamed of other romances elsewhere, on that other planet that she inhabited from time to time.

10

A MOMENT OF DRAMA

She was perhaps wrong to react in such a way, but it was now delightfully obvious to Rose Riley that Andy Ratcliffe was shamelessly attracted to Sandra.

Having never set foot in the place before the summer, he had now frequented Turner's at least four times in as many weeks and on each occasion, Sandra had been the barely concealed centre of his attention.

And Sandra was now fully aware of the situation, too.

It was a Thursday in mid-July when he blessed all and sundry with his latest appearance and made for the serving counter, where Sandra was amid a transaction with another customer concerning a mug of coffee and an iced bun.

Rose watched covertly from the tabled area with dish cloth in hand, as he casually stared over the glass cabinet comprising gateaux, cheesecake, and éclairs.

His eyes traced Sandra's movements affectionately as she handed over the change to the teenage lad.

Finally, Rose could resist the game no longer and sidled up to where he was positioned with a pleasured expression of mischief.

'Would you like *me* to serve you, sir…or will the lady behind the counter suffice, today?'

Andy smiled sheepishly but as ever was armed with a witty repost.

'No thanks. This lady here is the one I want. But I appreciate your considerate offer all the same.'

He was dressed differently today.

The customary black jeans were now blue and the sweater and long coat he was previously attired in were now replaced by a white polo t-shirt and black leather jacket.

Rose was in no mood to resist temptation.

His arrival was duly announced to his unwitting, yet willing target.

'Ayup, Sandra! There's someone here with a special delivery for you!'

Rose chuckled and wandered off to attend to other chores as Sandra reacted to her visitor with an automatic smile that served to bathe her features with an incredibly enticing aura.

She had been making an extra little effort of late to ensure that should Andy make an appearance, then she would be in somewhere nearer pristine condition to greet him than she ever was before.

It was a woman thing, she figured. And she found herself revelling in the brief spotlight that he had occasionally been providing. By the same token, Corrine has resurfaced from her umpteenth cigarette break and opted not to speak to the handsome customer as he leaned desirably against the hot cupboard counter.

It was obvious who he had come to talk to, and Corrine had swiftly become bored with trying to compete with someone old enough to be her mother.

Andy's velvet tones carried across the trays of beef baps, mini quiche Lorraine's and scotch eggs.

'So…Sandra. How've you been? Missed me much?'

Trying her utmost not to blush, she remained calm and blushed.

But she was ready to engage in the casual banter.

'Of course, I have! Er…what's your name again?'

Laughter ensued, further breaking through the natural inhibitions felt by both participants.

He positioned closer to her, allowing his voice to convey an assuring quality.

'Well…I've certainly missed *you*. I'd hate it if you didn't feel the same. After all we've been through together.'

More chuckles resonated, alerting the distant attention of both Rose and Corrine. Sandra succumbed and felt her cheeks helplessly flushing bright scarlet, betraying her secret wish that she would give anything to stand and talk to Andy Ratcliffe all day every day.

'That's nice to hear. Is your daughter, okay?'

His blue-eyed gaze never left hers as he replied.

'Annette…she's fine. She's amazing, in fact. Your kids? Are they good, too?'

She wasn't aware of the fact that she had begun to play with the third finger of her left hand, twisting the rings that adorned it.

Subconscious body language, perhaps.

'Yes. Good. A few romantic hiccups with my daughter which is par for the course at that age isn't it? But generally, they're okay, I think.'

Andy smirked and looked around the shop.

'Romantic hiccups, eh? Well, we all need a few of those, don't we?'

'Makes the world go around…so they say.' came Sandra's teasing reply.

It was only a mildly suggestive exchange, but her banging heart was perhaps telling her differently.

She quickly ascertained the location of her two ever-inquisitive colleagues who, thankfully, were well out of earshot.

Suddenly her mind became strangely flooded by thoughts of Stuart.

She could not erase his image from her head, even though she was staring directly at another man.

The inner quandary caused her to giggle nervously again.

'What's so funny?' Andy enquired, somewhat puzzled.

Composing herself, Sandra cleared her throat.

'Oh…nothing. Just wondering what my husband would say if he could see what I'm doing.'

Andy feigned a pout of bemusement and looked around him.

His eyes widened as he spoke with a hint of sarcasm.

'Why, Sandra? What *are* you doing?'

The lure was irresistible. She rested on her elbows and moved her face closer to Andy's to afford her own voice a level of quiet.

'I'm being naughty, aren't I? I'm flirting with somebody I hardly know.'

His white teeth dazzled against the dark pigment of his movie star profile. She detected the arresting aroma of his distinctive aftershave once again.

'What? *You*, Sandra? Flirting…with *me*? Is that what you were doing? Well, I never…'

She laughed once more. Such a welcome release through genuine humour was most welcome remedy to her recent negative preoccupations.

She felt instantly contented when in his company. Perhaps, she might even say, *joyful*. She also felt distinctly feminine; she found that she greatly appreciated the male attention.

'I apologize, Andy. I'll slap my own wrist. It won't happen again. I promise.'

Now he pretended to be upset and threw Sandra a grimacing scowl, albeit performed.

'Well, there's not much point in me coming in here then is there if I can't show off to the best-looking woman in town? I may as well go elsewhere to eat now then, hadn't I?'

His unanticipated reference caused her stomach to lurch and encouraged a further quickening of the pulse. Then simultaneously, a pang of doubt intruded once more and attempted to interrupt her full submission to the moment.

A thought dominated: why would this man say such things if he perhaps didn't mean them?

But perhaps…just maybe…he *did* mean them?

'Listen, Andy. I'm certainly not the best-looking woman in town and if you keep on telling fibs I won't serve you your tea and toast!'

He playfully raised both hands and tried in vain to suppress his own revelry in the interplay.

'Okay! Okay! I surrender. Just tea and toast it is then, please. And I promise I won't pay you any more compliments or drool when I stare at you.'

Sandra winked her most rehearsed and hopefully most seductive wink, as she placed two slices of brown bread under the grill.

'Good boy. Now behave yourself and find a table.'

Turning to face her infinitely favourite customer once again, she was surprised to find him practically lounging across the counter next to the cash register.

With a slight jerk of his head, he beckoned her closer.

She willingly obliged, after checking around the shop for unwanted potential witnesses.

And she was also wary of being caught by Mick, who had been rather grumpy again for most of the day.

'What is it? You're not really allowed to hunch over the serving top like that.'

Their faces now only inches apart, he spoke into her ear, allowing her a fuller experience of his now very familiar scent.

'I may have promised not to flirt anymore, but I can tell you here and now…I would never lie about how attractive I'm finding you.'

Sandra was now truly stuck for words.

Standing speechless in her tunic, catering hat and apron, she felt about as enticing as a traffic warden, yet Andy Ratcliffe obviously saw a very different Sandra Bancroft beyond the work costume.

Maybe the true side of Sandra Bancroft that she had even forgotten about herself.

Or indeed…the side of herself she had never discovered.

Taken aback by his insistent and irresistible bravado, she simply opted to stick to the job at hand and poured boiling water into a small metal teapot before placing it gently onto his tray.

As she did so, she felt his eyes follow her every nuance.

Her every curve.

And it was an alien, delectable sensation that surged through her.

So unfamiliar; yet so instantly infecting and undeniably addictive.

She felt she was an object on display exhibiting herself for him.

A slave girl to the prince, no less.

She reached under the grill and flipped his two slices of wholemeal.

Sandra Bancroft; unwitting queen of the stage.

Exhibiting her spontaneous sensual routine.

And how the limelight intoxicated her so.

They exchanged glances once again with mutually inviting smiles of almost electric intensity.

Finally retrieving the toast from under the grill, she placed it on Andy's plate and added two packets of butter. Her confidence now fully returned, she felt completely comfortable with a return to the gentle swapping of suggestion.

'Well…sir…let me think about this for a moment…'

Andy's blue eyes lit up in anticipation of her next statement.

She pretended to muse over some delicate issue before releasing him from his suspension.

'Two toasts and a tea for one…that's one-ninety, my lovely!'

Again, the sound of laughter emerged between the pair, causing both Rose and Corrine to look up from their separate missions.

By now, Sandra could not have cared less.

'Would you like me to bring it to your table, sir…or can you manage?'

Andy handed over the correct money and picked up the tray.

'No, thanks. I think I can handle this alone! I'm a big boy, you know.'

Sandra sniggered at the innuendo and affectionately waved him away, as two schoolboys approached the counter signifying the commencement of the lunch-time influx.

Watching Andy walk steadily to a table, she smiled at the youngsters who peered through the warm glass at the savouries on display.

'Hi, boys! What can I get you?'

Their response was muted by a resounding clatter that echoed around the dining area, instantly followed by a deafening silence throughout the entire shop.

The schoolboys sniggered and pointed. Sandra was jolted by the disturbance and scanned the vicinity for the source of the commotion.

It became quickly evident that Andy had dropped his tray.

He stood motionless, staring down at the steaming pool of brown liquid and slices of toast on the floor as Sandra rushed to his assistance and gently grasped his arm.

107

'You alright, Andy? Did you miss the table? You daft bugger! Well, you've woken everyone up, that's for sure!'

His gaze remained focused at the mess on and around his shoes.

He did not utter a word as Sandra knelt to clear up.

'Don't worry. We'll get you some more. Sit yourself down, Andy. It happens to the best of us. It won't be a minute.'

Sandra collated the items on the tray and duly straightened herself up to face him once again. Despite trying to make light of the scene, she could see that Andy had been embarrassed by the accident.

Lifting his gaze, he frowned intently towards her, which instantly nullified her wish to continue with the humour and instead inject some female sincerity.

'Andy. What's wrong? It doesn't matter. It's only a tea tray. That's all. Soon be sorted.'

She placed the broken crockery on the counter and fetched a mop and bucket as Andy shuffled toward the front door of the shop and the smirking throng of school children that had gathered to spectate on his misfortune.

Within seconds the incident was over, and Sandra approached him as he stared vacantly through the window into the High Street.

'Sit down, sweetheart. I'll put more toast on.'

His eventual response seemed tinged with anger.

His eyes met hers as though it were *she* that had committed some terrible sin. The words he spoke were not specifically hurtful or personal, but their bluntness hit her hard.

'Don't treat me like a child! I'm not a child, Sandra. I didn't mean to drop the bloody tray.'

She was taken aback by his curtness but pursued a peaceful conclusion to the episode as Rose observed from a distance.

'Of course, you didn't. It was an accident. I know that.'

'There you go again!' he snapped.

She felt a slight lump of trepidation begin to form in her throat as Andy's persona instantly adopted a more downbeat and frustrated air.

She also sensed a growing audience which featured Corrine on the front row.

And they could hear every word.

'I'm not an idiot, Sandra. Don't ever presume that I am!'

Her reaction was one of sheer bewilderment.

He seemed unduly perturbed by the whole thing, despite her comforting words of assurance.

'Nobody thinks you're an idiot, Andy. Now come on and sit down.'

With that, he threw a scornful glare towards the onlookers and pulled open the door.

'Yeah? Well, I reckon *that* lot do! I'm going. I've…got to…I've got to go…'

And then, true to his word, Andy Ratcliffe was gone.

Gone. Out into the street to mingle with the crowds and vanish from view, as though he had never entered the bakery at all.

Completely dumbstruck by the abrupt departure, Sandra attempted to scan his path from the behind the glass of the front window.

Even from a distance, Rose could sense the onset of emotion in her friend and moved to take charge of the imminent fall-out.

'Go and have a break round the back, Sandra. Take your time. I'll carry on serving for a while.'

Complying with her colleague's kind suggestion, she wandered toward the rear of the shop and pulled open the staff room door whilst exchanging a dubious stare with Corrine.

A few seconds later in the solace of the rest room, Sandra retrieved her handbag and a packet of tissues before making for the toilet.

She studied the cracked glass of the tiny mirror and observed her distorted, disturbed reflection.

It was only then that she realised she was crying.

Tears were literally rolling down her cheeks.

Yet, such an extreme response to a relatively frequent event was uncanny and most puzzling.

What was happening to her?

Similarly, she struggled to reconcile that such an innocuous occurrence as a spilled teapot had caused Andy to retreat so urgently and had caused her to feel so disconcerted.

She was not personally offended by Andy's outburst, but something, somewhere in her heart, was tugging relentlessly in response.

As she dried her face and re-applied some eyeliner, the cause of her unease began to dawn like a lead weight.

She stopped and looked at herself again and the ridiculous evidence of her undue distress. Further emotion smudged her fresh mascara as a double-edged realisation hit home.

It was now obvious that her flustered response was borne out of some incredulous yet genuine concern for a man she hardly knew called Andy Ratcliffe.

She wanted there and then to go and find him to check he was alright.

To see him smile that wonderful smile once more.

And for him to assure her that he was no longer angry with her.

And that he would be back.

And more importantly, that they would remain friends.

Yet her brimming upset was also engulfed by the harshest and even more unfathomable of likelihoods.

The possibility that he might keep his pledge that he earlier made in jest.

That she might never set eyes on him again.

11
ARRESTING DEVELOPMENTS

Yet another weekend came and went with Sandra now entrenched in winsome thoughts regarding a certain person. She hid the internal symptoms well, but when alone for long periods, her mind wandered back to the peculiar episode of the previous week.

If she were frank with herself, Sandra had little earnest motive for feeling so concerned. Yet the bemusing reaction could not be controlled by her. The emotions within would ebb and flow as they wished.

Whether the cause was comprehensive to her or not.

Monday reared its head and Sandra did not feel like attending for her shift at Turner's. She would have given anything to have rung in with some fabricated ailment but conceded that the alternative was to sit around at home and continue to dwell.

So, off to work she went under a subduing cloud of disinterest.

In truth, the hours passed quickly and there was little opportunity - or inclination for that matter - to stand and gaze at the passing scenery beyond the front window.

Rose noticed her friend was particularly quiet throughout the entire day. Not to an unsociable degree, but the customary effervescence that Sandra displayed at work was not in evidence.

At least…not until around four-thirty that afternoon.

As she commenced the daily clean-down of the ovens and trays, Sandra's furious attempts to deploy elbow grease onto stubborn burnt crust were interrupted by a tap on the shoulder.

She turned fully armed with Jif and brillo-pad, to see Rose standing behind her.

'What's up, love?'

Her friend said nothing and simply pointed to the front door of the shop, beyond which stood a vision to wash away all Sandra's recent sorrow.

Sandra felt suddenly short of breath.

Her unsettlement surrounding Andy Ratcliffe was immediately eclipsed by the glorious confirmation of his unannounced return.

Adorning his enticing smile, he curled a forefinger that beckoned her to him.

She glanced at Rose, who nodded in sympathy.

'Go on, San. Give me them rubber gloves. I'll do the trays. But take him around the back. Out of Mick's way. He's still here for some reason.'

Skipping out to the front of the counter like a teenager with a crush, Sandra pulled open the shop door to greet the unexpected visitor.

'We can't speak out here. Meet me around the back near the skips. You can get down the side of Cordon Bleu's.'

Sending Andy on a very necessary diversion gave Sandra precious seconds to swiftly venture to the toilet armed with handbag and a chance to touch up what the day had tarnished. She re-applied a little make-up and pulled a brush through her hair.

It was then that she felt her body sway under a physical reaction that she didn't readily recognise. Her chest heaved wildly and butterflies in her stomach felt like blackbirds. Her hands shook with anticipation as she replaced her handbag in the staff room and tentatively pushed open the rear fire escape.

And there he stood.

Waiting…just for her.

Just as she had so wished him to do for recent endless days.

Clasping her hands together to reduce the signs of her nervousness, Sandra strode confidently to him with that inviting smile that made her seem infinitely more striking to his eye.

It was at that moment that she realised the cause of her unprecedented bodily responses.

It was something called pleasure.

'Hello, Sandra.'

She lost herself in his sparkling blue eyes. Like hers, they too were edged with emotion, and he was obviously uncertain about his presence and her possible unwillingness to speak to him.

Nevertheless, he was there.

A combination of relief and anticipation flooded Sandra's very being as she deliberated on her opening gambit.

'Hi, Andy. You okay, today? You didn't seem a happy bunny the last time I saw you. I've…I've been worried sick that…well…I thought I might have upset you.'

The mutual concern was etched in his face as he shook his head and closed his eyes.

For his sheer proximity alone, Sandra felt consoled.

But he had a surprise in store.

'No…not at all. You didn't upset me. Don't ever think that. I reacted badly. I sometimes do. I can't help it. Please forgive me. I spoke in a terrible way to you. You didn't deserve it. I'm so sorry.'

Sandra's heartrate had begun to settle, yet she had now moved on to feeling like she was floating on air.

Just watching him speak to her was satisfaction exemplified.

The words he uttered were additional music to her ears.

'I'm so glad we're still friends, Andy. I'm growing to like you…a lot.'

She held no reservation with the sentiment.

Nor did she sense regret about openly expressing it.

He pursed his lips and swallowed a gulp of uncertainty before producing a bunch of twelve red roses from behind his back.

Sandra's eyes lit up at the gesture and she was overwhelmed by the obvious sincerity of Andy's contrition.

'These are to help my apology along…and to show my appreciation for your understanding. I knew you wouldn't judge me, Sandra.'

She smirked wildly before opting to tease him just a little.

'Well, I don't know. I'm not won over *that* easily, you know. I might have still been very angry and told you to shove your flowers where the sun doesn't shine.'

He moved his face close to hers, once more inducing her chest to thud like a drum.

113

A thousand conflicting responses erupted within her head.

She felt fragile; yet secure.

Vulnerable; yet safe.

Confused; yet assured.

'No. I never doubted you, Sandra. Never. Please forget about last week. I have. If I'm forgiven, can we start again? Friends?'

Sandra looked skywards and feigned a moment of indecision on the issue. Gazing at the scarlet petals, she then noticed the small greeting card amidst the bouquet, emblazoned with a pink heart.

'What's this?'

Andy did not smile, but merely encouraged her curiosity.

'Well, if you don't open it, you'll never know, will you?'

Sandra handed him back the flowers and removed the envelope.

With trembling fingers, she carefully tore the seal and retrieved the little card.

Her mouth dropped open as she read it.

Her head told her not to return Andy's persistent and inviting stare, but her heart so wanted to. The energy between them was once again irresistible and was already luring them both to dark, undiscovered, yet wondrously exciting territory.

A place so dangerous and inherently sensual.

Strictly forbidden and yet so welcoming.

Finally, she succumbed and gazed deep into him.

'Andy…this…this is…your telephone number?'

He nodded without word, as words were not necessary.

'But…I…*can't*…what am I supposed to do, Andy?'

Offering her back the bunch of flowers, he cradled her hands in his as she gingerly clutched the card with the number written on it.

Bearing even closer to her, he spoke softly, in total command of the woman in his grasp.

'Listen. I'll give you two weeks. Think about it. If you don't ring me, I won't bother you again. Okay? I'll understand, Sandra. I'll totally get it. But I can't help this. Believe me. I want you. From the first time I saw you. I knew.'

Sandra now felt deeply concerned, whilst inside she churned in a search for a viable solution to this most idyllic of potentially disastrous problems.

'But…Andy…I'm married…I have a family…this…what you're suggesting…it can't be right…can it?'

He released his hands from hers and stepped backward, admiring the fearful, beautiful woman wavering before him.

'It might not feel right at this moment, Sandra. But ask yourself this: does it truly feel so *wrong*? As you stand here now…looking at me, do you wish you *weren't*? Do you honestly wish you'd never met me?'

Her attention nervously alternated between the flowers, the number on the card, and him.

Gorgeous, wonderful him.

This person she did not know, who had entered her life and changed her whole existence. In the past few days her mind had transposed from the regularity of organised wifely duty into a tumbling mess of relentlessly sporadic thoughts.

Yet it was immersion into a new dimension; the like of which she had never previously experienced. Not even when courting Stuart did attraction seem so tangible.

So spiritually and physically moving.

The very image of Andy Ratcliffe soothed her so much.

Her turmoil and anguish regarding their meeting dissipated just by resting her dark brown eyes upon his demanding, irrefutable form.

'I…don't know…what to say…I need time…this is…crazy…I just don't know…'

'Don't say anything. Think about it. Two weeks. I'll hope to see you soon.'

Sandra observed Andy's departure.

Dumbstruck. A torn woman.

Only a short while ago, her life was humdrum; routine; ordinary.

Yet flames of wanton unrest had been ignited and were now lapping fiercely within her core.

The reality of the scenario was brilliantly debilitating.

Crushing her long held sense of security yet simultaneously liberating her soul.

She could not register the inconceivable fact.

She was desired by another man.

It was not a situation to be ignored, yet she was at a total loss as to how to even begin dealing with such a prospect.

Setting foot back into the staff room, she closed the fire door and gently laid the roses on the table. Studying the card once more, she tried desperately to pretend that she was not holding a strange man's telephone number in her hand.

Yet the number was indeed there.

In her hand.

And the man was a stranger, no more.

12

A FRIEND IN NEED

Closing time for Turner's had never been quite like this. Sandra and Rose had been left to clean up and lock up as usual, yet end of shift today felt anything but normal for Sandra Bancroft.

Rose switched off the interior lights as they both retreated to the staff room. The bouquet remained on the table where Sandra had left it an hour earlier. The flowers would have to remain there overnight. There was no way she could take them home and pretend to her family that they had been given to her by some old couple who were thankful for their hot soup and bread roll.

Sandra changed out of her tunic and slipped on her jacket as Rose readied a welcome cigarette between her lips and checked that she had selected the correct key to shut the front door.

Her opening comment about the afternoon's events was nonchalant, yet direct.

'You'd better get those in water first thing in the morning, San. They'll dry up quick in here.'

Sandra offered a discomforting half-smile. She was confused as to how to reply to such a genuine, if telling, observation.

Out front, Rose set the burglar alarm and secured the large glass door behind them. A warm yet blustery breeze welcomed the pair onto the street, causing Sandra's jacket to fly open as she fought with the zipper.

Rose lit her smoke and gazed fondly at her colleague and friend as she battled with the elements. She shook her head slowly, eventually inducing a mild grin from Sandra.

Her natural curiosity finally breached bounds of honest respect for her friend's privacy.

'Them flowers…they from your new mate, I take it?'

Sheepishly, Sandra reluctantly nodded and decided to confess her troubles.

'Yes…yes, they are.'

Rose detected the emerging unrest within Sandra as they wandered along the street in the direction of the bus stop.

'What is it, San? You look worried, girl.'

Sandra stared straight ahead as she strode.

Uncertain that any further revelation was a wise idea.

'That's not all he gave me.'

Rose's eyes widened and her mouth slackened, causing her cigarette to droop from her lower lip.

'Oh yeah? What else, then?'

Sandra stalled as she reluctantly summoned the truth from her barely concealed depths.

'I've got his phone number in my locker.'

Rose almost choked as she inhaled on her smoke.

'Christ on a bike! Friggin' hell, Sandra! What on earth are you *doing*? This isn't the school playground, you know! Come on. I'll drive you home. We can chat. I'm parked around the back. The bus will be ages, anyway.'

*****

The two women sat in the front seats of Rose's silver Austin Metro, with a cloud of uneasiness enveloping their typically upbeat union. The car was Rose's pride and joy - a fiftieth birthday present from her family. She inserted the key into the ignition but deferred from starting the engine.

The silence between them endured, but Rose was not one likely to allow that to last for long.

She flicked her ash out of the window and commenced the inquiry.

'So, what now then, lovebird? What's on your mind? We can all tell you fancy him. And it's bleeding obvious he fancies the knickers off you! But this is dodgy ground for a happily married woman. Not to mention whether he's a married *man*!'

118

Sandra stared blankly through the windshield, feeling the elevated heat of the sunlight as it penetrated the glass.

'I don't know if he's got a wife or not. We've never even had a proper conversation, yet.'

Rose simply sighed in sympathy as she drew on the last of her smoke and extinguished the nub end in the over full ash tray.

'I don't know what to do, Rose. I honestly haven't a bloody clue!'

Rose laughed out loud and lit another cigarette.

'Well, that's fellas for you, ain't it? They don't leave you with much of a clue at the best of times, do they? But you've got to make your mind up. He's obviously keen. You can't play games, San. This is big time grown-up stuff!'

Sandra tried to acknowledge her friend's expression of concern. Rose could not offer much reassurance, but it was a relief just to discuss the quandary and off load a little of the burden.

'But…he's lovely, Rose. Drop dead, isn't he? And the thing is…he's in my head.'

'Bloody hell, San…you *have* got trouble, haven't you?'

Again, there was a soundless pause as the women pondered life and all therein.

Suddenly a familiar figure passed behind the car from the housing estate beyond and made his way down the side alley onto the High Street.

Sandra was instantly alerted to the characteristics of the middle-aged man in pin-stripe suit trousers, running shoes and carrying a briefcase.

'What's up, San? You look like you've seen a ghost! Don't tell me old Charlie's after you as *well*!'

Intrigued by her friend's commentary, Sandra probed for answers.

'He gets on my bus every day. Do you know him then?'

'Yes! It's Charlie! He's works at the components factory next to the park. Davies Incorporated.'

'Is he a director then or something?'

Rose guffawed as she drew on her fresh nicotine.

'What? *Charlie*? Not really, San. He's the labourer. The company gopher. Odd job man. Cleaner. You know…'

Sandra continued to debate the puzzle with herself.

'So…what's in the briefcase he carries all the time?'

Rose's chuckles were now getting the better of her and were beginning to lift Sandra's spirits into the bargain.

'Would you believe…his sandwiches?'

'His *sandwiches*?'

'Yes, San! His bleeding lunch! Apparently, he found the briefcase in one of the skips at work! He's a right dreamer, but harmless enough, bless him. Likes to pretend he's a manager. Anyway, never mind him. Let's get you back to that husband of yours!'

*****

The journey through town was slowed significantly by rush hour traffic and intermittent road works. However, Sandra was pleased for the ride home. It took her mind off matters regarding Andy.

At least it did, until the silver Metro eventually pulled up outside Number Twelve, Orchard Road.

Sandra fixed her attentions on the scene beyond the windscreen, as though reluctant to get out of the car.

She sighed heavily and scratched the side of her head.

'Bloody hell, Rose! What can I do about this mess?'

Placing a hand on her friend's knee, the elder woman offered some logical advice.

'That's the whole point, San. There *isn't* any mess yet is there? So don't go making one, neither! Do the sensible thing, eh?'

This wasn't the kind of advice Sandra wanted to hear.

'But why did he have to walk into our bloody shop and play with my head like this?'

Rose leaned across and presented a wily glare of sincerity to her trusted colleague and confidante.

'It's called *fate*, Sandra, my love. You can't control it. It makes its own decisions. The reason he came into your café…is because he wanted something to eat. It just so happens that you work there. It's as simple as that. Now for God's sake don't go complicating things any more than you have to. Now get out of my car and get Stuart's tea on!'

Sandra leaned across and gave Rose a peck on the cheek before unlatching the passenger door.

'Thanks. Thanks for listening to me.'

'Okay, love. Sleep on it. Mum's the word. I shall not say a thing to anyone. See you tomorrow.'

The silver Metro pulled away, leaving Rose observing her friend in the rear-view mirror.

The vision of a somewhat hesitant Sandra Bancroft gazing vacantly at the frontage of her home, before fumbling in her handbag for the front door key.

Finally, Sandra ventured along her garden path as she in turn watched Rose's car navigate the corner and disappear.

13

NO SIGN OF THE HERO

Sandra counted down every minute of every hour of the following fourteen torturous days. Time had veritably stood still since she last set eyes on Andy Ratcliffe.

Her inner confusion was hidden adeptly from family and colleagues, yet the doubt and indecision regarding her forbidden potential liaison with such a tempting specimen of mankind, had manifested in varying odd and inexplicable symptoms.

Corrine had found it particularly pleasurable to remind her workmates of Andy's absence every single day. Whilst annoying for Sandra to listen to, she played along with the joke until Rose found her in a fit of pent-up frustration in the staff room one afternoon and calmed the storm.

Then unannounced, the joking finally ceased when Rose held Corrine up by the lapels of her tunic and threatened to feed her limb by limb into the dough machine if she didn't stop rabbiting on about Nick Kamen.

At home, life with Laura and Daniel continued in its customary conflicting ways especially with the school holidays in full swing, whilst Stuart was just plain old reliable Stuart.

Stocks and shares; cricket and vegetables.

His foundation for the perfect life.

Away from the fast lane, Sandra had secretly begun to experiment with her appearance in those quiet bathroom moments.

After serious self-analysis, she decided that changing her hair style was an immediate priority, but visiting a salon would perhaps be too obvious a move and may create suspicion.

Even though at that juncture, there was nothing for anyone to be suspicious about. Bathing and sleeping with her hair in curlers counted as a first-time experiment, just to see what it looked like in a morning after the curlers were removed.

In short; not a good solution to re-styling.

Instead of giving her hair more body and shine, the top of her head resembled a deserted bird's nest that had then been ravaged by a cat.

Miss Jones could offer little in the way of constructive opinion and could only observe in tentative sympathy, as Sandra yanked the plastic rollers from her scalp to the accompaniment of intermittent yelps of pain.

Anatomical inspections had been resumed in full and were now deemed a daily must, but only when the rest of the household had been evacuated.

However, there wasn't much to report in terms of progress on the boob and bum front. Her legs were still shapely and stomach relatively flat. Slight inhalation still gave the impression of a larger chest, which mildly appeased her. Same old story.

And still Miss Jones still gazed on in singular bemusement as she yawned and purred whilst reclining contentedly on the bedclothes.

Over the fortnight, Sandra secretly tried on once-worn dresses that didn't fit anymore because she wasn't twenty-years-old, anymore.

She inserted her feet into shoes that looked ten years out of date.

Because they *were* ten years out of date.

Tights were an absolute no-no, although stockings were perhaps a little too garish for a first meeting. After considered deliberation, Sandra concluded that a good leg wax wouldn't go amiss, but a daily shave would continue to suffice for now.

Different applications of make-up were attempted, yet she found herself limited by the limited amount of make-up she possessed.

The lipsticks that still worked properly were either orange or bright red whilst the gentler pastel colours that she preferred to employ crumbled like chalk as soon as they protruded from the tubes.

In all, it felt like a generally unsuccessful venture into the realms of a partial makeover.

Yet she never once stopped during such frantic fashion trials to ask herself *why* she should be so intensely occupied with presenting her physical form in a different way.

After all, Andy Ratcliffe fancied her when she was donned in her baker's tunic and catering cap!

For instance, on her day off, she visited her mother with the shopping as usual and received sharp criticism for walking around in bare legs and two-inch heels.

And of course, the supposedly fresh bread was too hard.

But the self-scrutiny was swiftly becoming an almost obsessive pastime.

One Friday morning as July gave way to August, she was caught red-handed by Stuart in front of the bedroom mirror analysing the texture of the skin under the folds of her buttocks.

Rather than offering a jovial assist in the unprecedented hunt for cellulite, he took one look at his wife as she strained elastically on the edge of the bed and commented that he thought he would have Shreddies for breakfast instead of the usual fried option.

He then left her in peace to continue the futile exploration of her backside.

It was when Stuart invited her to a growers' convention at a local stately hall that Sandra decided to shine in earnest.

He encouraged her to dazzle by claiming that she shouldn't wear her typical garb but should dress to impress.

Whilst mildly insulting, the opportune offer was far too tempting to disappoint. It might well have been a full day's discussion on fertilizer and soil nutrients, but it was also scheduled to be interrupted by a lunchtime finger buffet with complementary wine.

Sandra tried to make the relevant effort and attired herself in a knee-length red dress that clung ever so slightly to the right places. Black heels and matching handbag completed the ensemble, which even encouraged Stuart to put his arm around her at one point.

Mind you, that was in posing for a photograph.

However, her renewed enthusiasm in searching for a diverse new image seemed to be waning as time lingered on. And the following Monday morning signified that a total of twenty-one days had come and gone.

Twenty-one days since Andy Ratcliffe had last appeared to light up her day and make her heart leap with a bouquet of roses.

The absence of revelry in her own household was now frighteningly noticeable. Stuart rarely made her smile even by accident these days, let alone giggle to herself anymore.

And despite her personal efforts to submerge herself in distraction from the numbing domestic schedule of old, her life had steadily reverted to its customary cycle of going to work, feeding the family, and going to bed.

Yet in her mind she had far from resumed old habits.

As time continued to pass, her mental anguish only increased. Frustrated by the vacancy left by Andy, Sandra gradually found herself feeling increasingly despondent about the situation.

By the culmination of the fourth week, the distinct lack of Andy Ratcliffe had led Sandra within touching distance of her wit's end.

Rose had decided not to bring the subject up in the hope that the incidental attraction between her married friend and the handsome newcomer would remain purely that.

However, Sandra eventually realised before it was too late that Andy, despite her inner despondency with the entire issue, had remained true to his word.

The rules had been laid down for her very simply: if she didn't contact him, he would never come and see her again.

Such a situation was becoming unbearable for her to live with.

It had taken nearly a month for Sandra to confidently establish in her own mind that she *needed* to see him again and that the ball was firmly in her court.

Just to observe his abiding, mysterious features in her eye-line would satisfy her agonised yearnings.

A raw desire to have him simply talk to her once again, hopefully before he forgot about her completely and went off to meet somebody else and love *them* forever instead.

But that nagging premise was unthinkable.

He was *her* Andy. Wasn't he?

She was his serving friend and his flirting partner.

And he said…or gave her the distinct impression…that he wanted to be *her* friend and flirting partner.

Friday evening finally brought the working week to an end.

It was a relief to strain out the floor mop up for the last time until Monday.

The staff room was empty when she entered.

Without a semblance of indication to anyone as to the imminent plan, Sandra opened her locker door and noticed the dried bouquet of roses in the footwell below. They never did make it into a vase of water.

She then slipped on her jacket and nervously retrieved the card with Andy's number written on it.

On saying her farewells to Rose as the shop alarm was set, she declined the kind offer of a lift home, preparing instead to embark on a journey of her own.

A path she would never have dared to tread before.

But her mind was made up.

She could not bear the thought of not making the jump.

A jump from the predictable life she had made for herself.

A jump into an enticing new world.

The lure of the unknown had finally proved irresistible.

14
MAKING THE CALL

Sandra had never felt quite so apprehensive about anything in her entire life. Getting married and giving birth were child's play compared to the imminent mission she had opted to undertake.

As she watched Rose walk toward to her car, the late summer wind seemed to take a calmer turn, which served to allow the sun its rightful place on stage.

Clutching the small card in her jacket pocket, the first hurdle was to decide on the most appropriate location from which to contact Andy.

Walking along the nigh-on deserted High Street as her brow became slightly moistened by the humidity, she reached the telephone kiosks in the centre of the precinct and tentatively selected a vacant booth.

As the door enclosed her in the glass chamber, the only sound she could readily identify was the resumption of the thumping in her chest. She took a moment of composure and in doing so noticed the varying messages scrawled in marker pen around the interior of the booth.

Teenagers evidently carried a far more vivid imagination than her generation ever did. One particular caption even encouraged a crimson hue to her cheeks.

Pulling the card from her pocket, Sandra carefully observed the hand-written digits. She then suddenly halted her progress as her mind became flushed with thoughts of her priorities.

Matters such as her home, her husband, and her children.

Yet at this most delicate of moments, they helplessly paled into secondary consideration.

Torn between wifely duty and wanton wish, Sandra briefly contemplated forgetting the whole reckless idea. Her secure lifestyle should never have been disrupted in this way.

She should never have taken the card with the number on it.

She should never have entered that telephone kiosk.

By now she *should* have been getting on the bus.

By now she *should* have been on her way home to Number Twelve, Orchard Road.

But as much as she told herself what she *should* have been doing, it was not what she desired. What she *wanted* to do, more than anything in the world, was to dial the number on the card.

Delving into her purse for loose change, she opted to use a pound coin as opposed to juggling with a palm full of tens and twenty pence pieces.

With a visibly shaking hand, she reluctantly dropped the coin into the slot - which then promptly fell into the return tray at the bottom of the telephone unit.

Reading the instructions inscribed near the cradle, she followed the guide and dialled in Andy's number, carefully double-checking each figure on the card before she pressed it in.

With the complete number inserted, she listened intently as it registered and eventually connected.

Then the ring tone sounded.

And her throat became suddenly parched.

And her pulse raced untamed as though dangerously out of control.

Her hand jolted with anticipation causing need for her to steady her wavering form against the glass wall of the booth.

Checking briefly beyond the kiosk windows again for passers-by, her concentration was instantly distracted by a wonderfully familiar voice in the earpiece.

'Hello? Andy Ratcliffe speaking.'

Sandra struggled with swallowing a hardened lump of trepidation before taking a deep, hopeful breath and dropping the money into the slot.

She had no script prepared.

No grasp of any idea what she wanted to say to him.

Another deep breath.

Another pang of guilt.

Another attempt at restraining her unbridled joy.

'Andy?'

'Yes...'

'Andy...its Sandra...Sandra...from the bakery...'

The vocal hiatus lasted for only a few seconds but seemed to endure for a desperate eternity.

She waited longingly as the deafening silence continued to threaten with a potential to punish.

Had she left it too late?

Was he no longer interested?

Could Sandra Bancroft already be committing the biggest mistake of her life?

'My God! Sandra! Great to hear from you! I'd given up all hope!'

His reaction of evident glee was music to her ears.

The ball was now well and truly rolling.

Smashing its way downhill.

Demolishing obstacles and gathering relentless speed.

'I...I'm sorry I took so long. It's...been...well...difficult...'

She looked through the grimy windowpanes of the phone booth once again to satisfy her fears that some covert witness wasn't watching her from the shadows.

'Sure...of course. Look, Sandra...I shouldn't have left this down to you. It's not fair. You shouldn't have to chase me like this. You've got your own life. I don't...'

'Andy...'

'What?'

Her voice quaked with both fear and with courage.

With doubt and with anticipation.

With hope and with abandonment.

Did she truly wish to say the next words?

'Andy...Andy...I've really missed you.'

Again, the exchange came to a temporary halt as both parties examined their role in such dubious yet exhilarating dialogue.

129

'I've...I've really missed you too, Sandra. God...I've missed you too. But when I said two weeks, I didn't mean take an extra two just to tease me!'

She laughed heartily. A relieving, cleansing emotion that she had sorely missed in the recent days. The tension of moments earlier tumbled out of her and immediately evaporated.

'So, Andy...what have you been doing...without me?'

'When...today? Well, I visited a massage parlour this afternoon before coming home to get ready for tonight's cannabis party.'

Sandra giggled again.

'No...seriously...what have you been up to?'

'I just told you...well, okay...I didn't go to a brothel...but I'll be smoking a spliff or two later, for sure.'

'You're an idiot, Andy Ratcliffe.'

'Yep! And you phoned me! So...what does that say about you?'

'It says that I'm an idiot too!'

'Okay. So, we are both idiots. Now that we've sorted that out, what can I do for you, madam?'

Now the easy comedy found cause to cease for a moment as it made way for plain honesty.

Now it came down to the brass tacks.

And they were sharp and unyielding to the touch.

'I want to see you, Andy. Soon.'

'Okay...I'll just check my diary...'

Sandra expected to chuckle, but she also wanted a serious response to a heart-assaulting declaration.

'Stop being silly! I need to with meet you. I've missed you so bad.'

Again, the pause.

Again, the danger of the pending scenario encroached.

'That's...good...really good...when is best for you?'

Now she was really becoming worried.

The situation was rapidly becoming irretrievable.

She had wilfully made her choice as a responsible adult.

And yet she now felt eighteen-years-old all over again.

As such, there was no hesitation in establishing the details of their private arrangement.

'Tuesday night. I've already got it covered because I usually play bingo. Where we meet…I'm not bothered. Just somewhere out of the town.'

Now it was Andy's turn to laugh out loud.

'Why…you're not scared of your husband finding out…are you…Sandra?'

Andy's tone sounded mocking, but of course it was a question that she had yet to ask herself.

It should have made little difference that Andy had been the one to broach the subject.

Nevertheless, an answer was required of her at some point.

'I…I don't know…I don't know what the hell I'm doing to be honest…it's all a bit scary…'

'Okay. You know the Priory Inn? Near the city's main police station?

'Yes.'

'Can you meet me there? In the lounge? Tuesday evening? Eight o'clock? Is that okay?'

'Yes. That's fine. I'll get the bus.'

'Great! Tuesday at eight. Can't wait to see you, Sandra.'

'Me too. See you then.'

As a beautiful toxin began to infuse her bloodstream and settle her fitting heart, Sandra felt as though she needed to offer one more thought to end the conversation properly.

The seconds passed as her mind raced, searching frantically for the correct parting message.

'Sandra…are you alright? You still on the line? Have you changed your mind already?'

Once more she looked beyond the grease-encrusted glass of the telephone kiosk and glimpsed the lengthening shadows of the High

131

Street, as the verification of their rendezvous assembled in her ragged brain.

'Andy…are we…am I…I mean…is this really the right thing to do?'

Now there was a pause at his end.

A long, unwelcome soundlessness that began to tear at her soul, as though she might await inevitable disappointment.

But how she dearly wanted him to say all was fine.

'Sandra…tell me now if you don't want to continue with this. It's not a problem. You'll break my heart forever…but I'll understand.'

More laughter; more silence.

More doubt; more courage.

The final decision was assured.

'See you Tuesday. Andy. Eight o'clock.'

Sandra hung up, not wanting the intensity of the moment to fade.

Leaving the phone box and heading for the bus stop, this upstanding woman of stringent, unhindered principle, suddenly found herself confronted by an overwhelming feeling that her life had taken a turn of complete unpredictability.

No longer having to be content with the humdrum.

No longer having nothing to look forward to.

Yet she knew her road to self-indulgence would be fraught with potential peril.

But the danger felt absolutely incredible.

15
KEEPING THE SECRET

In the days that followed, Sandra had no choice but to ensure that her intended meeting with Andy Ratcliffe was concealed from everyone. And that *everyone* included her unofficial moral mentor in the matter, Rose Riley.

Sandra's mindset during the weekend had gradually renewed itself as firmly upbeat and jovial. She even had Stuart laughing as she danced haphazardly around the kitchen whilst cooking breakfast to the sound of Five Star on the radio.

Can't wait another minute, indeed.

The plan to see Andy was well and truly under wraps, but the sad reality was that maintaining discretion in the Bancroft household was not a true challenge anymore.

These days, Laura and Daniel were always preoccupied with their own lives and arrangements, so any possibility of arousing their limited suspicions regarding anything beyond their individual radars was minimal.

On Saturday afternoon, Sandra went shopping with Laura as usual.

Whilst knowingly playing with fire, she had decided that roles should reverse for once. Sandra would treat herself to some new shoes and a new dress and that her daughter would be the one to convey some expert advice regarding the final choices.

The selected garment would hopefully be utilised as the outfit to impress Andy. Laura was understandably taken aback by her mother's sudden desire to upgrade her wardrobe.

'What's it in aid of then. Mum? Are you and Dad going out somewhere?'

Sandra smiled inwardly at her daughter's innocent curiosity.

'No, love. I just fancy spoiling myself for a change. No problem with that, is there?'

Laura shook her head in mild dismay as the bus pulled to its final stop at the city terminus.

'Come on, girl. A few try-ons and a few opinions from you. Then coffee and cake! I'll deal with the front-end reflection, but I need your honest opinion on the rear view!'

'Okay. Mum. You're in charge today!' chuckled Laura, whilst covertly noticing the distinctly happier demeanour that her mother had adopted of late.

But if it was all in the name of retail therapy, then who were either of them to question the motives?

*****

It took three hours ten minutes and nine clothes shops to finally make the ultimate final decision on a respectable, black knee-length design, plus a matching pair of suede sling-back heels with a closed toe.

A resounding thumbs-up from the daughter told the mother that her shopping expedition had been a worthwhile if lengthy success.

Sandra was positively brimming inside as she and Laura embarked on the journey home. She covertly studied her daughter's blemish-free and youthful features as the bus arrived. And then the guilt rained down about the fact that her first born remained oblivious as to the true nature of her mother's intentions.

If only that beautiful, loving seventeen-year-old knew of what her Sandra had conspired to do.

Back in the bedroom at Orchard Road, she tried the new dress on again and slipped her feet into the shoes.

Having uncovered a small black handbag from the depths of her chest of drawers, the ensemble was pretty much complete and, according to Laura, instantly effective.

'Wow…Mum…you look so…different…sexy, even…*younger*…'

Performing an unsteady pirouette in front of the full-length mirror, she turned to see the misplaced yet earnest pleasure in her daughter's eyes. And then reality once more descended on the moment, causing Sandra's head to spin and stomach to knot involuntarily.

A mother's personal anguish tore in rabid fashion at her very core, questioning the decision by such a respected woman of duty and responsibility to involve herself in such a devious act.

Even more painful was the sight of her angelic daughter, giving positive appraisal on the new outfit.

The new outfit that would soon be used to charm another man.

The idea suddenly felt so completely terrifying.

Instinctively repulsive and utterly, unavoidably wrong.

She continued to preen and pose in front of the dress mirror.

What on Earth did she think she was getting herself into?

Sandra's inner doubt swiftly drowned her clear conscience like a thunderstorm in summer. There was surely no way that she would be able to commit such an unforgivable deed.

The guilt would likely erode her personal wellbeing for the rest of her days. She would never be able to look at her dear, beloved family in the same way again.

And similarly, if the imminent treachery was ever discovered, her family would have just motive to disown her forever.

Sandra Bancroft contemplated the possibility that after next Tuesday night, her life may well be altered irreparably.

The path she wished to walk was one way only.

No return was possible once she took those steps.

Thankfully, a daughter's kind words distracted Sandra from her torturous confusion.

'A great choice, Mum. You look *wonderful*.'

'Thank you, sweetheart. Though I'll think I'll get changed and put my pyjamas on now! I feel a bit silly. Don't know why I bought the dress, really. Waste of money.'

Dumbstruck by her mother's untimely proclamation, Laura glanced at her watch.

'Mum…it's six-thirty on a Saturday night…and you're getting ready to go to bed? You're in your *forties*…not your *seventies*! God! I bet even Grandma stays up later than you!'

Sandra smiled as she kicked off the sling-backs and replaced them with her comfy white fluffy slippers.

'Well, yes, maybe…anyway, what are you doing tonight?'

'Oh, going to the cinema with Craig and another couple…you know them. Gemma and Ian. In fact, I'd better go and get changed, myself!'

As she oversaw her daughter's exit from the room, Sandra slumped dejectedly onto the edge of the bed. Having been so full of zest only hours earlier, she now contended with some very distracting second and third thoughts.

Perhaps it would be the best thing to do to ring Andy back on Monday and tell him to forget the entire thing.

To forget that she'd ever contacted him.

To forget that they'd ever met at all.

To forget that he ever existed.

Pulling her make-up mirror from the dressing table, she examined the frowning features of a troubled middle-aged woman.

What had she become?

How had she evolved into this seemingly heartless and selfish cow?

A heartless and selfish cow that was apparently willing to throw her whole marriage down the drain based on the premise of a little frivolity.

She studied the minimal lines around her eyes and lips.

The upturn of her nose and the smoothness of her neck.

And her mindset switched once more.

It was possible that some other man could find her attractive, she supposed. But did that mean she had to risk all she depended on in response to such vague and shallow flattery?

Perhaps a little more attention from her husband would remedy the problem. But he was more interested in his greenhouse these days than affairs of the heart.

And even worse than that, the ultimate tragedy was that Stuart innocently presumed his wife was actually satisfied with life.

Such was the growing chasm between them nowadays.

And maybe, just maybe, she would have carried on regardless with her life, if Andy bloody gorgeous Ratcliffe hadn't arrived on the scene to upset the apple cart.

Yet truthfully, all he had done was open her eyes to how discontented she had become after twenty years of marriage.

She should really have been counting her domestic blessings and relishing the cosy, reliable nest that her family had built on Orchard Road.

But she was not going to wallow in such an ethical argument.

For she was no longer so joyous about the finer or indeed the basic details of her daily existence.

Not really. Not with hand on heart and a gun to her head.

She was bored rigid with being a mother and a housewife.

Their was a yearning woman inside of her who was desperate to take the stage.

Yet, such demons had not been present until her attention had been diverted from what she knew and trusted.

These were unsettling considerations, for sure.

But they were also brutally and painfully honest admissions of what lay within her heart.

The process of self-psychoanalysis was interrupted by a familiarly comforting sensation around her legs and feet. Miss Jones had appeared in the room, no doubt wanting replenishment of her empty bowl.

Then Sandra heard footsteps ascending the stairs which no doubt belonged to Stuart. She listened and watched as he inquisitively poked his head around the door and smiled.

'Here you are, dear. Family Fortunes has just started. You make yourself comfortable downstairs. I'll order us a take-away if you want. Do you want the usual rice and ribs?'

Sandra smiled back at the man she thought she loved with all her might.

And the agony crucified her inside.

'Yes please, darling. Sounds lovely. I'll be down in a minute.'

137

Stuart exhibited a broad grin and promptly departed the bedroom.

And to her seismic disappointment, he played entirely to form.

Once he had journeyed back downstairs to the lounge, she heard him making the call to the Chinese restaurant as she gazed aimlessly in the bedroom mirror.

And he never even noticed the new dress.

*****

Monday was accompanied by wave after relentless wave of self-doubt.

Which was then followed instantly by absolute conviction.

And eventually concluding with the return of terminal indecision.

Three times during her shift, Sandra had very nearly left the shop to make the phone call that would nullify the source of her torment.

The phone call that would relinquish her of the guilt and leave her free to resume the normality she knew best of all.

And yet three times she dissuaded herself from doing so for some crazy, unfathomable, illogical, totally self-absorbed reason.

Rose had not mentioned Andy at all during the previous couple of weeks. Sandra was thankful for her friend's respectful lack of curiosity, but of course as her closest ally, Rose Riley would eventually be told everything there was to know.

But not just yet.

*****

That evening, Sandra completed the household chores by seven-thirty and with her head ricocheting amid the maelstrom of conflict, she decided to try on the new dress and shoes once again.

Stuart remained oblivious to the activity upstairs as he indulged himself in the latest episode of Coronation Street with a mug of tea and some ginger biscuits. Sandra donned her new attire and padded across the landing into the bathroom to apply some make-up.

A gentle smudge of foundation; a touch of gloss for the lips and light mascara to accentuate her brown eyes.

Maybe some blush to give a hint of colour to her face, but not too much.

Indeed, less was definitely more, and she was mightily pleased with the overall effect.

She just hoped that Andy would feel the same.

Suddenly her inner bubble of whimsical satisfaction was disturbed by a presence beyond the door.

Daniel's muffled tones travelled through the wood as he knocked.

'Mum...are you in there? You've been ages! I need my hair gel. I'm going out in a minute!'

Sandra began to panic.

The last person she wanted seeing her in such attire was her *son*.

He could invent and exaggerate stories for England.

'Hang on, love. Five minutes! Then I'm done!'

She hastily removed the dress and replaced it with her pink dressing gown. Rapidly removing her make-up with the swish of a damp flannel, she checked her image in the mirror.

Content that she had seemingly eradicated any possibility of arousing suspicion, she unlatched the door to reveal Daniel's frustrated features.

'Thank God for *that*! I thought you'd had a funny turn or something! I'm going to be late, now! I can't go out without my gel on!'

Sandra smiled maternally as she passed him on the landing and duly hung the dress in her wardrobe, checking for any marks or snagged threads before she did so.

With the trial run now accomplished, she would simply await the passing of the next twenty-four hours.

Trying to hide her renewed inner enthusiasm from Stuart, she need not have concerned herself. His head was now buried in the latest monthly edition of Garden Kitchen magazine, and he barely even acknowledged her as she perched in the armchair opposite.

Finally diverting his gaze above the pages, he offered an expression of mild concern as all truly concerned husbands would surely do.

'You were a while in the bathroom, love? What was it? A bit of tummy trouble?'

Sandra shook her head as she picked up the television remote control.

She considered conveying the threads of her alibi for the following evening.

'No…I'm fine now. By the way…I've…I've got bingo tomorrow night as usual, you know.'

She waited nervously for some kind of overly inquisitive reply from the other side of the room. To her relief, the resulting response from her husband offered no underlying suggestion that he believed her story might just be a complete and utter lie.

'Oh yes, of course. Do you have a lift arranged or do you need me to drop you off?'

Swallowing a gulp of trepidation, Sandra was assured in her answer.

'No. I'll make my own way on the bus, love. It's okay. Honestly.'

'Okay, darling. Whatever makes you happy.'

16

THE BIG NIGHT

'A bit glammed-up for bingo aren't you, Mum?' observed Daniel, grinning from ear to ear as though he might just possess an inkling of the sin that his mother was about to commit that evening.

Of course, such commentary was unavoidable.

There was little chance of Sandra evading discovery in her newly purchased outfit, especially with a nosey, sarcastic fifteen-year-old male in the house.

Stuart, on the other hand, did not share his son's views. Indeed, his eyes widened as she entered the lounge, even making him suspend fascination in his latest novel for a minute or two.

'I think you look lovely, darling. You show yourself off if you want to. Let the world know how lucky I am!'

Her husband's ironic if complementary summary could not have been more poorly timed. On the verge of betrayal, Sandra forced a half-smirk that felt ever more like a grimace of guilt.

'Well…I'm just saying, Dad. I thought all that bingo stuff was for fat women in cardigans and jeans. That's all.'

Again, Stuart leapt vehemently to his wife's defence.

'Yes. Thank you. That will be all, Dan. Haven't you any homework to be getting on with?'

'No, Dad. It's still the school holiday until next week, remember? That's why I've been hanging around at home a lot more lately.'

'Oh, right. Yes, well, you can still spare us from your rapier-like wit for once.'

That was all the instruction required. After kissing his mother goodbye through his immovable grin, Daniel trudged up to his bedroom.

But not before issuing the traditional parting shot down the stairwell.

'Have a good game, Mum. And make sure you get hammered on lager like last time! You're hilarious when you're hungover!'

Sandra instantly gauged the disapproving look on Stuart's face.

A mother could still chuckle at a son's playful observations, but her mirth was restricted by her intensely overwhelming anxiety.

Standing in her own lounge with the knowledge of what was to come began to tear at her conscience like a lion ravaging fresh quarry.

She had to get out of the house soon and get to the bus stop.

Under the protection of privacy where it was safer.

Free from the binding love for her family.

Free from duty.

Free from the raging guilt.

Stuart appeared in the hallway to see her off.

'Enjoy yourself, darling. You are quite sure you don't want a lift?'

Sandra nodded in tortured silence, throwing her lightweight jacket over her shoulder in fumbling desperation for an escape route.

Her husband continued to observe her admiringly as she checked her purse.

'You do look stunning Sandra, love. Have a good night.'

Again, she forced the grin of an amateur actress before performing the obligatory peck on Stuart's cheek.

Stepping onto the driveway and listening to the front door close behind her brought welcome if uneasy relief.

Outside, she breathed in deeply.

Outside, to liberation and onward into an entirely new world.

*****

Sandra was alone at the bus stop. She checked her make-up in her compact mirror and played with her hair a little more. Her eyes scanned up and down the street to ensure no one was around to acknowledge her departure.

She was most grateful she did not have to wait too long for her chariot to arrive. Luckily, she did not recognise the driver and even better still, he did not recognise her.

142

But he eyed her appreciatively as he handed back her travel pass.

The mildly surprising thought occurred to Sandra that she was turning heads already.

Taking her seat of choice in comfort without being catapulted along the aisle was also a pleasing alternative to the usual procedure.

She noticed nothing beyond the bus window as the adventure began. Her mind was awash with thoughts of the man she was about to encounter.

And the other man she had left behind at home.

It was a twenty-five-minute journey into the city which eventually brought her almost to the door of the designated destination. She stood and stumbled slightly in the new shoes, clumsily regaining her balance as she advanced to the driver's shoulder as her indication she wished to alight.

More doubt encroached as the vehicle made a smooth entry to the bus shelter and pulled to a stop. Now it truly was crunch time. More questions pummelled her prevailing inclination.

There was still time to bail out.

Was this the right thing to do?

Should she get off the bus and meet Andy?

Should she stay on board and go back home to her husband and family? Yes…of course she *should*.

But she did not wish to.

Then just as the driver invited her exit with a hiss of the doors, a calamitous thunderbolt crashed her down to Earth.

She had not mentioned the date to Rose.

She had not secured her alibi.

And tomorrow was Wednesday - her day off.

Would she take the risk?

As the situation stood at that moment, she was about to ride on a trapeze for the very first time and with no safety net in place.

Her chest heaved wildly, and her legs became weak as she hurriedly pondered the potential nightmare.

'Are you getting off here, love? Or are you a bit lost?'

The inquiring voice of the driver only served to heighten the urgency of her predicament.

More seconds passed as she tried not to panic.

Then, a judgement arrived of its own accord.

Fuck it, she thought.

It was too late, now.

She would have to see Rose on Thursday at work.

Things would be fine.

She hoped.

Reacquainting herself with the warm evening air as she stepped onto the pavement, Sandra remained under the bus shelter and in purposely delaying the pending manoeuvre, checked her purse once again for money and keys.

The twinkling lights of The Priory public house looked attractive from across the road, softening the unforgiving harshness of the scenario evolving within her mind.

And so, Sandra continued with her inaugural journey into another galaxy.

Crossing over with a quickened walking pace, she approached the front doors of the pub. The aroma of ale barrels was an unusual test for her senses as she and Stuart had hardly frequented such places in their time as a couple.

In fact, if her rapidly assembled theory proved correct, this was probably the first time she had entered a public house alone for twenty-two years, if at all.

Breaking new ground all over again was infinitely thrilling for her.

The initial noise and bustle created by the patrons inside was welcoming, unlike some of the leering stares of the pool players that halted their game as Sandra strode past.

A fruit machine attracted the loud attentions of a small throng of young men in the corner as they gambled with their remaining beer money in a futile attempt to win more.

An overweight man with a moustache who she presumed to be the landlord presented a mildly lecherous expression as he observed her sidle nervously up to the bar counter.

It quickly dawned on her as she scanned the seats in the room that there was no sign of Andy. She quickly became distinctly queasy with the uncertainty of the situation.

Double checking the clock on the wall in comparison with her own watch, she confirmed the time to be eight-thirteen.

'Yes, love? What is it to be?'

The request from the barman startled her somewhat.

She was not accustomed to ordering her own drinks, either.

'Erm…oh, I don't know.'

The bar tender's expression remained glum and unmoving.

'Well, it's gonna be a long night if you make me guess.'

His humourless attitude was not helping to suppress her unease.

'Well, just a half of lager then, please.'

A loud shout went up as the pool table supplied a victor, just as a simultaneous holler arose from the group of frustrated gamblers.

'There you are my love. Sixty-five pence, please. Are you okay, darling? You look a bit confused. You're not a regular, are you?'

Sandra's eyes darted around the room again in search of her would-be hero.

Instinct was beginning to encourage spurts of negativity.

'I'm supposed to be meeting someone, but he's…not here…'

With that, the walrus-faced server came to her rescue.

'Hang on a mo. Is he a tall chap? Good looking? Dark?'

Sandra's eyes lit up as the overweight man readily depicted her supposedly mystery date.

'Next door, love. He's been there half an hour or so. It's quieter in there. Through that door there, look.'

Paying for her drink, Sandra lifted the glass from the bar top and steadily followed her guide's direction.

The sign above the door indicated the lounge.

Of course, this is where Andy said he would be.

The gradual relief welling inside her was contenting.

As she struggled to put one foot in front of the other.

Like a child on Christmas morning, she slowly pushed the door open…and revealed a vision to eclipse any remaining speck of reluctance within her soul.

Sitting in the corner snug, Andy's instant smile was a gilt-edged assurance that she was doing the right thing. He rose to his feet with one hand on the table and shuffled toward her around a chair.

His eyes veritably bulged as her full form honed into view.

'Hello, you! Jesus, Sandra! You look bloody amazing! All this…just for *me*? Or have you got a date later?'

Of course, she laughed without hesitation.

An earnest, relieving, enjoyable release of tension which seemed to eradicate all the reticence and pressure that had mounted in her mind over the previous days and hours and minutes and seconds.

Yet being light-hearted was so easy with Andy Ratcliffe.

Her responsive wit flowed readily, as if it had been stemmed for so long. Like an enormous river suddenly freed by the removal of a dam, she allowed the vibe to enswathe her, and she unshackled herself to reign free over the moment.

'Yes…well…I'm supposed to be meeting a sex god in here tonight, but I don't think he's turned up. So, I suppose *you'll* have to do!'

They both sat down in the same bench seat with a mutually engaging expression of excitement, whilst maintaining a respectably civilised gap between them.

Sandra glanced warily around the otherwise vacant room. She suddenly felt oddly at ease with the completely alien venture.

Andy fingered the rim of his glass as he lost himself in her gaze.

'I really didn't think you'd want to see me again, Sandra.'

She looked deep into his blue eyes as he sipped some beer.

'Well, Andy…it was a hard decision…you know…but not *that* hard…'

Now he chuckled and again sampled from his glass. She watched attentively as he sat with his back against the chair and folded his arms.

'So, Sandra…I'm intrigued…is your alibi convincing?'

She pulled a face of mock concern and leaned closer to him, furtively placing a hand lightly on his shoulder.

'I haven't got one! I forgot to set it up! What's yours?'

Andy nodded as he drank some more.

Then he shook his head as he swallowed.

'I…er…I don't really need an alibi, to be perfectly honest with you.'

Naturally, Sandra became instantly confused by the statement.

'But…why? What would your wife say? Wouldn't she mind?'

Andy stared at his drink, contemplating the most suitable response.

Sandra was becoming more bemused by the second.

'No. She…er…she won't mind. Well, she *shouldn't* mind. She left me three years ago.'

He chortled amidst another intake of ale, yet he could see that the revelation had come as something of a shock to his companion.

'Oh…I…didn't…realise.' stammered Sandra, herself now needing a sizeable intake of lager.

'There's no reason you *should* have realised. It's the first time we've ever discussed the issue. So anyway, what about your hubby? Is he the suspicious type?'

Sandra found herself at a loss for words.

She was somewhat thrown off kilter by Andy's nonchalance regarding the subject.

Having presumed that they were both taking a great risk by arranging the rendezvous, it rapidly dawned on her that she was the only one who was walking a tightrope with her future and all therein.

Feminine bravado came to the fore and disguised her revived reservations.

'No! Stuart? No. He trusts me. After twenty-one years of marriage, can you believe! He still…he…still…*trusts* me.'

Andy didn't show any emotion aside from a slight pout of the lips, which then issued another query.

'How about your daughter? Does she know about this?'

'Hell, no! Though, my son had a bit of a surprise when he saw me going out tonight! Especially when I told him I was playing bingo!'

Andy sniggered and rolled his eyes to the ceiling. He could sense Sandra's evident discontentment at lying to her family.

Despite his upbeat mood, the position he had willingly placed her in did not sit easily on his shoulders.

'Look. If this is too much for you, please say so. We'll stop it now. If you want to, that is. There's no pressure, Sandra. Honestly.'

She stared into his perfect, enticing face, losing herself in his deep, azure eyes.

Despite the nagging complexities, the inert danger of the moment was irresistible.

Logic quickly offered her a palatable solution.

He was a heavenly creature who desired to be in her presence. For a woman who had felt uninspired and neglected for so long, she was not about to offer him a rebuff.

'No…Andy…this is fine. It was *me* that made the call, remember? So, anyway. About you. Why did your wife leave you?'

His demeanour altered visibly, as though he had suddenly been placed under investigation. Evidently, the scars of separation still had not healed. He sipped some more beer; his hand noticeably shaking as he held the glass to his lips.

'Well…we just weren't suited, I suppose. Just a shame it took us so long to realise.'

Natural sympathy washed over Sandra as her desire to learn more grew by the second.

'And what about *your* daughter…Annette, isn't it? Does she know you're here tonight…seeing *me*?'

He fell silent once more and stared at the table as the question burned in his mind, leaving him seemingly scouring for the truth.

There was little other option but honesty.

His gaze firmly addressed hers as he spoke.

'Yes…yes, she does know I'm here. And she remembers you from the café.'

Once more Sandra was surprised by Andy's latest confession.

'And what does she think? Does she approve of her dad seeing a married woman?'

He smiled, as though expectant of Sandra's scrutiny.

'Thankfully, yes. I have her blessing to enjoy myself.'

Another question pressed to the fore.

One that had intrigued her from the first time she saw him.

'How come we've never seen you in the café before your recent visits? We know most of the regulars. But a regular you most definitely *weren't*!'

Andy crossed his legs and placed his beer back on the table. She carefully observed his body language, struggling to ascertain the depth of his responses.

He certainly wasn't overly uncomfortable about supplying such information, yet she sensed that he was possibly withholding selectively.

'Well, I'm from the city scape, aren't I?'

'Oh right. So, one day you just felt like a change of scenery then?'

'I guess it's not unusual for me to have visited cafes in and around the city instead of the outskirts. Annette wanted to try something different. For the shopping, mainly. So…here I am!'

Sandra finished her drink, encouraging Andy to empty his own glass and fetch some more. He appeared to struggle to his feet, giving cause for Sandra to assist his stance.

'You, okay? Bit of a wobble on there for a minute!' she smirked.

'Yeah…I know…I can never pace myself with the beer…I've overdone it a little maybe…nervous about seeing you!'

She observed his rear view as he ventured to the bar for replenishments. For all the anxiety she may have endured regarding the evening, her own nerves had all but dissipated.

149

She knew there and then, as she vainly endeavoured to avoid blatantly staring at Andy's backside, that she had definitely made the correct decision.

One way ticket.

No return.

*****

The remainder of the evening seemed to endure for about ten seconds. Andy effortlessly made Sandra giggle with every other word. Her jaw ached and her stomach strained from the relentless line of patter and witty stories that he conveyed at his disposal.

All her concerns of earlier that day had been duly diluted with lager and then forgotten about completely.

What was unacknowledged by both parties is that they gradually sat closer together as the night wore on. They had also become confident with briefly touching one another as they swayed in their amused union.

Fortunately, the room was virtually theirs alone and as time elapsed the welcome seclusion served to protect them from the harshness of normality beyond the windows of the inn.

She wanted the secret occasion to last forever.

A blunt reminder of real life came crashing back in with the startling ring of the bell for last orders.

Sandra checked her watch, struggling to focus through an alcoholic mist.

'Jesus, Andy! Its half-eleven! I'd better get myself back home! Stuart will be worried about me! And I might have missed the last bus!'

Adorning coats and staggering outside into the unseasonably chilly air, they made their way toward the bus stop.

In such proximity she could smell his aftershave and he wallowed in her distinctive scent. As Sandra turned to glance at him, she noticed that he was walking at a significantly more laboured pace than she, as though struggling to keep up.

'Come on slowcoach! Do you want me to give you a piggy-back?'

Andy wheezed as he chuckled.

'Might be an idea. I think my legs have gone to sleep.'

Together in the unpredictable shadows of night, they wanted nothing and no one to part them at that long-awaited moment of togetherness in the bus shelter.

In a shielding embrace that deflected the prying eyes of the world, he rested his chin onto her shoulder.

'Well, Sandra, your last chariot is due any minute. Just made it.'

With his mouth covertly nuzzling into her neck, Andy then whispered a carefully considered offer.   '

'Listen, I don't live too far away from here. Come back for coffee and I'll get you a cab home. No funny stuff.'

Sandra felt as though she were watching the scene from afar.

Akin to viewing a romantic Hollywood movie.

As if it were not Sandra Bancroft being enticed by this handsome stranger, but some other, incredibly lucky lady.

The invite to his house was a sorely tempting offer, for sure.

Perhaps *too* tempting, however.

But it was far too soon in the infancy of their growing bond for her to consider such a proposal seriously.

The temporary contemplation was halted by the distant approaching engine of the last bus of the day.

Now her heart quickened once again in wilful expectancy of the creeping, enticing unknown.

Then, as her dream deliriously evolved into actual real time events, he pulled her toward him and placed his face close to hers.

His soothing tones conveyed everything she needed and wanted to hear in that blissful instance.

'It's been perfect, Sandra. Thank you. I want to see you again.'

Her mouth hung slightly open as though her words of mutual desire had already been spoken, yet she could not summon any appropriate response at that precise moment.

Shifting ever closer in the murk of the cool summer night, they dared one another teasingly and finally touched lips to immerse themselves in triumphant, physical unification.

The embodiment of a forbidden friendship was completed.

Her body shook from head to toe as the blinding unfamiliarity flooded her veins and took complete control of her being.

The delicate yet asserting kiss ended all too soon.

The bus came to a grinding, squealing halt.

The sliding doors gaped open as though to call time on the intimate, delectable exchange.

Yet he still held her strong and ever closer as if his life depended on it.

'Andy...I've got to go.' she whispered. 'Come and find me. At the shop. Soon. I'll be waiting for you.'

Showing her pass and taking her seat, the bus doors closed on an evening of sheer, unadulterated exploration.

Craning her neck, she avidly watched the forlorn silhouette of Andy Ratcliffe disappear into the shadowy distance.

Watching her coach vanish around the corner into the amber-hued twilight, Andy roused himself to commence his own journey home.

He winced as uncooperative limbs fought against the brain's command to guide him. His mind now focused only on one person as he walked away into the night.

*****

Sandra turned the key in the lock just as the hall clock touched half past midnight.

Floating on air and on an untypically overindulgent intake of beer, she nearly tripped over a very curious Miss Jones in the hallway, slightly straining her ankles in the new heels.

Creeping upstairs, she made sure not to disturb the rest of her family as the cat flitted awkwardly about her feet.

The warmth of Stuart's body had rendered the bed a welcome retreat from the shrill damp shroud outside.

Her head slowly lowered into the pillow, accompanied by the strangely comforting soundtrack of a husband's oblivious, contented snores.

But he did not interrupt her own pleasured descent into slumber, for it was time once more to dream of planets far away.

17

A MOTHER'S OPINION

'You're a cheerful so and so this morning! What's happened? Has that husband of yours packed his bags and left you at long last?'

Sandra ignored her mother's worryingly inciteful observations as she unpacked the shopping and laid it out for scrutiny on the worktop.

Her skull thudded very slightly due to the lateness of the previous night and the associated intake of lager. It had been a few weeks since Sandra's last hangover. And the way she felt at that moment in her mother's kitchen, it would be another few weeks before she encouraged a repeat performance.

'Oi...what date is on them eggs? You can't be too careful, you know! So come on! Spill it, girl. A mother knows when something's happened to her own daughter. That's what makes us good mothers!'

Of all the people in the world that Sandra would never readily confide in at any level on any subject, her mother was usually top of that list. Especially regarding issues of domestic and emotive pertinence.

This was by no means a callous approach on Sandra's part.

Her mother had rarely been prone to bouts of warm understanding and doses of healing sympathy, particularly when it involved her own relatives. In short, Phyllis Baxter was a hardened spirit, shaped by a life that had not gone to her plan.

Her typical reactions to hearing general family bulletins would be, to say the very least dismissive and cynical. Subsequently details were always kept to a minimum.

As a matter of habit, Sandra would convey any business at hand and receive instantaneous disapproval and criticism. Often both at the same time and usually directed at her, her children, or her husband.

One subject that always acquired unwelcome scrutiny was Sandra's appearance. According to her mother's ever-ready gospel of goodliness, Sandra's clothes were always scruffy and unfashionable and apparently, she always appeared fatigued.

But not today.

Today was different.

Today, she had dressed to impress.

'That a new top, love?'

'Yes. Mum. Do you like it?'

'Not your colour, is it. But quite nice.'

Sandra was also privy to the regular and unnecessary reminders that her job at Turner's was demeaning and the shopping she had purchased for her mother was invariably too expensive.

All were minor issues and carried little detrimental effect on anyone's existence, yet Phyllis would rarely fail to bring such trivia to the fore.

But not today.

Today was different.

Today, Phyllis was genuinely alerted to a very untypical aura surrounding her only offspring.

'Is the new top for work, then? Been promoted, have you?'

Over the years, Sandra avoided relating any relatively important news as it really wasn't worth the price of disparaging consultation.

But not today.

Today was very definitely unusual.

Something instinctive was pressing Sandra to buck the lifelong trend of secrecy that she had adopted when dealing with her mother.

On awaking that morning and relishing the memory of the idyllic previous night, she decided that for the first time in her life, she wanted to shout from the rooftops.

She felt confident in the prospect of revealing her new friendship.

Why she felt so compelled to involve her mother in the matter remained unclear as she stood aside from the table, waiting patiently for the weekly grocery inspection to commence.

Ordinarily, it would have been tantamount to suicide should any member of the Bancroft clan discuss personal and confidential matters with Phyllis.

She was renowned as the estate gossip.

Nothing and no one were sacred. The local gazette struggled to keep up with the neighbourhood news as efficiently as Phyllis Baxter seemed to.

But not today.

Today, Sandra would be the one to announce the newsflash.

Sandra truly believed in her heart of hearts, in this instance, that her mother could be trusted implicitly to listen quietly, and then maybe offer a considered and thoughtful response.

It was certainly a risk, and in truth she had no idea how to begin the conversation. But the very fact that Phyllis had become immediately aware of the positive shift in her daughter's disposition, encouraged her desire to disclose recent developments.

But of course, Phyllis being Phyllis, the weekly rigmarole tried desperately to rear its pointless head as Sandra pondered the correct moment to strike.

'That label's ripped! Hope you got it cheaper! Leave it at the front. I'll use that first. What's this? Minestrone? I can't stand Minestrone! Why didn't you get chicken?'

Sandra filled the kettle and flicked the switch as her mind churned its conundrum.

'Mother…'

'No toilet rolls again! Lucky you got me double last week…'

'Mother…I need you to listen to me for a moment.'

Phyllis continued to rummage among the edibles on display.

'Pork pie? I can't abide the stuff! It's that white jelly! Why do they stick that in it?'

'Mum! Yes, you *can* abide pork pie. You *love* it! Anyway…forget the shopping for a minute. I need to speak to you. Properly for once. With you paying attention to what I'm saying without interrupting.'

Phyllis was not even hearing her daughter, let alone listening.

'Any soap? I'm all out, I think.'

Oblivious to Sandra's calling, she continued to rustle among the carrier bags.

Sandra's impatience finally got the better of her.

'MOTHER! STOP WHAT YOU'RE DOING AND JUST LISTEN TO ME!'

At last, a daughter's voice finally breached the barrier.

Phyllis ceased her inspection, turned, and stared inquisitively at Sandra, feigning an expression of puzzlement.

'You *never* shout at me! What are you shouting for? I'm not deaf, you know!'

Sandra pulled two mugs from the cabinet and made coffee.

'Mum…go into the lounge and sit down. I'll bring these in.'

'Bring those custard creams with you too, our San.'

A minute later, mother and daughter sat facing one another in the front room with drinks in hand.

Sandra suddenly felt uneasy about the imminent discussion, but she had to confide in somebody before she burst.

She gazed at her mother's wizened features, white hair and curious green eyes that studied her as if expectant of some grim revelation.

'Come on then, girl! Get on with the bugger now I'm sat here!'

Sandra smiled and sipped her coffee before taking a deep breath.

'Mum…something's happened to me…'

As ever, the reply was instant, judgemental, and unhelpful.

'You're not *pregnant*. Not at *your* age, surely? I never did believe in all this menopause crap that the quacks drone on about…'

Sandra raised her palm to interrupt.

'Mother! I'm not pregnant. Shut up and let me speak. Please.'

Phyllis nibbled on a biscuit as her mind worked overtime.

'Are you ill then?'

'NO!'

Phyllis put her lips to the rim of her mug in weary resignation that she might just have to let someone else talk for a while.

Sandra fidgeted in her armchair before recommencing.

'It's hard for me to speak about, Mum. I need you to be gentle with me. I'm a bit confused.'

'Well...you always have been a bit feeble haven't you, my girl? Now get to the point or we'll be here all blessed night!'

Sandra inhaled deeply again before unleashing the announcement.

'Okay. Mum...I've...I've met...another man.'

Phyllis swiftly swallowed a mouthful of caffeine before an enormous grin spanned her angular jawbone.

'You've done *what*, my love?'

'I've...I've been out...with...another man. Last night. We arranged a date. Out of town. A secret date, like. You know.'

Placing her mug on the lounge table, Phyllis leaned forward, her emerald eyes now wide as saucers and her expression akin to the Cheshire Cat's.

'Yeah? Honestly? How have you met him, then? You never bloody go anywhere to meet any fellas!'

The daughter remained determinedly composed as the mother became increasingly excited.

'I know, Mum...don't remind me about it! He came in the café about two months back. He took to me straight away. He eventually asked me out...and I...I said...yes...'

The momentary peace was suddenly shattered by the raucous laughter of Phyllis Baxter as she swayed back and forth in her chair, false teeth protruding ungainly until her tongue hooked them back into place.

'Bugger me, my girl! Who'd have thought it! Eh...what's he like, then? I always liked Rock Hudson. Kirk Douglas too. Well? Well?'

Sandra's confidence was building with her mother's unbridled enthusiasm in the subject becoming increasingly more vigorous as the seconds passed.

'He's...the full works. He's called Andy. Tall, dark, handsome. Blue eyes. Just...bloody *yummy*! I still can't believe he wants to go out with me.'

Phyllis cackled sarcastically.

'No! Neither can I! How old is he, then? And don't say mid-fifties like that damned husband of yours!'

158

Now it was Sandra's turn to become enthused as her mother's appetite to learn more grew beyond all previous anticipation.

'He's about forty…I think.'

Phyllis' eyes swiftly narrowed with due suspicion.

'Hang on a minute. What about his wife?'

'She left him…three years ago…'

The elderly woman swayed back and forth once again, clapping her spindly hands in appreciation of her daughter's exploits.

'Bloody hell fire Sandra, my love! Was he a bad boy to his wife back then as well, then?'

It was an innocent yet very potent question.

That particular consideration hadn't even crossed Sandra's mind until her mother threw it quite innocently into the exchange.

'No. I don't think so. He said that they just grew apart…simple as that. He's got one daughter. Annette…she's nineteen…at university.'

Phyllis sat back in her armchair and looked upon her daughter with a definitive fondness that had been largely absent in their relationship.

She had always known that Sandra was an attractive woman and that she had put a lot of effort into her ordinary life, yet somehow had received comparatively little reward in return.

Needless to say that Phyllis Baxter was very pleased to hear that something positive had happened to her solitary child at last.

She could barely conceal her smile as she enquired further.

'So, you *naughty* girl. Now you've had a date with him…what's next, then?'

Sandra shrugged her shoulders, raised her hands, and feigned an expression of bemusement.

And a tone of concern accompanied her speech.

'Mum…I haven't the foggiest idea…'

'Well…you know how he feels about you, don't you?'

'…yes…'

'So how do you feel about *him*, then? God you're hard work at times, our Sandra. And another thing…I hope you're being careful!'

159

She drained her coffee mug and set it down whilst recoiling from her mother's blatant assumption.

'Mum! We've had one date! One! In a pub! With one goodnight kiss!'

'Well…I'm just saying…that's all. Some blokes leave it all down to the women you know. Okay…carry on talking, then.'

Sandra thought carefully about revealing her true feelings about the situation.

Again, an area she had not covered in any detail until now.

'I'm…excited…scared…worried…pleased…all sorts of things, really.'

Phyllis thrust her angular visage forward once more and it evolved into a stern glare.

'What about that husband of yours?'

'What do you mean?'

'What I mean is…if you continue as you want to with this fella…things could turn sour on you, Sandra, my girl. You know what I'm saying, don't you? You've got a home and children to think about. And money in the bank. Don't forget that!'

Of course, the potential consequences of her dangerous liaison with Andy had been at the forefront of Sandra's mind for many days.

No surrounding issue was being taken lightly. But she felt that a burden had been lifted even during the five-minute confessional to her mother.

And as Sandra had perhaps justifiably expected, there was not an inkling of disapproval from Phyllis.

In fact, quite the opposite.

But then, Sandra knew somehow that her mother would support her. The whole idea was uncanny and perverse, yet ultimately satisfying.

'Like I said…I've only been out with him once, Mum. There's nothing too serious about it at the moment. It's all a bit of fun, really.'

Phyllis raised a bony forefinger and maintained her stony-faced assessment.

'*Fun*? Well, God knows you deserve some of *that*, love! But the fun will pass. Things *will* get serious…no matter how much you try and avoid it. You'll be in love before you know it. You mark my words, Sandra. Even worse than that…*he* might fall in love before *you* do! That's when you've got *real* problems!'

Sandra started to snigger as the maternal prophecy registered in her clanging conscience.

'Me? In *love*? Don't be daft, Mum. I'm nearly forty-three for lord's sake!'

Having rebuked her mother's timely and foreboding forecast, Sandra suddenly grasped an undeniable strand of truth in what the older woman meant.

She had already felt earnest sufferance of longing during Andy's absences. She had already been subjected to strong emotions concerning Andy Ratcliffe that could not be suppressed.

Phyllis Baxter was absolutely spot on.

That premise *alone* made Sandra chuckle again.

'Don't laugh about this, my girl. It's serious business. How do you feel now, sitting here? What if he phoned you tomorrow full of regret and called it all off? You might have escaped the trouble that's coming later, but I know you, Sandra. You'd be hurting like mad. You've always been a soft 'un!'

Sometimes, a supposedly loving mother could be unequivocally and impressively correct in her assumptions. Sandra Bancroft realised at that moment sitting in her mother's lounge, that her feelings for Andy indeed ran far deeper than she had previously imagined.

She hardly knew the man, yet her heartfelt passion for him was helplessly on the point of controlling her every thought and action.

Phyllis relaxed her posture and continued to sip her drink.

'Well…I can't say a deal more to you, love. You're old enough to make your own decisions. But I'll add this much. If you find happiness with this fella…then grab it with both hands whilst it's there, because I'm bleeding sure that husband of yours doesn't make you happy!'

The matriarchal truths were unrelenting as they rained down like hot hail, dousing Sandra in common sense.

Her mother's views on the issue were uncharacteristically persuasive and philosophical. It was a side of Phyllis Baxter that did not emerge very often.

In fact, Sandra didn't believe that such parental reassurance had ever been conveyed to her before now.

'You keep me posted, mind. Mum's your guardian…and Mum's the word! And Sandra…'

Phyllis left her seat, moved closer to her little girl, and placed her arms around her.

Their faces were only inches apart as a cautious whisper confirmed an undying, affirming bond.

Phyllis' green eyes seemed to moisten as she spoke, evidently fuelled by an ill-placed pride in her daughter's reluctant admissions.

'What is it, Mum?'

Phyllis placed her lips next to her daughter's ear and her voice began to quake as she whispered softly.

'Thanks for trusting me. I'm so sorry I'm a miserable old bat. You know…I do love you, Sandra. You do know that…don't you? I do love you so much.'

'Oh…Mum…'

They embraced for a few silent seconds of mutual solace.

When the moment to part intruded, mother and daughter wiped their eyes and smiled.

'I don't know Sandra, love. We're a couple of daft buggers! Come on. Let's get that shopping put away!'

An inner tranquillity had developed within Sandra as she accompanied her mother in locating the rest of the food to the cupboards.

Today, it took them only minutes when it may have taken an hour on another, customary, ordinary day.

But no day seemed ordinary for Sandra anymore.

Every rising dawn sun brought with it a new story to be discovered.

Every night-time moon gifted a new opportunity to dream.

Never more had she appreciated the love of her own mother than when they stood together in the kitchen that day.

And untypically, departure from her mother's home would be a strangely bittersweet experience for Sandra.

Phyllis had presented several entirely novel facets of her personality.

Compassion. Empathy. Encouragement.

A previously undisclosed capacity for dealing with what truly matters in life, as opposed to immersing herself among bitterness and minor, futile detail.

It was most heartening for Sandra to think that after all these years, she might finally be getting close to her own mum at long last.

Phyllis spun to face her daughter once again as she pointed to the fridge, causing anticipation of further pearls of wisdom.

But sadly, the content of the maternal offering was back to form.

'Ayup, our San! You forgot the Branston's…to go with me pork pie!'

18

ANOTHER TASTE OF PARADISE

It was Friday morning when Andy re-appeared at Turner's and discreetly positioned himself at the table in the far corner of the dining section.

Sandra's elation was barely concealed as she took him his regular order, under the distant scrutiny of Rose and Corrine. Once out of her colleagues' earshot, she neglected her need for secrecy and brazenly sat opposite him, figuring that those paying a passing interest might well be able to see, but could certainly not hear.

But Rose was now fully aware of the likely nature of the conspiracy occurring in the corner.

She wasn't overjoyed at being used to cover Sandra's tracks from the previous Tuesday evening, but when a friend asks for help, she figured that a friend could do nothing less than oblige.

It mattered little, anyhow.

Trying to avoid being part of the situation was now impossible for Rose Riley. She was effectively involved as much as Sandra. But she could keep a secret for her country, and she knew Sandra would be ever grateful for the fact.

'How have you been?' Andy grinned whilst spreading butter on a slice of brown toast.

She lost herself within him, smirking inanely as she watched him crunch.

'Good. Really…*good*! You?'

Nodding and chewing simultaneously, he lazily glanced around the room.

'Are you sure you are alright sitting here? You might get into trouble.'

Sandra chuckled and waved at Corrine, who was making a poor fist of pretending not to be fascinated by the mysterious rendezvous.

'Oh…I'm *already* in trouble, Andy. I'm right up to my bloody neck in *trouble*! Thanks to *you*!'

They laughed together.

And they weren't necessarily being careful not to make their amusement too audible for the surrounding audience.

'So…what about another date, Sandra? You up for it? Or was one night more than enough?'

She pouted and looked longingly into his eyes. She had been dying to see him for three days. Now he was sitting across from her, and it caused immense frustration that she even couldn't so much as hold his hand.

Nodding her head furiously, she beamed at him through glinting hazel eyes.

'You must be joking. I'm *desperate* for another date. I've got a lot more to discover about you. I'm quite sure of that! The other night was so…relaxing. And funny! I *loved* it. So…when are we going out again?'

Andy poured tea into his cup, never averting his gaze from hers.

'What about next Tuesday, then? Your so-called *bingo* night. Can you keep your alibi sweet, though?'

Sandra checked over to the serving counter where Rose was attending to a customer.

'Oh…yes…she'll be fine.'

'You are sure they won't mind covering you again? It's important.'

'Ask her yourself…she's behind you…over *there*!'

Nearly choking as he swallowed, Andy spun around in his seat to see Rose offering a nod of acknowledgement which was reciprocated by Andy with a gentle wave alongside a nervous smile.

'*Her*? Your workmate…over there? *She's* your alibi?'

'Yes. Don't look so worried! She's a bloody good mate, too. So be nice to her! Anyway, what about next week? When and where?'

She noticed his hand tremble as he lifted the teacup from its saucer.

'Are you alright, Andy? Adrenalin, is it? The thought of being inches away from my heavenly body!'

He rolled his eyes before sipping some tea and unsteadily setting the cup down with both hands.

165

'Meet me at the Priory again. Then after a quick drink we'll go into the square and watch a film…if you'd like to.'

Sandra wanted to squeal with absolute, inflating euphoria.

This couldn't be happening to her.

It must be happening to somebody else.

She felt she was living inside a dream.

'Wow! The *pictures*! I haven't been for *years*! How romantic of you, dear!'

Andy winked before crunching on toast again.

'Yeah…I should warn you, though…I'm a *back row* kind of guy!'

She leaned closer and whispered teasingly into his ear, purposely exhibiting a sultry grin.

'That's good…because…I'm a *back row* kind of girl!'

They laughed louder than before, just as Mick emerged from the kitchen with a tray of fresh savouries.

'*Shit*…the boss! I'd better get up and look busy!'

Sandra jumped to her feet and kissed the inside of her hand which she then playfully placed on Andy's cheek, before moving to serve a trio of teenagers that had just arrived.

It was a titanic struggle to concentrate, knowing that the man of the moment was in residence only a few yards away.

Rose exchanged a knowing look with her friend and colleague which was followed by a reluctant wry smile as they passed each other behind the serving counter.

'You're a very bad girl, Sandra Bancroft! No doubt you'll be coming to bingo again on Tuesday?' Rose whispered.

Sandra nodded shyly, chuckled, and continued to pour coffee into a filter jug.

'If that's alright with you, of course!'

Taking every opportunity that arose in the following half hour, Sandra would grab a sneaky look at Andy as he quietly read the paper in the corner.

She was not sure if she would be able to cope without seeing him until Tuesday.

How she so wanted tonight to be that next special night.

But the seemingly endless wait would only sweeten the eventual reunion.

Finally, Andy finished his snack and left the table, but not before winding past Sandra to confirm arrangements as she purposely wiped down trays near the front door.

'Tuesday, then. Seven sharp! At the pub. See you there!' he muttered as she opened the door for him.

'Thank you, sir. PLEASE do call again!'

Hanging from the doorway, Sandra watched avidly as the object of her rapidly reawakening feminine desires slowly made his way into the distance beyond her viewpoint.

He left behind only a tempting trace of his scent and a poignant, lingering image that she would cherish for the next four days.

19
THE FLICKS

'Which film do you fancy? I've brought the local paper with me so we can scan together!'

Sandra and Andy sat in the same seats of the pub lounge as they did exactly a week ago.

Seven days had passed since their mutual journey into undiscovered country had commenced.

The excitement was tangible.

The amusement never ending.

'I'm really not that bothered, Andy. It's just great to sit here and have a drink for now.'

He sat back in his chair and giggled.

'Well, if you don't want to go to the cinema, that's fine cos it'll save me a few quid!'

Responding with a playful slap on his thigh, Sandra snuggled herself closer to her handsome companion.

'You know what I mean! Let's have a gleg at that paper, then!'

A few seconds of silence elapsed as both studied the listings for the three city picture houses. She felt like a queen, revelling in the closeness, and letting his aura flow within and around her.

His very presence gave her mental strength and such diverse feelings of womanhood that had evidently been missing for the longest time.

Linking her arm within his, it was simple bliss just to have a man treat her as something very special. It was a sensation of warmth, consideration and unity that had been unwittingly eroded and eventually forgotten through the years of marriage to Stuart.

Andy averted his gaze from the page to set his full attention to her.

Her deep, doe eyes drew him inward.

Without word, she stared back in response for a few lingering seconds before eventually continuing with the search for a movie.

He, on the other hand, could not take his gaze from the beautiful woman perched beside him.

'You look great again, tonight, Sandra. Really…elegant. Perfect, in fact.'

Almost embarrassed by the complimentary critique, she felt her cheeks blush slightly.

'Well, thank you. But it's the same dress as last week. I've just thrown a cardigan over the top. That's all.'

Andy chuckled before recommencing his close inspection of her form.

'Yeah…I know. That's why I like it.'

He gazed around the room as he finished his lager. Again, the lounge was empty beyond their snug. They felt marooned together on some fantasy island where truth and reality mattered little, and whimsical opportunity was everything.

He took his chance as she concentrated on the newspaper print.

'Sandra…'

'Hang on…I can't decide. I'm not really clued up on the film world these days. It's been years since I took the kids!'

He turned in his seat to place his body directly facing hers.

'Sandra…'

Finally, her eyes resumed engagement with his.

'What is it, Andy?'

'Just…just…kiss me.'

There was little need for further deliberation.

She knew their intimacy would not be witnessed as she placed her lips onto his.

It was better this time.

More controlled; governed by premeditated will as opposed to frantic, impulsive instinct.

More sensual; far deeper and more asserting.

The union was extended; and the longing continued after they finally drew apart, flushed with the anticipation of an imminent repetition.

169

Then the overweight landlord with the drooping moustache appeared behind the counter and bellowed across to them.

'Ayup, you two! Same again, is it?'

Andy and Sandra glanced at each other before bursting into fits of giggles. He squeezed her hand under the table whilst conveying his polite reply to Walrus Face.

'No thanks, barman! Me and this gorgeous thing are off to the pictures.'

*****

They eventually departed The Priory and again linked arms against the August evening air which had adopted a milder feel than of late.

'Bus or on foot?' enquired Andy.

'Erm...we'll walk, I think. I seem to spend half my life sitting on or waiting for bloody buses!'

The city centre was not more than fifteen minutes away and the conversation on route withered the time down to about fifteen seconds. It had been an age since Sandra had been out in the town for an evening.

She felt glamorous and revered.

She felt like a woman should feel when on the arm of her man.

Approaching the inviting glass frontage of the cinema, Sandra felt a burst of irrepressible exhilaration emitting from her very core.

It was like being a teenager on a first date all over again.

Entering the crowded foyer, they joined the lengthy queue for tickets. Unreservedly, she leaned into Andy and confidently whispered in his ear.

'Hey...you...give us another kiss...*now*!'

He glanced over, but for some reason looked a little on edge.

Naturally, she withdrew slightly as her ready smile faded to match his expression.

'What? What's up, Andy? You look worried.'

To her relief, his pleasured expression resumed.

Without need for further word, as per her request, he kissed her full on the lips.

'I'm fine. Just wanted to catch you off guard…that's all!'

Immersed in contentment and sated by an inner peace, she took a firmer hold of his hand as they neared the front of the throng that clamoured for show tickets.

'Come on, then! Which film, Andy? That gruff-looking woman behind the desk is going to ask you in a minute!'

A feigned look of dismay spread across Andy's face.

'She won't ask *me*, Sandra.'

'Why not?'

'Because…*you're* paying!'

He ducked as a playful fist rose to touch his chin.

Sandra's attention temporarily wandered as she gazed around at other couples in the immediate vicinity. They too looked so happy, revelling in their joint little worlds.

And Sandra now felt a part of that scene.

The uninitiated observer would not pause to question her or Andy and their friendship. The soothing mantle of closeness that had seemed so distant to Sandra Bancroft for a lifetime was now hers to share with the rest of the world and feast upon.

Only a few short weeks ago, she could not have expected in her wildest fantasies to be in such a heavenly state of fulfilment.

Yet in that heavenly state she most certainly was.

And now her palate had accustomed itself to the flavour of loving companionship once again, she never wanted to let the feeling go.

'Yes, please?' the box-office attendant snapped.

Andy shuffled his weight from foot to foot and from his coat pocket retrieved his wallet, which he then duly dropped on the floor. Wincing as he knelt, he motioned to Sandra to select a film.

'Hurry! You pick! Quick!'

'Erm…do you fancy the new James Bond?'

'Yes. Anything is fine.'

'Two for The Living Daylights, please.'

Andy finally straightened himself up and paid.

Again, she noticed that he appeared distinctly uncomfortable, but this time did not question him as they moved to the food kiosk.

Then in an instant, his mood altered once more, and positivity resumed.

'Okay, Sandra. When you come to the pictures with me, a large popcorn is obligatory!'

She observed the paper buckets being munched upon around the foyer as people waited in line for various screens to open.

'But…they are bloody *enormous*! I'll *never* finish one!' she squealed.

'It's okay. I'll help. I love the stuff.'

Sandra perched close by Andy's side as he studied the menu behind the counter and fingered the notes in his wallet.

'Let me get these, Andy. You've paid for the movie.'

His responsive glare was stern, considerate, and authoritative.

'Not at all. It's *our* date…but it's *my* treat. No arguing. Right?'

The attendant was ready to serve the pair and presented a half-hearted smile from behind the large glass cabinet filled with goodies.

'Yes, please?'

'A large, sweet popcorn and large Pepsi, please…and the lady will have the same!'

Mouth agape, Sandra's concern at the potential size of the order just requested caused her to give him a sharp nudge in the ribs.

'You are doing *nothing* for my weight, Andy Ratcliffe! Think of all those calories! I have to watch my figure carefully these days as it is, you know!'

Grinning incessantly, he winked and gave her another kiss on the cheek as she pretended to sulk, whilst mentally licking her lips at the treats being presented on the countertop.

'Don't worry about that! You've got *me* to watch your figure now!'

Her doting brown eyes lovingly met his as he retrieved money from his wallet.

She barely noticed that his hand movements had become suddenly awkward. She watched him grasp the note, as his arm then began to visibly twitch.

Sandra quickly looked up at his face, which was now etched into a mask of utter dread.

Then a split-second passed before he rapidly moved both hands onto the counter to steady himself, in turn careering into the bags of popcorn and drinks.

Suddenly aware of the audience of dozens behind him, Andy began to fluster as Sandra watched the attendants attempt a rapid clean-up operation. Fizzy drink and yellow popcorn flakes littered the entire serving area as the crowd became congested, curious, and gradually impatient.

Backing away from the mess, Sandra tried in vain to ascertain what she had just witnessed.

Looking across the milling throng, she was then alerted to the fact that Andy had disappeared from the resulting melee. Her eyes darted from strange face to strange face.

She became immediately engulfed by concern and made her way back through the tightening crowd in a desperate search.

Now beginning to panic, she frantically scanned every single person in proximity, but to no avail. The seconds quickly evolved into passing minutes as her heart rate increased with fearful anxiety.

Yet there was no sign of him.

It was as if he had vanished into thin air.

And in turn, had apparently deserted her.

Now total bewilderment developed in tandem with her growing annoyance.

Two more circuits of the foyer elapsed, as she was jostled by the happy couples and bombarded with the sound of loud chatter which only moments earlier, was her privilege to enjoy also.

But it soon became alarmingly evident that Andy had left the premises.

And the undeniable truth revealed itself; that she was now completely alone in the heaving mass of movie-goers.

Resigning herself to the somewhat brutal and incredulous fact, she pushed open the glass door of the picture house. The warmth of the foyer was instantly eclipsed by a potent reminder of encroaching night outside.

She stood in the street, desperately looking up and down as she did so. But the evolving darkness hindered her hopes of success.

She was on her own in the middle of the city.

No protection; no guardian.

No companion; no date.

No Andy.

Suppressing her verging upset whilst checking the clock on the dome of the Council House, its large hands displayed the time to be just after eight-thirty.

They should still have been together.

Watching a film together.

Enjoying one another's company together.

Yet she suddenly, inexplicably, found herself to be totally isolated and alarmingly vulnerable.

And still longing for a sign of a man whom she craved; yet evidently had much to learn about.

Regretfully, she relented to the obvious next move.

With brimming emotion pushing her every step of the way, Sandra walked quickly to the city terminus and boarded the waiting bus which thankfully was ready to leave.

Dismayed as to why the evening had ended so unexpectedly, she huddled on the seat, now with only one longing.

To be back within the haven of Number Twelve, Orchard Road.

Where she knew she should have been all along.

*****

On entering the hallway at nine-twenty, Sandra was immediately greeted by the sight of Miss Jones who weaved in and around her ankles as a much-appreciated gesture of welcome.

Then Stuart appeared from the lounge doorway, unsurprisingly inquisitive as to the possible reasons for her premature return from the weekly bingo night.

'Oh…I didn't feel very well, love. Thought it best to come home and get to bed. Be alright tomorrow. Just tired, I think.'

'Yes. You do look a bit peaky, love. Do you want some cocoa putting on?'

Removing her shoes as she closed the front door, Sandra declined Stuart's offer and shuffled upstairs as her throat flexed with the pain of her concealed and constrained disappointment.

Slipping on her Paddington Bear nightie, she switched off the bedside lamp as her mind buckled under the unwarranted weight of confusion and an unyielding sense of loss.

Finally, back in the protective solace of home, Sandra forced her face deep into the pillow and wept quietly for someone currently beyond her reach, until slumber finally came to the rescue.

20

FOOD FOR THOUGHT

Nearly three weeks had passed since the incident at the cinema.

Twenty days since Sandra Bancroft had laid eyes on, or heard the voice of, one Andy Ratcliffe.

Yet despite the justified belief that their enticing dalliance with each other was over before it had barely begun, her thoughts never veered away from the subject for a single second.

Despite a daily three-pronged contest between anger, bafflement, and an overriding sadness, Sandra had soldiered on through the unwelcome hiatus in her recent rollercoaster ride.

Ironically, she was now secretly thankful that the routine she once considered to be so sterile, now served as a competent distraction from the encroaching realisation that her all too brief friendship with Andy was possibly at an end.

Within the walls of Number Twelve, Orchard Road, she wallowed in the mealtime arguments at the table between Daniel and Laura. She relished the prospect of pending housework. She even feigned wifely enthusiasm for Stuart's green-fingered ambitions.

She upheld the act of positivity, whilst quietly crumbling inside.

She even managed to maintain a false demeanour in front of her mother, whose unprecedented thirst for knowledge on the matter predictably knew no bounds.

Sandra told untruths to deflect her disappointment.

Phyllis Baxter continued to exhibit elation at the prospect of her daughter conducting an illicit affair.

The entire situation was now bordering on the insane.

However, the outer façade that she fought to present to the world disguised deep sufferance.

Sandra was hurting badly.

And she now felt more neglected than she ever had, even before Andy Ratcliffe walked into her life.

Not just because of his abandonment of her on that fateful and strange night, but because she had no inkling of what had happened to cause it or why he fled in such a state of distress.

Sandra had no option but to pin the blame on herself and carry on regardless.

But relentless questions burned in her heart and soul.

And yet, whilst time passed slowly and the pain of their lengthening estrangement gradually eased, the desire to have her fully warranted questions answered only seemed to grow.

Rose had been informed very briefly as to the unfolding events of the second date, but due to the hectic nature of Turner's daily business, authentic divulgence of Sandra's sorrow was given little opportunity for proper attention.

Until that is, one Tuesday evening, as closing time beckoned.

The cleaning had been accomplished.

All customers had gone for the day.

All nosey colleagues - namely Corrine - had long been despatched homeward.

Sandra sat alone in the staff room, flicking through an old copy of Woman's Own, when interrupted by Rose carrying two mugs of coffee.

'Oh…you're a star. Thanks, love. Just what the doctor ordered.'

Rose pushed the fire door ajar and lit a cigarette. The tepid air of late summer felt refreshing after a full shift in the bakery.

The moment was nigh.

And both women knew it.

Rose duly folded her arms and commenced the inquiry.

'So…what's to do then, Sandra? You heard anything from him?'

She screwed her face into an expression that signified a combination of upset and despair. A slow shake of the head confirmed her perplexed stance on the issue.

'Nothing at all. I don't know what to think, Rose. He's not been in the shop, has he? So, I presume he's had enough of things.'

Rose drew on her smoke whilst pondering the puzzle.

177

'No, San. I don't buy it. There's something else going on.'

Sandra looked up to her friend in genuine curiosity.

'What do you mean? What don't you buy? If he's fed up with me, then he's fed up with me. It's not rocket science, is it?'

Sandra could tell by her friend's mulling expression that other options were about to emerge for consideration.

'But it doesn't add up, Sandra. *He* spent time chasing *you*. You were playing along with it. Blokes don't just lose interest in a second and piss off. Christ! You haven't even been to bed with the guy! So, it's not like he's even *used* you or anything, is it? No! There's got to be something else.'

Sandra tasted her coffee as Rose continued to debate the subject with herself.

'Are you sure he's not with his missus anymore? He could be telling porkies on that score. That might explain his panic with the popcorn. Did he say anything before he left the cinema?'

Standing up to join her friend at the open fire door, Sandra stared hopefully into the blue September sky, wondering where Andy might be and what he was possibly thinking at that precise moment.

'He just…knocked everything flying and…vanished…and that's all I can tell you. I know it sounds barmy, but that's how it happened.'

Now Rose offered a look of suspicion as the cigarette hung loosely between her fingers.

'What? That's *it*? No argument? No squabble? Nothing at all to give him the hump?'

The mournful shake of the head confirmed Sandra's desperation.

'Well, San…it's a weird one and that's a fact. Maybe it's all for the best. Maybe fate has decided the end needed to come sooner than you expected. Don't beat yourself up about it. You've still got your life, you know. You've still got Stuart!'

Sandra listened dejectedly as she squinted into the lowering sun.

Her turmoil was not likely to be allayed by the notion of being thankful for what she still had.

Her cravings concentrated solely on that which had been inexplicably taken away from her.

'I know I should count myself fortunate, Rose. But…ends have been left untied. I'm left dangling, here. And…I'm finding myself feeling worried about him.'

Rose was evidently perplexed by her friend's last comment.

'*Worried*? What is there to worry about?'

'It happened here in the shop a few weeks back…when he dropped his tray. He just took off. Not a word of explanation.'

Rose stubbed out her smoke and slammed the fire door shut.

'Well…if you're *that* bothered…and I'd say it's obvious that you *are*…it looks like you're going to have to make the first move…doesn't it, Sandra, my little love bird? Anyway…coats on! Let's get home!'

Pulling her jacket from the locker, Sandra glimpsed the card with Andy's phone number written on it and considered Rose's final sermon.

Discreetly slipping the card into her pocket, she closed the locker door and helped her confidante and sometime romantic mentor secure the premises.

She declined the kind offer of a lift home and said goodnight.

She had made her mind up.

Sandra's destination was the High Street.

To the telephone kiosk.

To the same booth she had called Andy from seemingly another lifetime ago to arrange a first date.

Now as the glass door slowly enclosed her in a cocoon of uncertain privacy, she wasted little time in dialling his number.

Destiny seemingly compelled her.

With a confidence borne out of curious annoyance, she waited impatiently as the ring tone sounded.

And she waited.

And waited.

Until it became clear that no one was going to pick up.

Resigned to defeat, she reluctantly replaced the handset.

Staring forlornly beyond the scratched and graffiti smeared panes of the booth, Sandra pondered an alternative course of action.

But realistically, there was no alternative.

She had no idea of his address.

And in truth she had no intention of trying to locate his home.

She possessed only his number scrawled on a piece of card.

A number that she defiantly punched into the keypad once again.

Instinct suddenly demanded that she didn't give up.

Not just yet.

And she waited again with coin in hand, just in case.

And still she waited on the verge of a final, conclusive submission to what had seemed inevitable for a fortnight or more.

And then, a distant voice broke her from such a resolution and answered her persistence.

'Hello?'

Fumbling the coin into its slot, Sandra caught her breath before stammering in disbelief with her spare hand anchoring the rocking ship.

'Andy?'

The resulting pause was overlong and awkward.

'Andy…its Sandra. Please talk to me.'

There remained a subdued absence of speech.

Until finally, Andy Ratcliffe acknowledged her contact.

'Sandra. Jesus. What must you think? I'm so, so sorry. Please don't hold it against me.'

Alarmed by the evident distress in his tone, Sandra conveyed a few words of earnest concern.

'Andy…I still miss you…like crazy…but I don't know what to do now. We need to talk.'

More momentary hesitation ensued between the pair.

Sandra sensed sorrow on the end of the line but could not fathom its reasoning. She pushed for some kind of response.

'Andy…please…say…*something* to me. *Anything*! Tell me what I did wrong. I'm hurting so bad. Things were getting so good. What have I done to upset you?'

She thought for a moment that she heard him sob but could have been mistaken as the noise of the evening rush hour traffic hummed just beyond her kiosk.

Still listening carefully, she opted to remain deathly quiet as Andy took time to compose himself.

Yet still he maintained an odd reluctance to speak.

'Andy…please listen to me. I've got to see you again. Just to check that you're okay and we can at least part as friends. What do you say? I'm free all day tomorrow. Please, Andy. Please say yes.'

She waited…and hoped…and continued to endure the endless deliberation at the other end of the line.

Then, at last.

'Sandra. I need to talk to you, too. Can you meet me tomorrow, then? At the bandstand on Bradham Park? Two o'clock tomorrow afternoon?'

Sandra's heartbeat began to resonate with glorious anticipation once again, as the recognition of relief and success anointed her soul.

'I'll be there. Definitely. Two o' clock. I can't wait to see you.'

Despite her inner joy at being granted another audience with him, Andy's parting tone was far from upbeat.

'I'm sorry, okay? Sorry for everything. See you tomorrow. Bye!'

With that, he hung up, leaving Sandra hanging on feelings consisting of subdued expectation and a disturbing air of apprehension as to what the next day's encounter would bring.

Under an ironic shroud of solemnity, she edged dejectedly from the phone box and made her way slowly to the bus stop.

21

A REVELATION

Wednesday soon beckoned recognition. Sandra had not slept a wink, her head filled with varying fabricated possibilities concerning the impending reunion with Andy.

Performing duties at her mother's was once again a relatively painless experience which she managed to cut short with a fib about having to be at work for the dinner time rush because Turner's were short staffed.

Standing before the dress mirror in the bedroom, she examined the uniform carefully selected for the mission of mercy. Miss Jones perched on the quilt to offer a yawn of approval, her ponderous feline reflection in the glass causing Sandra a moment of mild amusement, but this was quickly erased by the overriding presumption of Andy's despondency.

Nothing made sense at that moment.

The short-lived joy they had nurtured between them had given way to a cloud of mutual doubt, confusion and maybe even, distrust.

Sandra figured that looking good for him would at least create the appropriate conveyance of her interest, even though the prospective conclusion of the meeting was still very much in the balance.

She stood with back straight and stomach pulled in, appeased by the functional yet fashionable attire on display in the glass. Dark blue jeans; black leather boots; white cotton blouse and brown leather jacket.

A casual yet appealing presentation that might just ease the tension.

It was seasonal and yet sexy. She hoped he'd be impressed.

A carefully made-up face was underscored by a silver necklace she hadn't worn for at least ten years.

It was now one-thirty; high time to embark once more on a ride into unknown territory. Locking the front door behind her, the unrest began to stir in Sandra's stomach.

Instinct informed her that this might not be an encounter to relish.

*****

Bradham Park was approximately twenty minutes on foot from Orchard Road. The shy, late September sun hung in vaguely blue skies and with the breath of wind thankfully at her heel.

She hated walking against wind. It made her eyes water, which would invariably deposit annoying streaks of mascara across each cheek before she reached her destination.

Walking through the streets of the nearby estates, she wondered if any of the hidden residents had ever experienced what she was going through at that moment.

An apparently contented housewife, now going to meet her other man in secret.

It was a truly ludicrous scenario to the casual observer, as indeed it still was to her, but Sandra supposed that it was still a welcome diversion from the tiresome existence she had known before Andy Ratcliffe came along.

The underpinning thrill that had guided her through the events of the past few weeks was that she was not in total control of her own choices.

There could be no order to the spontaneity, and this presented a wondrous liberty within her psyche.

Maybe this was an authentic sign of fate being in charge.

For the first time in her life, Sandra was beginning to entrust herself to the power of destiny.

*****

The tall, lean poplar trees of the parkland peaked over rooftops in the distance, swaying in tandem with the stiff breeze. Sandra crossed the road and made for the wrought iron entrance gates, which once were painted black and now were largely rusted.

An aging portal to future memories.

In summer, the place was a sea of welcoming greenery, which seemed to dance in unison to the tune of the elements.

The schools had recently re-opened, so surrounding activity was noticeably reduced.

In truth, Sandra felt quite drained of energy as she trod gingerly through the narrow pathway toward the centre of the park, where the playground, lake and bandstand were situated.

In fact, she felt totally alone in her world during those few fearful minutes.

The park now lay so silent and still.

Aside the odd dog walker that flitted among the distant backdrop of branches, bushes, and tree trunks, it seemed the arena was solely hers to behold.

Why Andy had deemed this location suitable for such a meeting was yet another mystery to add to the growing list.

Yet there she was, nevertheless.

And soon, she would be with him once again.

Approaching the smattering of primary-coloured swings and slides immediately brought back pleasant recollections of Daniel and Laura's infancies.

Many hours had been enjoyed in this fantasy land of fun and frolic, and the screams of childish adrenaline from long ago once again came flooding from her memory. The pure innocence of a bond developed between a mother and her babies seemed to be from another life.

A recent yet almost forgotten time.

How she wished to be blessed by their childhood once again.

If only for a day.

Adulthood was infinitely more confusing and difficult.

And sadly, far more agonising.

The circular, red-tiled roof of the bandstand honed into view as she crossed the playground and clomped over the metal footbridge that spanned a trickling stream.

Striding with more purpose now, she navigated her way around the back of the rostrum and around to the front steps, where she was greeted by the vision that she had yearned to see for so many days on end.

He sat on the wooden steps, hands clasped and elbows on knees, looking every inch the model of male perfection that she had first encountered.

Yet his altered demeanour severely detracted from his appearance.

Sandra picked up on the signals instantly.

She halted her determined march and stood quietly some metres away, until finally Andy lifted his head and glanced her way.

His forced smile foretold of imminent anguish, but for now, she resumed her step to a more sedentary pace as he stood to greet her.

His unshaven face was riddled with angst, but she was glad only to be within his grasp.

No words were exchanged as finally, they embraced.

A meaningful, close, relieving contact that once ensnared to, Sandra never wanted to depart from.

But it wasn't a sensual touch this time.

Moreover, an acknowledgement of cautious respect.

She buried her head into his shoulder and once deep within his protective shroud she felt his body tremble with emotion as she fought to hold him firm.

A distinctly diluted flush of jubilation was with Sandra Bancroft once again.

But unbeknown to her as she let their belated re-acquaintance wash over her mind and body, the return visit to wonderland would be woefully short lived.

They drew apart and locked into each other's gaze.

'God, Andy…I thought I'd never see you again.'

His smile failed to melt her apprehension further.

'I know. Shall we walk a while?'

Together they ambled from the steps of the bandstand and made for the lake, which provided a glimmering threshold for a family of swans. He gestured to the water with a large brown paper bag clutched in his spare hand.

'I've brought some bread. I like to feed the birds. Its consoling, don't you think?'

Sandra nodded and caught a furtive glance of two young mothers and their toddlers in pushchairs entering the gates of the swing park.

At the bank of the pond, Andy handed Sandra the half-loaf. Casting morsels onto the surface, she giggled nervously as the unkempt cygnets raced their more cautious parents toward the feast.

Yet despite the mildly comical relief, Sandra detected sincere misgivings about the conversation she was about to have.

Andy seemed so withdrawn and unwilling to open himself to her as before. There was no light behind his eyes. He stared vacantly at the young swans as they fought for crust.

Andy's weakened tones broke her concentration away from the birds.

'I suppose I offer you an explanation for my last performance?'

Sandra continued to throw the bread as she formed a reply.

She did not feel sufficiently entitled to demand answers, yet certainly felt she needed to understand her role in the episode.

'I was just left feeling so confused, Andy. We were having a good time. It didn't make sense. I've heard of being stood up. But I've never heard of a bloke turning up and *then* doing a disappearing act!'

He positioned himself closer to her on the lakeside and followed her gaze to the flapping, squabbling cygnets, and their contest for food.

'The thing is, Sandra…I've not been completely open with you.'

Instinct told her that he was about to unveil the anticipated mystery surrounding his wife.

Rose was right. Andy was probably not a single agent, after all.

Not the free and easy hunk of legend. So, it *was* too good to be true.

The pipedream was never destined to become an exhilarating reality. She ceased tossing the bread as a dreadful expectancy hung heavily over the scene. As though to delay the inevitable that she had presumed, Sandra opted to encourage the disclosure.

'In what way, Andy? Have you lied to me about something?'

The absence of physical contact was buttressed by the insertion of his hands into his coat pockets.

The sheet of cold steel that had quickly evolved between them was now an unavoidable barrier.

'No…no…not lied. I'd never lie to you, Sandra. I just haven't told you something that you ought to know.'

Now enveloped once again by nervous expectation, Sandra delved back into the bread bag.

She furiously tore it into strips as though to distract her from the creeping numbness of disappointment.

Her tone of voice swelled with impatience.

'So…tell me then! I'm standing here. I'm listening to you. That's why we've met…to talk? It's your wife, isn't it? You're going back to her. That's it…isn't it? You've chosen your wife over me…haven't you! That's it isn't it? Well…*isn't it*?'

Andy could feel her understandable anger attaining momentum by the second.

Yet ironically, she was way wide of the mark.

The emerging hostility was tangible between them.

But it wasn't what he wanted.

Besides, as she would soon discover, there would be no necessity or grounds for such resentment.

'Can we go to that bench? Please, Sandra. I need to sit down.'

Now parked side by side, they both stared quietly at the same indeterminable spot in the middle of the lake.

After a few moments of purposed deliberation, he continued.

'Sandra…I'll be honest with you. I don't know if this is a good idea, anymore.'

Her moistening eyes remained firmly focused on a distant point of bright water. But of course, her entire attention was centred on the words of the man sitting beside her. Her heart twitched wildly as her stomach squirmed in revulsion of the story about to be disclosed.

Once more her rightful irritation reared its head.

'Do you mean…me and you? You want to stop it…between us? Is that what you're saying to me?'

187

He was now struggling to retain his own composure.

She observed his struggle but was powerless to assist.

'No Sandra…I don't *want* to stop it. But…I think…I believe…I *must*…'

She slowly turned to faced him as he began to quiver feebly beside her, visibly moved by the ordeal of his stuttered admission.

Her defensive approach softened as his disquiet increased.

'Why? What's *happened*, Andy? Tell me what I can do to put it right?'

He met with her deep, sincere, caring brown eyes.

In them he sought sanctuary and found it with consummate ease.

Torn by a need to confess, his words were strangled by long-held fear and the knowledge that he was possibly about to destroy something wonderful.

'You *can't* do anything about it, Sandra. Nobody can.'

She shifted her position on the bench once again and moved even closer to him.

Placing her hands over his, she willed the trauma to extract itself.

'What is it, Andy? Surely, I can help you? Tell me what I need to do. It can't be that bad that we won't survive it together. Nothing is so bad in life.'

He now wrapped her hands in his and engaged fully with her undoubted and heartfelt concern. It was a massive wrench for him to summon the announcement from his very depths, but this excruciating moment was inescapable.

And had been so since the day they met.

'Sandra…I'm…I'm not what you think you see. I'm…I'm not a…not a…well man.'

She studied his face as he spoke, unsure of what he meant as he strove to enlighten her further.

'Sandra…I'm…I'm ill.'

Her initial reaction was one of feeling stunned.

She demanded more information.

'You're *ill*? I don't understand. How? In what way?'

Andy gulped with deep reservation; his voice now quaking.

'In an…incurable way.'

He looked to the water. The swans now stared back at the couple in their united curiosity. Andy battled to hold himself together.

His hands tightened around hers, as though she were his last lifeline.

His expansion on the tale was not easy listening for Sandra.

'Five years ago…I was diagnosed…with an aggressive form of…of Multiple Sclerosis.'

She looked longingly into his sapphire eyes as the wholly unexpected disclosure began to register in her mind.

She looked at the man who had completely turned her life upside down without even trying. She had held him so close to her, and the thought cursed her that now she may have to watch him fall away once more. Yet she would deflect such potential with all her womanly powers.

'But Andy. This doesn't mean your life is over. They can do things for you…surely?'

'I'm on medication, yes. But there's no cure. No remedy. I had symptoms long before the diagnosis. For years I was physically aching…all the time. So…tired…all the time…even after sleeping for hours on end. I couldn't concentrate on work, so I had to tell them the truth and leave. To the point now where I am virtually unemployable.'

She sought solace as she spectated on the chasm that had just opened between them.

'But they can treat it, surely?'

He shook his head and offered an expression mauled by desolation.

'I have injections and tablets. But they just mask the symptoms to give me back some control. They don't take the problem away.'

In disbelief and desperation, Sandra attempted to appease his distraction.

'But Andy…I've never noticed your illness. Not a sign. Not a whimper of complaint have I heard from you…ever…'

His harsh grimace tore through the fragile fabric of her hopes.

'Sandra...what you have seen of me so far is the carefully honed act of a terminally ill man. You know what they say about a joint a day keeps the doctor away? Well...it's been working for me...'

Sandra gripped his hands like a vice as she mentally juggled her mixed reactions. What he had revealed was the last thing in the world she had anticipated.

'So...what for the future? What will happen to you? And...what will happen...to us?'

He paused, averted his gaze once more and inflated his lungs, as Sandra edged into his shallow, unfeeling embrace.

'I'm already on the downturn...it's happening already. My body isn't functioning as it should. My physical reactions are unpredictable. If I panic, I lose control. And by the same token, if I lose control...I panic. I can't rely on being able to do normal, everyday stuff anymore. Sometimes, even writing my own name down on paper hurts.'

Her thoughts turned immediately to the scrawled manner of the telephone number on the florist's greeting card. But he looked so flawless to the untrained eye.

Surely this handsome beast would not succumb to an unseen enemy. He looked indestructible. He appeared so strong and sturdy in posture.

Her denial continued.

'But you seem...fine. You seem...healthy.'

His tone now became irritable and more forceful as he bolted upright on the bench, pulling himself away from her touch.

'How can you say that? Jesus Christ! After the night at the cinema? And dropping my bloody tray in the shop? I'm an accident waiting to happen, Sandra...twenty-four hours a day! But I've been stupid. I thought I could hide it from the world. The drugs and smokes helped me keep it from you. I hoped I could keep it from *everyone*. So, they'd never have to know. So, you'd never have to see it for yourself.'

A sorrowful silence draped itself around the parkland.

Bells of doom tolled subconsciously in Sandra's mind.

Andy was becoming agitated by her futile scrutiny of his wilful admission. And she was at a total loss for a solution that might even partly appease the reality of his affliction.

'But…they were…*accidents*, Andy. No more, no less. Literally just spilt milk. Not worth crying over.'

Snatching himself fully from her weakening grasp, he stood to his feet and moved to the water's edge, now brooding furiously.

'You're missing the point, Sandra! Ever since Michelle left me, I condemned myself for my illness and swore that I would never entertain another relationship. Yet…from the moment I saw you, I wanted you so badly. But I'm kidding myself…because…I have no future. *We*…have no future. I'd be fooling you. You can't give up the life you've got for me…because I won't be around long enough to go old and grey with you.'

Sandra was stunned into silence, horrified by what she had just listened to.

Her presumptions of only minutes earlier proved to be to too close for comfort.

'Your wife…Michelle? Are you saying she left you…because you were ill?'

She detected his evident upset as he faced the lake.

But he would not let her see him wallow in self-pity. A slow nod of the head affirmed his reply as his attention remained centred on the shimmering surface of the water.

In tandem with his plight, she suddenly saw the tears travelling down his face. Utter disbelief now blanketed the scene, choking the air with fate's command.

This was not how her dream was supposed to conclude.

This was not how she imagined her little chapter of happiness to play itself out.

Forcing herself upright to stand behind him, it was obvious that Andy could not bear to be seen by her.

Contorted by the agonising scalding of emotion, she found herself similarly rooted.

Yet still she was in hope of some belated reprise from the latent murk that had ruined their golden horizon.

Her desperation now manifested itself in a pointless appeal.

'But I…I…could help you if I stayed with you! We could fight the illness together, Andy. Please.'

Now he turned to her and observed the cascading tears that doused her own cheeks and blackened her eyes. She was a beautiful woman, even in absolute, helpless distress.

'*How* can you help? The fight has already been won, Sandra! I'm finished. In a few short years I'll be incapable of going to the toilet by myself! They've told me what will happen to my body. And it's all beginning to come true! And just at the moment when I…'

Now his upset descended again in accompaniment to hers.

He broke down before her under the strain of shredding remorse.

That handsome, perfect, terminally ailing man.

Overriding her own pain, Sandra still needed him to talk to her.

'When you *what*, Andy? When you *what*?'

He averted his eyes from the floor and looked up to her angelic, splintered expression.

'…when I…allowed myself to…perhaps to love again.'

A momentary lapse of response was eclipsed by a torrent of grief that released itself at will for the world to see.

Shaking as she stood inconsolable, Sandra folded her arms in total despair at the sight of the forlorn specimen by the water's edge.

She so wanted to protect him as he cowered.

Yet she knew in her heart that the gesture would be refused.

'So…are you truly telling me this is what you want…that…this is it…for us? After today…we are no more?'

He looked upon her tortured visage once more and slowly shook his head.

'What I'm saying…is that…I *want* to love you…but I can't let myself…it won't be fair…'

Retaining a fragile composure, Sandra vented a final opportunity to rescue him.

'Really? And what if...what if I said...I loved *you*? What *then*?'

Transfixed by the stoic image of her sufferance, he moved toward Sandra as his features glazed over with an almost hateful sincerity.

Her hope was now all but gone as she awaited his whispered ultimatum.

'You can't possibly love me, Sandra. We barely know each other. It's just not meant to be. I'm sorry. We should never have met. You need to go back to your family and forget me. Forget you ever knew me. Just go. Don't prolong the heartache.'

His words were callous, yet definitive.

An unwanted prophecy; yet a truthful dictum.

There was no further room for ambiguity.

The situation was clear.

It was over between them.

The one light in her life that had shone like a beacon in the previous weeks had seemingly been extinguished for good.

But she was not quite ready to relinquish her inner resilience as her tones of anguish echoed across the lake.

She stood back, now wild with rage, vexed by what destiny had deemed upon them.

What the lord had given so readily, similarly the lord now wished to take away without warning or reason.

'Go? *GO*? HOW CAN I *GO*? IS THAT ALL YOU CAN SAY TO ME? Do you really think I would turn my back on you now? When you need me most?'

Alas, her fevered expression of stumbling torment was to no avail.

He had no solution that might buffer the blow for either party.

Andy turned attention back to the surface of the water, hopeful that the intensive resonance of her frustration would soon disperse like the ripples on the lake surface.

Now fleeing the scene, she purposely did not say goodbye.

Sandra's unrestrained wailing rebounded back into her through the tree-lined avenue of the park and followed her as she staggered beyond the large, rusted iron gates, like a hundred ghosts chasing away their unwanted intruder.

She did not hesitate or dare to look back, fearing that the unattainable future she briefly and foolishly dreamed of, might just be dissolving without trace with every step she took.

Although still free-falling at speed amid a black void of personal upset, it amazed Sandra how she was able to conceal her mental and physical agony from those closest to her.

During the weeks since Bradham Park, routine had never seemed so futile and unappealing, yet her female fortitude was seemingly able to cope with the untold distress and present a semblance of complete normality to a watching world.

Rose had been vaguely informed of developments, but the subject remained virtually untouched between them. Naturally, Sandra's duties at Turner's were almost unbearable to undertake, but she soldiered through her work with a false smile and wrenching heart.

The most puzzling aspect to the entire scenario was that despite her admittedly limited knowledge of the man, Sandra believed that she had somehow known him for an eternity.

She no longer willingly accepted that Andy was ever a stranger to her. She wanted to be fully acquainted with his personality and principles and be intricately involved with his existence.

She wanted to form a fuller relationship with him that would endure through future years.

Not this brief passing of ships in the night. It was a wholly unsatisfactory, unexplored conclusion. Besides being an encounter that might even diminish from the memory banks given time.

But such wanton, reckless desires were now relegated to mere ash and dust. Packed away as the annals of a vague daydream.

She did not reveal the details of supposed rejection to her mother, instead openly preferring to discuss the finer points of food packaging and a noticeable increase in supermarket prices.

In fact, Sandra would wilfully and capably enter any discussion to avoid the subject of Andy Ratcliffe. Her mind could not allow itself to dwell on her unfulfilled needs or the lingering agony of loss.

Her efforts to disguise the immense discontentment continued successfully at home.

Housework became something to appreciate during the quieter moments alone. The accomplishment when hoovering carpets was a veritable pleasure compared to analysis of a failed and forbidden love story.

Ironing was also a useful pastime, although under such emotional duress she capably burnt holes in several expensive garments whilst simultaneously amassing a perfectly formed pile of pressed bath towels.

Her family's comings and goings were always a reliable provision for comic relief, but inside she did not feel like laughing.

And with the Christmas rush just around the corner, she dearly hoped the festivities at hand would be inclined to help her forget what had occurred in her life that summer.

Incredibly, despite other matters serving to try and interrupt domestic priority, Sandra had somehow managed to amass all the family's Christmas requirements. Wish lists had been duly submitted and the presents gradually wrapped and hidden in various nooks and crannies of the house.

It was a week before Christmas Day that Sandra had instructed Stuart to retrieve the boxes of decorations from the attic. Having obliged her request, he left the collection of baubles, tinsel garlands, and a two-piece plastic tree in the hallway for her to decide when and where to display them best.

Wednesday. The day before Christmas Eve was chosen as the appropriate time when she would attack the task.

Having confirmed arrangements for Christmas dinner with her mother in the morning, Sandra returned home with the admirable intention of decorating the lounge with festive colour.

It was an annual job usually left to the women of the house and typically attended to far earlier in the month. But Sandra didn't want anyone else to touch the job, mainly because Daniel and Stuart would invariably end up breaking far more than they managed to hang or erect.

Commencement of the chore was undeniably difficult.

The absolute emptiness of the house was torturously unpleasant to withstand, so Sandra flicked on the kitchen stereo and purposely increased the volume as she rifled through the boxes of tinsel and coloured balls.

Assembling the tree, she feathered out its branches, slotted the stem into its base and chose a discreet position in the corner of the room. Miss Jones perched nearby just in case her talents for chasing baubles were required, but of course a cat's interest in Christmas trees typically begun once the thing was up and dressed.

Then of course it became an ordainment of feline genetics to try and chew it to pieces from the bottom upwards or, better still, defy electrocution in attempting to climb to the top branches before Boxing Day.

Sandra stroked the top of Miss Jones head as she contentedly purred beside her, finally sensing that her festive spirit was being roused and employed to a positive end.

She was determined the living room would look cosy for her family's return that evening.

The tree was swiftly completed. The radio continued to emit its mix of seasonal and popular tunes as Sandra scavenged the various rooms of the abode to retrieve the hidden gifts to place underneath.

Gradually, brightly wrapped presents begun to gather at the base of the tree, awaiting their shrieking recipients in a couple of days' time.

Sandra hung tinsel from picture frames and around the mantelpiece.

Miniature and plush Santas adorned every plinth and platform of the room. It was a scene to behold, and the mildly pleasurable afternoon had passed without hindrance or diversion.

Until that is, Sandra ventured into the kitchen to make a coffee and became suddenly transfixed by thoughts of *another* world she knew of.

A place that now seemed so far back in her history.

She stared beyond the window, up to the slate-grey winter skies, naked tree limbs, and matted, damp grass of the lawn.

Then, for the first time in a while, she began to weep gently.

The potent reminder of times past echoed from the radio speakers.

The sentiment of the song was unavoidably striking, as her emotions clawed her back into dreamland.

Miss Jones sat at Sandra's feet and looked up in complete bemusement. The tears dropped into her coffee mug as she clutched it tightly to her chest.

The track playing through the stereo carried every exact sentiment she carried inside her.

China in his hand. Indeed, she was.

The anguish of denial cut like a knife into her very being.

Taking the opportunity to let regret drown her soul, she placed her mug on the draining board and gripped the edge of the sink with all her might.

Attempting to dissuade her heart from taking hold, logical thoughts paraded through her mind to mask the fantasy she still yearned for.

She hardly knew the man; it could never have been.

She rocked with tearful release; an image of elusive male perfection embellished firmly behind her eyes.

Grief convulsed the scene, painfully doubling her body at the waist and as she cried helplessly into oblivion, the song played on.

Lifting her head momentarily, Sandra listened as a distant scream for help echoed.

Then she realised, it was her own calling.

The sound of her own, fruitless desperation.

Her own heart breaking into pieces all over again, as she mentally envisioned the damning portrait of a man she once met.

And loved so briefly.

Yet achingly, a man she now wanted more that even she could ever have imagined.

But she hardly knew him.

So, it *couldn't* have been love.

Could it?

The saltwater continued to rain down, forcing her once again to succumb to her sorrow. Many weeks of hiding her pain from the world had resulted in this.

An unwelcome curtain call of tragic implication.

The maelstrom endured for minutes on end.

Until, eventually, like a vessel that had passed through stormy waters, Sandra slowly retained an even keel and settled herself.

She maintained her fast grip on the reliable, familiar work surface, unsure as to her body's response should she let go of the stable anchor.

Then with some gradual resumption of composure, she dispensed with the risk of further distress via her false, whimsical belief.

And floated back into the emotionless state of the normality she had now come to resent.

23
A VISITOR

Despite all her prior expectations, Sandra could reflect on Christmas as being an enjoyable time for the Bancrofts. The naturally upbeat festive atmosphere within Number Twelve, Orchard Road served to erase her inner dysfunction almost completely.

The holiday period brought with it a teasing premise of snow, but in the event, produced little more than a powdery coating of ice each morning.

Daniel was most disappointed of all as his long-held aspirations to build a six feet tall snowman complete with genitals in the front garden and then bombard Laura with hundreds of snowballs just for the sake of it had yet again been thwarted for the foreseeable future.

Surprisingly, Phyllis had somehow elevated her popularity and similarly, Stuart's exhibition of almost earnest hospitality knew no bounds, as he strived to make his mother-in-law feel vaguely wanted.

A laborious performance that had been honed to perfection over many years.

Thankfully for Sandra, it appeared that her mother had forgotten about her daughter's confessional of a few months earlier. Not a welcome subject for the Christmas dining table.

The New Year brought with it a fresh hope and in turn implored a strict personal resolution from Sandra.

No more accepting offers of dates from handsome strangers.

It had been a hard lesson learned.

She was glad to feel capable of finally ridding herself of the past and looking ahead to the coming year. She and Stuart had even discussed the potential destination of their summer holiday and the very realistic possibility that they would be 'child-free' for the first time.

Perhaps man and wife were seemingly united in resuming the more invigorating aspects of their twenty-year marriage, after all.

*****

January evolved seamlessly into February and the cold snap of weather would not relinquish its hold.

Turner's seemed to be relatively busy, and Mick had managed to offset some warranted pre-Christmas worries about the increase in rent for the premises.

His mood had improved dramatically since the New Year, so Rose and Sandra could only presume between them that an upturn in his financial situation must be the cause.

However, as it soon transpired, Corrine had played the major part in Mick's more enthused approach to the business. Three weeks into February, she had been given notice that her services would no longer be required.

Her day of departure was one of mixed feelings. Corrine seemed disappointed yet fully understanding that Mick had been fair and honest in dealing with her.

Sadly, as the last to be employed, she was by default, selected as first and only casualty for redundancy. In truth, catering was not really where her talents lay.

In tandem with Corrine's farewell, Rose and Sandra were awarded a marginal pay increase to encourage their appetite to working a few extra hours per week.

In short, Wednesday was no longer Sandra's day off.

In all, the first two months of the year were comparatively satisfying for Sandra Bancroft. The utter disorientation she had experienced - and had admittedly encouraged - had seemingly been relegated firmly to the archives of history.

Or so she thought.

Occasionally during the working day, she would casually glance to the scene outside beyond the window and study the various passers-by just in case anyone familiar happened to be in the frame.

Yet slowly but surely as Nineteen-Eighty-Eight gained maturity, the gradual resumption of her revised routine was deemed complete.

201

But of course, fate always had other plans.

Sandra's even keel was about to be swayed once more.

The long overdue return of her emotional wellbeing was soon to be shattered.

*****

March was in its infancy.

It was an ordinary week-day morning at Turner's.

A steady stream of customers had kept the shop active and due to the recent streamlining of the workforce, Sandra now always found tasks to attend to that made her shift pass in the blink of an eye.

She was in the kitchen helping Mick roll pastry when a bemused looking Rose entered through the swing door. Her face was ashen as she stared at Sandra, beckoning her with a curled forefinger.

'What's up, Rose? You look like you've seen a ghost!'

She gestured with her hand for Sandra to come closer.

'I think I have, San! Look through the porthole. The woman at the counter.'

Mick looked up from his rolling pin, ever ready with the standard gaffer's quip.

'Oh…the woman that needs serving, you mean? Whilst you two are hiding in here, you mean?'

Confused, Sandra ignored the inevitable mocking contribution of the boss and peered through the circle of glass as she was instructed.

'What am I looking at, Rose? Yes…there's a woman waiting…so what?'

Adopting a sullen tone of suspicion, Rose whispered in her ear.

'Because…she's just asked to see *you*! Don't you recognise her?'

Sandra looked through the small round pane once again.

She tried to place the young woman's face, which was partially concealed by a fashionable black fur hat. She was certainly familiar from somewhere, but her mind toiled to fit the features to some episode of the past.

202

She was not a regular customer, but Rose had evidently remembered her. Tilting her head to look at her friend once more, Sandra expressed a need for further assistance in the guessing game.

'Well, I don't think I know her. Has she been here before, then?'

Now doubting her own mind, Rose pulled Sandra out of the way and reaffirmed her suspicions. Drawing away once again, she straightened up, her face beaming with anticipation.

'It's his *daughter*, isn't it? Can't you remember her? I know it's a few months back, but bloody hell!'

Sandra felt her legs begin to tremble as she quickly looked through the porthole to confirm Rose's deduction.

It was indeed.

It was Annette.

Sandra suddenly became very defensive as she looked blankly at Mick and Rose.

'You say she wants to see *me*? What on Earth for?'

'How the beggar should I know? Just get out there and find out, will you! I'll carry on in here! Go on!' blustered Rose.

Sandra's breathing became slightly laboured as she wiped her floured hands on a damp tea towel. Gingerly pushing the kitchen door aside, she made her way tentatively to the counter where Annette was standing.

The attractive young woman was distracted by the passing traffic and pedestrians beyond the front window and did not sense Sandra's approach.

Swallowing her trepidation and summoning an appropriate word of re-acquaintance, Sandra offered a hand of greeting.

'Hello? It's Annette, isn't it? You…you wanted to…speak to me?'

The young woman turned and smiled with a hint of affection.

She reminded Sandra so much of Laura. Her posture, colouring and femininity were very similar.

Annette's expression was friendly enough, but the motives for such an unexpected visit were somewhat concerning.

Her tone was respectful yet ordered in its mission.

'Hello. Pleased to meet you again, Sandra. I'm sorry to just drop in like this. I'm not even sure I should be here at all. Can I talk to you? If it's convenient? Somewhere…a little more private? Just for a few minutes. Please?'

Intrigued by the visit, Sandra saw no reason to refuse the request and duly obtained permission for half an hour's leave before venturing into the staff room for her coat.

A quick inspection in the cracked toilet mirror offered a vaguely passable reflection of a woman approaching middle-age but there was no time for make-up. As she left the shop, Rose offered a hopeful wave in concerned anticipation of her friend's imminent discussion.

Sandra joined Andy's daughter on the pavement and rapidly buttoned up her coat as the late winter sun carried a biting breeze. Still a little uncomfortable with the scenario, Sandra opted to let the younger woman lead the way.

'Where did you want to go and talk?'

She simply stared at Sandra before nodding her head toward the shopping precinct.

'We can just sit down on a bench in the marketplace if you like. It's a nice enough morning. I just didn't think you'd want to talk in the shop.'

Sandra couldn't immediately ascertain what there could be to discuss but followed the scent of intrigue. The two finally positioned themselves on a seat in the middle of the High Street.

Sandra suddenly felt apprehensive about the reasons for Annette's presence. She could think of only one subject that would be of common interest and wasted little time in augmenting the conversation.

'I suppose…this is about your dad…is it?'

Annette nodded, squinting into the hazy, gently warming sunshine.

Again, Sandra sensed the onus was on her to speak, but her line of questioning felt so inept and out of place.

'So…how is your father? Is he doing okay?'

Annette turned at the waist to face Sandra.

Her face exhibited a hint of worry, as though something bad had happened. Holding her own reservations within, Sandra decided to be patient and allow Annette to respond in her own time.

'Well...he's been better...obviously. But I had to see you. Just before Christmas...he told me about what happened between the both of you...'

Sandra allowed her gaze to wander among the throng of shoppers. She felt slightly embarrassed.

The negligible length of time her friendship with Andy had endured was almost farcical considering the immense shockwaves it had implemented in her mindset. Sandra offered a strand of humour.

'Yes...very short but very sweet, wasn't it?'

The women looked into each other's eyes in a game of mutual assessment.

Annette's tone became more sincere and perhaps mildly emotional.

'Dad...he misses you, you know, Sandra. Every single day. He's not been the same person since he stopped seeing you. He's become...well...down and depressed. He feels like a failure. He feels he's treated you badly.'

Sandra was now confused.

This was nowhere near what she had predicted hearing.

Her reply was fuelled by curiosity to know more, and a need to reinforce her position.

'But Annette...your father told me to go away and forget about him! Do you know how hard that was for me? It took a long time to get him out of my head. Even though we only knew each other for a very short while, he turned my world upside down. And even now... I've only just got my mind right again, to be honest.'

Annette's manner softened further, as though to try and draw Sandra into her concerns and create a more sympathetic approach.

'He's often mentioned you. You might not believe this, but you were the only woman he took an interest in since...well...'

'Since your mother left him?' prompted Sandra, curtly.

Annette nodded guiltily and let her focus settle on the distracting activity that bustled around the pair. The thought crossed Sandra's mind that she may be verging into business that wasn't strictly hers but figured that as Annette had come to talk to her then she had the right to venture opinion.

Honesty in the arena was surely paramount now.

'Is it true, then? Did you father's illness cause the end of your parents' marriage?'

It was a difficult subject, but Sandra felt assured that the moment was right to ask such questions.

Annette sighed as she contemplated her reply.

'Mum couldn't handle the fact that dad was ill. She knew that eventually…he'd need caring for. So…yes…off she went.'

Abject disbelief descended, temporarily stunting the conversation.

After the hurt he'd unwittingly caused her, Sandra now felt herself unavoidably jumping to Andy's defence.

'But…that's so *selfish*…so…uncaring…so callous.'

'Yes. It is. But that's my mother for you. It tore Dad's heart out. He was so low for months. But I made sure he was looking after himself at home. You know, eating and so on. Making his appointments okay. Getting his treatment every week. But he became a recluse. He needed to get out more and socialise, rather than give up and let the MS gradually take over.'

The dialogue was refreshingly earnest and surprisingly invigorating for Sandra to be a part of. So many issues that had burned within her were now being placed on the table to be ironed out.

'Annette…I must be honest. I don't know much about the illness or what it does. How bad will your father's condition become?'

Annette pondered once more, giving due consideration to her answers. It was an emotive subject that she had learned to live with for several years. Sandra admired her for appearing so strong in the face of her father's adversity. She was a daughter to be proud of.

Yet an overriding sensation loomed.

It was obvious that Annette had barely discussed the subject of her father's condition with anyone, let alone a practical stranger such as Sandra.

Yet she relayed the daunting scenario with stoicism.

'Well…the doctors have said that he may well live for another twenty years. But it's the most rampant form of the illness. The disease gradually destroys the nervous system. It causes lack of coordination and numbness in the limbs. He's so tired all the time. He can't be bothered to even get out of bed some days.'

Sandra diverted her attention from the pained explanation of the young woman sitting beside her.

She chose to stare blankly at the myriad of people, flitting in and out of shops, talking in groups and walking to varying, untold destinations.

Her mind was once more filled with endearing visions of Andy Ratcliffe. It seemed so surreal to be seated next to his daughter, discussing *his* future. Yet Annette was pleasant company, and her ready divulgence was a most welcome tonic.

Then the crux dawned.

Brass tacks time was upon the discussion.

'I'm still not clear, though. Why have you come to the shop to see me, today?'

Annette played nervously with her hands whilst summoning an effective answer to Sandra's justified and genuine query.

She stammered a response as tears begun to well in her eyes, which widened with the words of her wishful plea.

'I…I hoped that…perhaps…maybe…despite everything…that you might like to visit him? At his home…just as a friend? You were the only one that gave him any hope, Sandra. He can be a morose sod at times…but you brought him out of all that. I think he still wants you to be around him. But he can't admit it to me…or even himself. He's too bloody stubborn for that.'

The implication of the request suddenly hit Sandra between the eyes.

She smiled warmly at Annette's concern.

'Your father…he doesn't know you're here…does he? You didn't tell him you were coming to see me…did you?'

She shook her head, anticipating a negative and possibly angered reaction from Sandra. But that was not Sandra's inclination.

The way she saw things, she had suffered a great loss when Andy dismissed their friendship as unworkable.

His subsequent absence had proved excruciating.

Yet Annette was offering her a chance to reclaim that special something back.

A chance to persuade Andy all over again.

An opportunity to try and return his confidence in their friendship at the very least.

A hiatus in the conversation allowed both women some valuable time to analyse the proposition. Yet it didn't seem correct to arrange a visit to Andy's house without his knowledge. It wouldn't be fair to him. It might not be what he wanted.

Yet as the seconds elapsed, the idea became infinitely more appealing. Maybe it *would* be entirely fair if she should just turn up at his home and see him again.

Perhaps that *would* be the re-ignition of the mutual affection they had reluctantly extinguished. Sandra's self-doubt quickly evolved into a brewing enthusiasm.

'But…what if your father doesn't *want* to see me again? What if he decides it's the worst thing that could happen to him…instead of the *best* thing?'

Annette presented her watery gaze and looked with sincerity into Sandra's eyes as she spoke. Determined in her quest, she willed the conclusion to be a positive one.

'Sandra…the worst thing is *already* happening to him, isn't it? I'm looking at the best thing in his life…right now…right here…sitting next to me. Trust me. Just be a friend. Be that friend that he needs most of all in the world.'

It was a shock to the system for sure, but also a reviving shot for dulled senses. It occurred to Sandra that despite her utmost efforts, she couldn't fully let go of her memories.

They still resided within her heart. And this was potentially a chance to create some more.

The premise of seeing Andy again was too tempting to dismiss out of hand. It needed serious thought.

He sounded isolated and alone.

He certainly sounded like he secretly wished to see Sandra again.

So, perhaps it would be understandable to presume that her own whim for a reunion was mutual. Her mind ploughed the quandary over and over, until she reached a decision.

To hell with resolutions; there's always next New Year.

Annette's face expressed sheer joy as she reached into her handbag and pulled out a sheet of notepaper. Excitedly handing it to Sandra, she gripped the elder woman's hands as she did so.

'This is Dad's home address. There's nothing more I can ask of you, Sandra. But...please give it some thought. I haven't made this gesture lightly. You are someone special in his life. Besides me, he's got no one else. And I guarantee you one thing. Should you decide to go and visit him...it won't be the wrong decision.'

Sandra nodded in thoughtful contemplation of her words as Andy's little girl concluded the conference.

'I'd better let you get back to work, hadn't I?'

Annette rose to her feet, evidently now carrying a renewed feeling of accomplishment as she dabbed her eyes with a tissue.

Sandra also forced herself upward, carefully clutching the piece of paper. She placed a hand on the younger woman's shoulder who promptly turned to face her with a light of hopeful expectation in her drying eyes.

'Annette...'

The pain of a loving daughter was all too obvious as she bit her lower lip.

'…thank you for coming to see me. It means a lot. Your father…he does still mean a lot. Even though we barely got to know one another. I never forgot about him you know.'

A gentle yet meaningful embrace signified the end of the unplanned rendezvous.

As Annette gradually disappeared into the crowd, Sandra folded the piece of paper and placed it in her coat pocket, before making her way back to Turner's.

24

ABSENCE AND THE HEART

As was the case with all of Sandra's stringent routines, anything out of the ordinary that needed attention usually had to be planned to fit in with the arrangements already in place.

Having deliberated on the issue in her mind a thousand times over the following few days, Sandra finally decided that she would see Andy again.

Only it would have to be a covert visit, on a Wednesday, after she had tended to her ever-demanding mother.

Mick Turner wasn't overly elated to discover that she needed to take the day off and leave the bakery under-manned, but that was the position he had encouraged having dispensed with Corrine's services.

Besides which, in terms of priorities, Turner's was way down Sandra's list.

It was mid-March on the morning in question. Phyllis Baxter's every word completely failed to register with Sandra, whose concentration firmly centred round the mission planned for afterwards.

Even her mother's ritual complaints about the shopping items floated straight over Sandra's head.

Nothing could disperse her buoyancy.

She was elated inside.

Dreamland awaited her entrance once again.

As before, she had been careful to avoid arousing suspicion, which had been an unhinging but unavoidable factor in her brief relationship with Andy. But once back at home, the only witness to her hurried preparation was Miss Jones.

With the customary presentation of clothing and cosmetics being given final approval, she finally left Orchard Road to catch the bus for the second time that day, once more with a definitive spring in her step.

Having checked on the street map where she should be roughly headed, Sandra was surprised to discover that Andy's address - Ninety-

Four, Trafalgar Gardens - was only a stone's throw from the Priory public house, where their one and a half dates had occurred.

However, as the bus journeyed toward the city centre, her initial enthusiasm for the venture began to dissipate, leaving her requiring deep breaths of reconsideration once departing the bus and crossing the road.

Her gaze wandered back along the pavement to the shelter where they had first kissed.

The memory of that moment of stolen tenderness brought butterflies back to her stomach and served to lighten her mood in readiness to face the unknown.

However, there was a potential flaw in her plan that might just be detrimental to its success.

She had not telephoned Andy to say she was going to see him.

He had no idea that Sandra Bancroft was about to descend into his life once again.

It would be a surprise for him, for sure.

Hopefully, a surprise of the most pleasant kind.

The housing estate behind the pub and beyond was a basic mix of ex-council homes and blocks of flats. Not a particularly endearing area on the eye, its grave image made Sandra thankful of her own relatively upmarket abode.

Having mentally recalled the layout from the map, she finally located Trafalgar Gardens with trepidation. Second thoughts emerged that battled for prominence with subsequent and even more unnerving third thoughts.

But if Annette's forecast were to prove accurate, Andy would be delighted to see her again.

Sandra walked the pavement slowly, checking each house number as she counted them down, before finally stopping outside the desired residence.

The frontage of number Ninety-Four stood behind a partly broken brick wall, on which was perched an empty beer bottle and greasy food carton, both of which she presumed did not belonging to the occupant.

As a red brick end-terrace, the appearance of the house could best be described as uninspiring. Blistered brown paint adorned the front door and weeds were being nurtured around the doorstep for some future use. She carefully scanned the front windows, but blinds adequately concealed the picture within.

Once again checking the piece of paper given to her by Annette, Sandra confirmed she was at the correct place and briefly glanced up and down the street for potential witnesses to her arrival.

Finally, she stepped nervously up to the door and employed three audible, firm, concise knocks, before moving back slightly to scrutinise the unyielding front window for any sign of a response.

Greeted by twenty seconds of absolute nothingness, Sandra repeated the act on the front door, this time applying a little more pressure with her knuckles as they rapped the weatherworn wood.

Without a viewing porthole, it was impossible to establish if any movement was occurring in the hallway.

All Sandra could do, was announce her presence…and wait.

And still she waited, until her sixth sense suddenly detected a life form within.

When the door finally peeled away from its splintered frame, Sandra felt herself inflate with anticipation as she prepared for a return to wonderland.

Back to that world she had tasted all too briefly; that place where Andy had come from and where she so wanted to be again.

His initial suspicion as to the identity of the caller was replaced by a smile of such intensity and masculine power, that any doubts she may have harboured regarding the visit readily evaporated.

Leaning through the gap in the door, he partly emerged into the daylight and appreciatively looked her over for a few, uncertain seconds.

Andy and Sandra grinned at one another. It was a simple gesture of compassion that instantly anointed any previous hurt. No words were necessary to convey the mutual appreciation of their overdue re-acquaintance.

213

But of course, as was Andy's way, humour was readily let loose from his lips to douse the formality.

'Hello stranger. You could have said you were coming. I'd have hoovered up!'

Sandra's eyes narrowed with pleasure.

It was enough for her just to behold the image of the man she had dearly missed for so many weeks.

For her, the moment was one of sheer, diluting relief.

Relief that not only was he pleased to see her, but she also found herself immediately enraptured to be in his company once again.

And still his supply of natural and ready wit, continued.

'You'll have to take your turn, though. I've got another woman upstairs. Give me five minutes to get rid of her through the back door…then you can come in. Okay?'

Sandra giggled like a lovelorn adolescent.

She felt confident to unleash the words that she thought would never get the chance to speak again.

'It's really, *really* good to see you. How are you doing?'

The question seemed to puzzle him for a second or two. Whilst intended as a form of greeting, it was also a genuine enquiry as to his health. He pushed open the door fully and retreated awkwardly.

What he revealed was alarming and somehow totally misplaced.

He leaned heavily on the metal walking stick and held out his other hand for her to inspect the complete display. It was a difficult concept for Sandra to comprehend and her inner reaction was considerably guarded.

A fact betrayed by her astounded expression.

Thankfully, Andy relieved the uneasiness of the disclosure.

'Well, I've still got both legs…but I think one of them wants to retire early!'

She wanted to laugh along with the joke.

But there was nothing remotely amusing about seeing him utilising such a contraption, however commonplace or basic.

Again, he attempted to divert her understandable surprise.

'Well…are you coming in…or do you want to stand outside, and I'll bring the teapot out to you?'

Entering the hallway, Sandra closed the door behind her and followed Andy as he limped into the kitchen.

The ramshackle appearance of the house's exterior belied the clean, contemporary design inside.

'Wow…this is nice! Did *you* decorate it?'

He turned to her with a cheeky smile.

'Erm…not lately! No…it was done just before my diagnosis. Perhaps four years ago. Bit tatty now, though. Could do with a facelift, really. Do you want tea or coffee? Or something stronger?'

Sandra examined the sleek lines and colour of the kitchen and perched herself on one of the bar stools.

'I'll have a coffee, please. One sugar.'

It was such a strange situation. They were almost like two friends that had known one another for years. Yet of course, the complete opposite was true. But for all the emotive unpleasantness that had transpired, neither party seemed willing to dwell on the past.

The atmosphere was relentlessly easy and relaxed.

Sandra felt so comfortable in his company. It brought back memories of first seeing him at Turner's.

He had placed a spell on her at first sight.

And despite her efforts to break free from that spell, she was still well and truly under its control.

Andy leaned against the worktop and looked at her as the kettle began to boil.

'You look great, Sandra. How's life treating you? The family all okay?'

She nodded, not wanting to entice the subject of her loved ones into the arena.

It seemed wholly inappropriate, somehow.

Yet she was touched by his obviously genuine concern.

'And you, my sweet lady? How is life treating you?'

Sandra swallowed a hard lump of reservation as she placed her handbag in front of her on the breakfast bar.

She could only ever be earnest with him.

Covering the truth was pointless.

'I am okay, now. But I wasn't, no. I was very upset for a while. Christmas was particularly hard. But you know, slowly…I suppose…I got over you…eventually.'

He smirked that smirk again.

The Andy Ratcliffe forerunner to a jovial quip.

'I don't believe you! *Nobody* ever gets over *me*! Just ask the ex!'

Sandra suspected that laughter would be the correct reaction, but Andy's words were tinged with a sadness that she could not ignore.

Perhaps she was not yet ready for his frivolity.

After all, the blunt culmination to their friendship had scarred her slightly.

A fact he duly recognised.

'I wasn't happy about how I handled things myself, Sandra. To spurn you…so thoughtlessly, like that. But as you can see…*I'm* the one with the problem…not you. I was putting on a good act which was bound to fail eventually. But I've thought about you every day since. Knowing I'd let go of something very special hurt me. But also knowing that letting you go was the only solution.'

He placed a mug of coffee onto a coaster in front of her.

'You didn't have to hide anything from me, you know. I am a grown woman!'

'Oh yes…I know! Biscuit? Rich Tea? Arrowroot?'

Now she conceded to the need for mirth.

'No expense spared, then? The most tasteless biscuits in the entire world saved up just for *me*.

A hearty, raucous, relieving expression of gratitude for their reunion took a while to subside. Once over her prolonged attack of the giggles, she wiped her eyes and focused on him once again as he settled on the stool next to hers.

'I'm impressed by this place, Andy. Its…lovely…smart…homely. You seem…well…pretty settled.'

He slurped his drink whilst letting his azure gaze pierce into her.

'I've missed you, Sandra. I really can't believe you're here. How did you find me?'

Her face concentrated briefly on the steaming mug before her, not knowing if it was a good idea to unveil the secret messenger that had descended a fortnight earlier.

Her uncertainty over the revelation was quickly diminished by Andy's intuition.

'Don't tell me. *Annette*. It was, wasn't it? Has she been telling you how sorry for myself I've been feeling lately?'

Sandra placed a hand over Andy's and gently squeezed.

It crucified her to think of him all alone in his battle.

'Well, Andy…have you been feeling sorry for yourself?'

He nodded before indulging in another sip of coffee.

'I've been…down, yes…and up…you know. What else did she say to you?'

The intensity burned from her hazel eyes into his, as the conviction of reconciliation washed over them.

'She told me you needed a friend. And that I was the friend you needed most.'

He smiled and sampled more of his drink.

She noticed his hand shaking as he lifted the mug to his mouth.

'That girl of mine! I don't know. She never fails to show her concern. I'm spoiled by her. I really am. She's a great kid. I must remember to thank her when she visits again.'

Once more his eyes bore into Sandra, and she embraced the acute sensation. His expression adopted a stern edge.

'But she's right, Sandra. I *do* need you. I'm so glad you're here. Life has been pretty empty since I…well…since...'

She placed a forefinger to his lips, which felt soft and tender to the touch.

'Don't talk about it, Andy. This is our effort to make amends. A chance for a new start. Let's be happy. As friends.'

Transfixed by her naturally striking appearance, he wallowed in the proximity of the woman sitting beside him, which acted as a soothing balm to his intermittent reminders of physical affliction.

An uneasy silence prevailed momentarily.

It was high time for humour once again.

'Well, I don't know about you…but I think I did pretty well just now…even if I do say so myself!'

She observed him, both bemused and amused by his commentary.

'Oh really? In what way?'

'Well…I gave you your drink without managing to throw it around the room first, didn't I?'

Sandra uttered a minor chuckle, reflecting on Andy's self-deprecating attitude.

It was admirable that he could mock his own increasing frailty.

She glanced piteously at the ugly walking stick propped inappropriately against the fridge door. Mixed emotions cursed the moment once more.

It was certainly not the suitable time to convey pity, but she could not help but feel so sorry for the vague future of the gorgeous man perched before her.

Life just wasn't fair.

Destiny's hand had not been even with him.

And as he continued to make her laugh, she felt like holding him forever and crying for his cause. Her contrary feelings were interruptive and would not abate.

They clouded her judgement, whilst ironically to Andy, everything in his life had gradually attained sudden clarity.

There was perhaps a comfort to be gleaned from some other unseen force taking control of one's life, but even as he appeared quite relaxed about what might lie on his horizon, Sandra viewed the situation with reluctance and had natural misgivings.

He offered to show her more of the house, which she gladly accepted and guided his arm to steady his step. His aftershave affected her all over again.

Even though only slightly touching his body, the connection served to fire her senses, whilst the regularity of his voice provided instant assurance.

Once in the lounge, she helped him settle onto the settee as he looked upon her endearingly.

'Well…now you can finally see where I spend my days! Trapped in this castle of pleasure! Well…I go for injections twice a month now, but hospitals aren't much fun really, are they?'

Positioning herself next to him on the black leather sofa, Sandra smiled at the continuing jests as she observed the modern furniture and stylish décor.

'Does Annette not live here with you, then?'

'Oh, no…well…not full time, anyway. She stays a couple of nights when I must go for my steroid boosters. Other times she stops at her boyfriend's place. He's got his own flat somewhere on the other side of the city. Mind you, from what she told me at the weekend, I don't think I'll be here much longer.'

Sandra thought she heard him correctly but needed confirmation.

'Why do you say that?'

'Because apparently, Michelle wants to sell up and split the country! She needs the money to emigrate with her new fella…according to Annette, anyway. I don't think I'll be hearing it from the horse's mouth.'

Sandra became roused at the latest example of self-indulgent behaviour from Andy's ex-wife.

'So…what about *you*? What say do you have in the matter? Has she spoken to you about this?'

His expression was blank and the tone gracefully accepting.

'Not yet. But I don't get a say. It's *her* house! Not mine. I'll eventually need respite care which she says she'll fund from the proceeds of the sale, but as for a home of my own…it could be a thing of the past pretty soon.'

Sandra's vexation bubbled within as she tried to create a supportive argument for him.

'But you're still a fit man! You don't *need* care! She can't do this to you, Andy!'

He looked forlornly at Sandra.

This once strong man, whose faith in fighting fate's ordainment was severely diminished.

'She *can*…and she *will*. And I don't really care, anymore. It all seems so…so secondary…so meagre. Anyway, listen…let's forget about all the depressing shit. I've got an idea! Why don't you let me cook dinner for you one night? Bus it here…I'll get you a cab back home. Bingo night next week sounds good! The faithful old Tuesday night alibi! Sort of a…I don't know…a reunion date with a difference?'

Sandra thought about the offer for a second.

And a second was all it took to be convinced into accepting the invitation.

'Yes. Okay. Great! But just one thing. Can I have my toast separate from my beans, so it doesn't go soggy?'

She started to chuckle at her own sarcasm as he adopted a look of feigned offence. Moving gingerly across her, he placed both arms around her shoulders and whispered softly.

'Listen to me, you…ravishing thing, you. I can cook, actually…and it'll knock your socks off! And another thing, what's your favourite tipple when you're in the mood?'

Her eyes widened in enticed response to his implication.

'In the mood for what, may I ask? Don't forget…I'm a respectable woman!'

'Oh, we'll soon knock *that* out of you! I meant …when in the mood for a nice evening, of course!'

More laughter resonated as she leaned warmly into his embrace.

'Oh…wine with dinner, of course. White and sweet. Cheap and effective!'

220

He drew away and winked at her as she continued to writhe with amusement on the settee.

'Brilliant! Next Tuesday, then! Here. Seven. Okay?'

Nodding with excitement, she winked back.

'By the way. Just one thing, Andy. You know you said the food will knock my socks off?'

He nodded in full expectation of further culinary abuse.

'Well…does this mean I have to wear socks? Because…if it's all the same to you…I'd much rather wear stockings…'

The simultaneous reaction of amusement soon ceased.

The unspoken expectations of their arrangement now proved almost too much.

He leaned into her as she welcomed his advance.

The kiss lingered and left them both wanting more.

But not now.

Now was only to savour the renewal of companionship.

Overseeing her departure, Andy hung excitedly from the door frame as she buttoned up her coat, grinning inanely.

'Next Tuesday, then.' she smirked, knowingly.

'Oh yes, Sandra. Can't…bloody…wait.'

Then, with a final peck on his unshaven cheek, she embarked homeward, away from her temporary island paradise.

Leaving Trafalgar Gardens, Sandra felt like a new woman all over again.

Consequence mattered little, now.

The hole that had developed in her life was now filled once more by a man who she would give anything to make well again.

And maybe in another life, another place, another time, perhaps aspire to make him hers entirely.

25

A FRIEND INDEED

'No chance! Bloody hell fire, Sandra! Don't you think you sailed a bit close to the wind last year with this? Mates or not, I'm not sure I want to be a part of things again.'

Rose's prickly reaction to the latest revelation caught Sandra off guard. Evidently, her presumptions had been woefully misaligned.

And Rose Riley wasn't finished with the lecture, either.

'You've left it bloody late to rope me into this! I thought you'd got over the need for all this romantic tripe! I thought you were relieved when it finished and were content to stick with the bloke you've already had for twenty years! Remember him, do you? Your husband?'

It was five-twenty p.m. on Monday afternoon.

Nearly closing time at Turner's.

Sandra sat at the table in the staff room as Rose let her cigarette smoke escape from the rear fire door.

Not unlike a juvenile in the throes of puppy love, she explained to her elder confidante the positives of rejuvenating the recent past.

'I know, Rose…I know. And meant what I said about loving Stuart. But things have changed…I feel…*different*, now. I can't put my finger on why.'

Drawing on her nicotine in frustration, Rose sighed as she exhaled more fumes into the air.

'Sandra! Listen to yourself, will you? You hardly bloody *know* the guy! What can you tell me about him? Just one thing. Okay. So, he's gorgeous. Okay…so he's officially on the market. And he's not very well! It's a powder keg waiting to explode in your face, Sandra! And I for one won't back you up when it does!'

Sandra felt deflated by Rose's attitude. Mainly because she knew that her friend was speaking the undeniable, exacting truth.

She gazed at the table-top, struggling for further words that might make the proposition sound even mildly palatable.

But she couldn't summon any and so resorted to begging for an alibi.

'Just one more time, please. For me. One last favour for tomorrow night. For your best mate. What do you say?'

Lighting another cigarette out of irritation, the older woman looked disapprovingly at her winsome younger colleague.

It was very hard to say no to Sandra Bancroft.

And whilst professing concerns for her headstrong plan to meet the man of her daydreams again, Rose also concealed a pang of envy about the fact that Sandra had the courage to follow her desires, as opposed to quietly conforming to wifely duty for the rest of her days.

But of course, as her mentor and adoptive beacon of morality, she would never admit such sentiment to the over eager forty-two-year-old.

She observed her friend's gloomy, doe-eyed expression and began to soften.

'You know what you are? You…are a frigging nuisance, Sandra Bancroft! But I've noticed you seem happier of late. Ever since his daughter appeared the other week.'

Leaning on her elbows, Sandra gazed into space, with a childish grin gradually emerging and eventually spanning from ear to ear.

'I think it's because…I missed him coming in the shop. But I only appreciated him when he wasn't around. He's special, Rose. I can't just forget about him. I tried so hard to pretend we never met…but it didn't work.'

Rose tossed her half-finished cigarette butt onto the back yard and pulled the fire door shut. She perched opposite Sandra, trying in vain to make her friend see some common sense beyond the thrill of her idealistic whim.

'I'm terrified things will go pear shaped on you, San. If Stuart ever found out…you'd destroy him. He adores you. And what about the kids? Think about them.'

Sandra interrupted sternly.

A policy of self defence came to the fore.

223

'Yeah? That's all I've ever done though, isn't it. The husband. The kids. The bloody cat! The cleaning. The washing. I was so bored and so dead inside, Rose. But Andy changed all that. He's breathed life back into me again.'

Rose shook her head, astonished by what she was listening to.

'You've been on one lovely drink with him and one disastrous visit to the pictures. Hardly grounds for chucking your life on the scrapheap, is it? If your family knew what we were even talking about, I'd expect them to string us both up on the spot. You're being a stupid overgrown schoolgirl! You're away with the bloody fairies again, aren't you?'

Sandra's dulled visage suddenly brightened.

'Yes…and it feels *amazing!*'

The friends held hands across the table as the debate drew itself to a close.

'But Sandra…poor Stuart. What if he…'

'He *won't* find out! He'll *never* know! Because I'll be *careful!* And you know how grateful I am for your help, Rose. It won't be a regular thing. Just tomorrow night. Then I'll think of something else. But he asked me…and I don't want to lose him again. I must be there for him. I can't walk away from this.'

Rose slowly lifted her gaze toward the overhead strip light and mentally scrutinised her friend's words.

She had severe misgivings about Sandra's current state of mind and disability of judgement. But figured that she would plough on recklessly with the mission even if she *didn't* have a concrete alibi.

'Okay, San. I'd do anything for you. You know that. I don't mind covering for you one more time. But I can see upset ahead. That lovely smile he puts on your face…it can't last. These things never do. Now think on. Remember what I've said.'

The friends stood up and pulled coats from their lockers.

'Rose…I don't expect you to understand what's going on inside my stupid brain. Even I don't know that anymore. But I do know that this would be far harder without you. I just want you to know that I won't be silly. It's just a dinner date at his house. No more. I'll be tucked up in bed by eleven p.m.'

Rose laughed heartily as they emerged from the staff room and flicked off the lights.

'Yes love! I'll bloody bet you will be!'

The humour of the retort was shrouded by sudden concern that manifested quickly within Sandra.

In all her presumed innocence she had not suspected for one moment that Andy's invitation would lead to anything more than dinner, drinks, and laughter.

Whilst giving her cause for deliberation, the premise was also tremendously enticing.

Keeping such euphoric thoughts to herself, Sandra opted to say nothing more about the issue.

Ushering to the front of the shop, Rose took one last look around before setting the alarm and closing the front door behind them.

She looked to the grey-hued sky and retrieved car keys from her coat pocket.

'Lighter nights are coming, San. Hope it's a nice summer this year. Last year's was crap!'

'Yeah…well…me and Stuart were thinking of going abroad this year…get away from the rain…'

Rose observed the naive yet undeniably attractive younger woman standing beside her and offered a quizzical expression.

'Oh yeah? Just the three of you? That's a Ménage a Trois, isn't it?'

Sandra slapped her friend lightly on the arm.

'Don't be disgusting, Rose!'

'What? I wouldn't put anything past you these days, my girl! Do you want a ride home or have you got somewhere else to go first?'

Sandra shook her head, smirked wryly, and scanned the snail's pace of the rush hour traffic.

'No thanks. It's not cold. I might walk some of the way, tonight.'

Rose hugged Sandra and ambled towards the side of the shop.

'Well…tread carefully you daft bugger. Know what I mean?'

Laughter was the resonant accompaniment to friends departing, as Sandra turned on her heel and slowly made for the bus stop.

Tuesday. Six p.m. Even by her recent encouraging attempts to impress with an improved image, Sandra's reflection in the bedroom mirror demonstrated nothing less than pure sex appeal.

Miss Jones sat silently on the bedspread which was bestrewn with discarded dresses, relegated shoes, and the contents of two handbags. She had carefully and curiously watched her adoptive human mother, registering every stage of the transformation.

Thanks to her eternal and sometime maternal guardian Rose Riley, Sandra left work early and had spent the best part of thirty minutes gripping her hair up to reveal a teasingly slender display of her neckline.

The previously lost art of effective cosmetic appliance had now been renewed and perfected after what seemed like a thousand trial runs over the previous few months.

Finally confident in her appearance, she ran her hands down the front of the dark brown suede dress, which hung just below the knee and outlined her curves with triumphant modesty.

And despite the recklessly pre-emptive nature of the purchase, underneath the inviting outer layer was hidden a set of brand new, white lace underwear.

Just in case of emergency, she had told herself at the cash desk.

Of course, a tempting amount of cleavage was mandatory for the occasion if a little unsettling in practice, but unlike before, she now felt sufficiently justified in presenting her long-concealed wares in such a fashion.

Matching heels completed the ultra-contemporary look, which ironically had been compiled with some haste on her usual Saturday afternoon jaunt to the city shops.

Thankfully, Laura could not be in attendance during the latest retail clothing selection process due to a pre-arranged commitment to a school friend, but on seeing her mother in readiness to depart the house that night, she could do no less than praise the choice of outfit and tasteful way it adorned her feminine frame.

'God…are you *really* my mum? Or is somebody else living here, nowadays?'

Sandra smiled in appreciation of her daughter's flattering appraisal but said nothing as she winked in response.

'Mum…you look *stunning*. It's a shame Dad's not here to see it.'

In another timely slice of fortune, Stuart had been delayed at the office to attend a monthly managerial meeting. He had claimed on the phone that his return home would be timed at around six-thirty. Of course, he had little idea that by such time, his wife would be out and waiting to catch a bus.

The personal boon for Sandra was that his prolonged absence would not incur any shred of suspicion.

'Bingo's getting a bit upmarket these days, isn't it?' Laura chirped.

Sandra chuckled at her daughter's commentary as she selected and attached a pair of earrings before checking the contents of her handbag.

Pulling a waist-length black leather jacket from the wardrobe, she glanced at her watch to affirm the time as being just before six-fifteen.

'Well…thanks for the vote of confidence, love. But I'd better go. I'm meeting the girls early tonight for a drink. Wish me luck for a full house.'

Still entranced by the striking image, Laura followed her mother down the stairs.

'Oh…by the way, love. When Daniel gets back from swimming, tell him there's a dinner ready in the microwave. A minute on full should do it. Your dad can sort himself out. Oh…and feed the cat for me, please? I forgot earlier.'

With a final check in the hallway mirror, she kissed Laura softly on the cheek, conveying a considerable sample of the scent she was wearing.

'Wow…perfume as well! You really are out to paint the town red aren't you, Mum! Don't worry…I'll make sure everyone is fed and watered. Have a great night. See you later!'

Sandra casually waved and fastened a couple of studs on her jacket as she marched excitedly up the street.

Miss Jones covertly witnessed the brief ceremony from the front bedroom window, before bounding downstairs and into the kitchen to the sound and aroma of food being placed into her bowl.

*****

Trafalgar Gardens. Number Ninety-Four. Andy's eyes nearly popped from their sockets as he pulled open the door and revealed the welcome vision of loveliness that decorated the front step.

He stared almost dumbfounded for a few pleasurable seconds before opening with his greeting.

'Did it hurt?'

Sandra looked at him quizzically.

'Did it hurt? Did it hurt, when?'

He smirked and held her hand.

'When you fell from Heaven?'

Immediately inducing mirth into the fray, she followed him into the hallway and closed the door behind her.

'Andy…that is the cheesiest line ever invented by mankind! Even *I've* heard it before! Little old *me*! Who never even gets chatted up!'

He held up his hands in a gesture of concession before taking her coat and hanging it on the banister rail.

'I'm sure you *have* heard it before. But the difference is…I *mean* it.'

Her mind assessed the surroundings as a myriad of thoughts bombarded her re-acquaintance with Andy's house.

She immediately detected his delectable aftershave.

Tonight, he also looked truly amazing in his white shirt and blue jeans and the mutual effort to affect was instantly successful.

The lighting was low, accentuated by several carefully positioned candles. She could smell something cooking but couldn't quite identify the recipe.

And to her astonishment, the most amazing sight of all was to see Andy walking without the aid of his stick.

'You wanted wine if I recall. The cheap, white, and strong sort if I remember, yes?'

Preoccupied by the ease with which he shuffled around the kitchen, she barely heard his question.

'Sorry, Andy? I was miles away.'

He chuckled whilst uncorking the bottle, also becoming aware of her focus on his lower limbs.

'Oh...yes...the legs. Well, I had injections yesterday morning. Which certainly helps for a few days. It's a simple plan, really. If I can't feel the problem, it doesn't hinder my stride. But there is another little secret remedy which I might show you later if you're a very good girl. Here you are.'

She sampled a little of the wine as bubbles fizzed into her nostrils.

'Wow...sharp stuff! A few of these might turn me into a very *bad* girl!'

With a glass now in his own hand, he moved his face close to hers and uttered a splendidly tempting proclamation.

'Well, then...I'll just have to punish you...appropriately and severely...won't I?'

Lost for a second in one another's gaze, they drank some more. Now alone and together in their own private world, they felt that nothing could touch them.

The clandestine meeting promised to be a consoling joining of minds. So far, their protracted and intermittent journey together had served to enlighten their lives and twist the normality they both knew into something pleasantly alien.

For Sandra and Andy, tonight would be a wilful, consuming affirmation of their bond of friendship. Nobody else mattered at that moment, aside the two people present.

Swayed by the alluring prospect, Sandra quickly emptied her flute and offered it for replenishment.

'I suppose I should take my time with this stuff?'

Topping her up, Andy was rapid with a mischievous reply.

'Oh…I hope not! There are four more bottles in the fridge to get through! Besides, I rather like the idea of you being a very bad girl!'

He placed the refill in her hand and moved coyly and slowly further to her, forcing her to support herself against the fridge. Something so primitive as feeling his body close to hers was a sensation so irresistible that Sandra felt like she would either faint or explode on the spot.

Her body reacted of its own accord with willing expectation.

She fully anticipated the passionate and unexpected embrace to evolve further as he softly whispered into her ear.

'You do realise…there's something I have to be sure of…before we continue…'

Sandra gulped more wine before nervously answering in kind.

'Oh, yes? What might that be, then?'

The hiatus in his reply was immensely naughty, yet immeasurably arousing. His sensual tones washed over her again as she wallowed in secret, wanton desire.

'I need to know…do you…if you…*would* you…'

Now frustration got the better of the exchange as her patience withered slightly to encourage the suggestion at hand.

'If *what*, Andy?'

He lightly kissed her neck, which instantaneously induced goosebumps everywhere and encouraged her legs to tremble. Such intensity of the human touch, she had never known.

The next temptingly elusive stage, whatever that might be, could not come soon enough for her.

And still he continued to tease as he smothered her with his pure male dominance.

'If *what*, Andy? Tell me! Just *say* it to me.' she gasped.

Draining her second glass to swiftly numb the rough edges of her conscience, she looked deeply into his soul and breathed his scent, looking for more guidance in this subversive guessing game.

Then at last, he revealed his earnest intentions.

'I need to know…if you…only if you want, mind you…if you like…spaghetti bolognaise.'

The silence that succeeded his query indicated a severe switch in mood. From a moment of overwhelmingly erotic promise, she had been led into a punishing let down that punctured her undisclosed hopes.

She drew away to see him cover his mouth to hide the giggles.

Naturally, her own similar reaction followed suit, despite a firm attempt to feign anger.

'You are a bastard, Andy Ratcliffe! A gorgeous bastard…but a bastard, nonetheless. And yes…I love spaghetti…and also…my glass is empty…again!'

*****

With unspoken ambitions put aside for the time being, they eventually sat down to eat in the soft glow of the lounge. Music floated on the soothing air as they exchanged long, meaningful glances across the table.

The banter was typically playful and complementary.

They were in an idyllic cocoon of intimate dining, gradual inebriation and a purposed avoidance of harsh reality that served to convince both parties that they were somehow destined to be together.

The evening passed without mention of absent families.

Without the painful rueing of unwarranted loss.

In truth, the hours endured without any due consideration for what truly mattered.

Such formal things would only serve to detract from their shell of solace. It was a time for selfish thought and action.

They exchanged opinion on personal ambition, both achieved and unfulfilled. They swapped memories of that first moment in the bakery, when the air crackled with undiagnosed chemistry.

And they cast prediction as to what lay ahead for their lives as they ran the gauntlet of a waiting, unsuspecting world.

But both agreed that any ensuing aftermath was, at that juncture, unknown and equally unimportant.

The evening evolved as an almost poetic recreation of what had been unplanned in the minds of two strangers. Now engulfed by mutual attraction, the meal was duly completed, and their thoughts diverted.

'Here. I'll take the plates. Hope my cooking passed the test.'

Now keenly pouring her own wine, Sandra kicked off her heels and lay back into the welcome embrace of the sofa.

'Well, I wouldn't say you were the best male cook I've ever known, but you're in the top one!'

Both armed once again with alcohol, they merged on the cooling leather of the settee. She rested her legs across his lap, revelling in the semi-darkness that enclosed the pair within their land of dreams.

In the background, music continued to quilt the atmosphere, giving both parties a confidence to explore thoughts regarding the one subject that had not been previously covered.

Their immediate future together, as man and woman.

'You know, Sandra...I've rarely been this happy. In fact, I can't recall the last time I felt so at ease with anyone.'

She watched as he stroked her bare feet, knowing that such sentiment would induce pressure on her honest response.

How she welcomed the frankness. It was refreshing.

There was nothing to hide from one another.

And seemingly, nothing to fear.

'My heart bursts every time I think of you, Andy. It's like...electricity...flowing through my body. It was there from the first time we met. It's stronger than ever...especially...right now.'

He chuckled to himself and swallowed some wine.

'That's because you're a little bit drunk. The senses are sometimes more receptive after alcohol.'

The sincerity in her responding expression was telling.

She focused obligingly on him, slowly moving her head from side to side in a protracted motion of denial.

'If anything…Andrew Ratcliffe…I'm not even nearly drunk *enough…*'

His attention was diverted by a change of song on the record player.

Enthusiasm fuelled a sudden inclination to stand up.

He took her hand and engaged her forcefully.

'This track is amazing. Dance with me.'

She squirmed in her seat and drank some more.

'No! I can't dance! I'm rubbish! No way!'

Giggling in mild yet relenting embarrassment, she slowly followed his lead and padded onto the hearth rug as the guitar-led intro of the song immersed them into a smooth joining of minds and bodies.

They moved slowly and as one, flirting with the flickering shadows on the walls.

The soft words of the ballad cast a beaming prophecy on what had transpired and maybe, they hoped, of what was still to come.

Her head rested gently on his chest as he guided her back into a wondrous oblivion.

Andy pulled her as close as possible and let his gentle breathing caress the curve of her face and neck.

His next words were effectively a shot in the semi-darkness.

A shot that could not fail to make its target.

'I've got to let you in on something.'

Floating with the soft, slow melody, she listened intently as he whispered.

'I'm…not going to be able to let you go home tonight. You do know that…don't you?'

Sandra looked up to him, completely embroiled within his addictive, commanding authority.

She had little doubt now as to how their special night would conclude.

So far as she was concerned, she was his to behold; to imprison.

Completely at the mercy of his masculine will.

And she was now totally convinced; dreams did come true after all.

234

As ever, mirth guided the reply as she stared deep into him.

'I should hope so too…I was a good girl…I ate all my dinner…'

He tightened his hold on her waist and back, encouraging her shape to fit with his. They slowly encircled the room, round and round, lost in a blissful haze of processed seduction and suppressed passion.

'Terribly naughty of me to suggest such a thing, Sandra…I know…but you are simply…irresistible.'

She smiled inwardly and lowered her head into his guise of comforting safety once more.

An endless, unwelcome silence signified the dance to come to an end.

They looked into each other, almost searching each other's souls, looking for some undefined confirmation or assurance of where they were and what was happening to them.

'Thank you, Andy. That was…magical. So…spontaneous …I've never done anything so romantic before…'

He now became a little nervous but concealed his trepidation competently.

'Do you need another drink?'

Sandra felt her head spinning slightly as she slowly recovered composure to resume her position back on the sofa.

'No…thanks…you feel free, though.'

'No…I'm fine, too. What about…a smoke?'

Puzzled by the unexpected gesture, she frowned at him in request for an explanation.

He offered a distinctly confused assurance.

'Oh…I don't mean cigarettes. Horrible habit!'

Now she was completely dumbfounded as Andy reached behind him and opened the drawer in the lounge cabinet.

Retrieving what *looked* like a cigarette - only thicker and slightly longer - he casually rested it between his lips and lit the end. The garlands of residue begun to hang in the air like a ghostly wreath, depositing a sweet aroma which quickly began to occupy the room.

'I didn't know you liked to smoke.' she proclaimed, still dubious as to his motive for doing so.

Andy smiled and placed the roll-up between his fingers, intermittently blowing and inhaling as he explained.

'It's not tobacco…it's…cannabis. It numbs the senses. Eases the symptoms. I shouldn't be doing this in front of you really, but hey…share and share alike…you want to try?'

With her instinctive reticence dulled considerably by alcohol, Sandra stood up and took the spliff from Andy.

'Draw very gently. Don't inhale if you don't want to. It won't harm you. It'll just…lighten the load of life a little…'

Spluttering on her first drag, she began to giggle.

'You sound like a bloody hippy! Where did you get such a thing?'

He raised a finger to his lips as he listed gently from side to side.

'Well…put it this way…not from a chemist…but I couldn't do without the stuff. Prescribed shots from the surgeons are not as pleasurable…or effective! And I can do this in my own time!'

He took the smoke back; his hand wavering as he gingerly removed it from her lips. The drug had little immediate effect on Sandra, aside leaving her with a renewed thirst.

'I've changed my mind…I need more wine…'

As the minutes passed, Andy's mood mellowed slightly as she in turn embraced the ensuing carelessness. He left the roll-up to burn itself out into a saucer before clasping his fingers around her hand. Drinking from her glass, he swam in her deep brown eyes.

Both were now in subconscious acceptance.

The moment of truth was upon them.

Nothing more was said as he kissed her gently on the lips.

Guiding her from the lounge, they ascended the stairs. His determined lead left her helpless and wanting as they entered the bedroom.

The gentle aroma of flowers enhanced the feeling of freedom and excitement.

He sat her down on the edge of the bed and flicked on the lamp, which bathed her profile in a soft pink glow. Now she looked unerringly divine, as he perched next to her and placed his face close to hers.

Euphoria engulfed the pair as their pumping hearts raced in tandem to the rhythm of intimacy. He graced her neck and ears with the softest traces of his lips, which messaged her body to respond with unpredictable and uncontrolled impulses.

Setting her on fire with his tongue, he drew back slightly and faced her again.

'Tell me now…we can stop if you want…'

Her unspoken response to his gentlemanly concern was to pull him closer to her, engaging fully with his needs and hers. They frantically intertwined and gradually de-clothed each other, before burying themselves in the warmth of the sheets to fully explore the hidden pleasure of their nakedness.

She was pleased to observe that he was toned and muscular, yet the sensation of touch in the half-light was far more alluring than any visual stimulus. He mouthed her all over, causing her to submit with a reluctant and flinching ease with every kiss.

Her involuntary whimpers only served to encourage his pursuit of fully enjoying her femininity. The growing tidal wave of wanton physicality and heaving arousal began to ascend to heights that she had never experienced.

A willing prisoner to his strength and hungry natural instinct, she resided in her vulnerability as the intensity mounted from deep within her core.

Never had the bedroom provided an arena for such incredible release. Free of all restraint, she now fully embraced the abandonment and forcefully grappled with him to increase the fuelling of her unconcealed lust.

Every inch of her body was now alive to his careful control.

And the unstoppable ride was climbing ever higher.

Past the point of no return.

As she rose with him, Sandra looked down upon the fathomless dark depths, clinging to him for a secure hand and a firm lead to the ultimate of peaks.

Then, in the throes of discovery, he stopped and reached over to his bedside drawer.

Panting with pleasured anticipation, she grasped for him in the semi-murk, not wanting his delectable tirade of exploration to end.

'What are you doing?' she mumbled.

Hunched over to one side, he concealed his preparation from her eyes, not wishing to spoil the unblemished moment of their final, all-consuming union.

He whispered a muffled reply that seemed tinged with frustration.

'I'm...taking the responsibility...well trying to. Either I've got bigger...or these bloody things have gotten smaller!'

Her physical wants were suddenly eclipsed by the incessant grip of laughter, and she held herself infirmly as Andy continued to wrestle with precaution.

Finally, he rolled back to face her.

'Right...that'll do...where were we?'

Looking directly at the ceiling, she placed her hand on the back of his head and pressed him into her loins.

'You...were...there...I believe...'

Acquitting themselves to the journey into paradise once again, the welling momentum began to build beyond previously known boundaries.

Now finally she would take him completely.

Full, and strong and straight, he slowly entered her, as they finally adjoined in the ultimate act of closeness.

They writhed and bucked, unrelenting in their ordained quest and began to gallop toward the halcyon summit of their primitive affections.

Physically, mentally, and emotionally they unshackled themselves.

No more were they under constraint from the long-standing inhibitive shrouds.

They laid their bodies free and wide to all that may come forth.

Reaching for the skies, Sandra hollered uncontrollably as she sailed above the clouds into that other elusive world, where ecstasy was the currency and dreams were the lifeblood of existence.

Descending from her climax, she then guided Andy to his, until together they touched down and rested peacefully on the quilt.

Spent, entwined, and relieved.

Fully sated and deliriously happy.

Slightly doped and absolutely drunk.

In the wake of their passionate storm, they drifted freely in recovery.

Gradually, slumber stole them from their lustful dementia and protected them within the folds of night.

*****

Sandra stirred as the early spring sunshine peaked through the curtains and illuminated the bedroom. Her mind could not register her whereabouts immediately. But a furtive glance across to her snoring companion soon reminded her of the current location.

The loud bump back down to Earth did indeed hurt like hell.

Squinting at her wristwatch, the time appeared to be about six-fifteen.

Six-fifteen - the next morning.

At that moment, several intimidating factors encroached upon her throbbing head.

She should not be in Andy's bed.

She should be at home, in her own bed.

Next to her husband.

Her kids would soon be up and wondering where she was.

The dream of hours earlier could turn into a nightmare within minutes.

Bounding from beneath the bedclothes, she sheathed her nakedness with Andy's bathrobe and scampered downstairs.

Double checking the time, her state of panic reduced a little.

It was only a quarter *to* six.

There was time for coffee.

But maybe not time for a proper goodbye.

Returning to the bedroom, she placed the mug of steaming caffeine on the dressing table and sat on the edge of the mattress. The dawn's watery sunrise began to display its presence around the room.

She smiled as she observed her crumpled dress, new lace underwear and empty wine glass on the floor at her feet.

The abandoned remnants of a plentiful feast.

Then her attention rested on the man who had provided such pleasures. She observed his peaceful expression and kissed him on the forehead as he slept.

Then her gaze rested on the chest of drawers in the corner of the room.

To a family portrait in a small silver frame.

A husband, a wife, and a child.

A father, a mother, and a daughter.

Together and happy as they posed for the camera.

The photograph of Andy, Michelle and Annette looked to be around ten years old, judging by the younger appearance of the teenager.

An image of life, taken before the heartache intruded.

Before the illness began to erode.

Before the split finally divided the loving circle.

The image stung Sandra sharply as she studied its unbearably potent symbolism. The strength of a family unit could never truly be broken by outsiders - only from within.

Her mind lurched as reality quickly encroached along with the protruding daylight outside.

Her wondrous escapade of a few short hours earlier had been a gloriously fulfilling mistake and left her with an intensive need to vacate the situation.

To fly back to her own nest.

To try and fend off the attacks of remorse and guilt that now repeatedly wounded her very soul like poisoned daggers.

Within a minute, she was dressed and passably presentable.

Finishing her coffee, she entered the kitchen and scrawled a note onto a piece of paper, which she left on the worktop for Andy's scrutiny.

Its words were inscribed clearly, even if the message conveyed was uncertain.

Thank you for last night.

Had to get home. I'll call you.

Love Sandra xxx

Checking her handbag, she slipped her feet into her new shoes and opened the front door. The bright spring air was shrill, and she was thankful of her coat, which was duly wrenched from its position on the banister rail.

Closing the door quietly behind her, she threw on her leather jacket and embarked on an uneasy exit from the scene.

Trotting quickly away from Trafalgar Gardens, Sandra Bancroft considered whether the family life she had left behind yesterday would still be waiting for her when she got back.

The anguish of desperate hope was crucifying as she boarded the first bus of the day and sitting quietly, she tried in vain to calm her tearing heart.

27

THE RETURN TO ORCHARD ROAD

'You had me worried sick. love! Overdo it on the lagers again last night, did we?'

Sandra's searing trepidation as she entered through her front door was quickly settled by the arresting vision of Stuart in his vest, underpants, and socks. Her hangover had become more inflamed during the bus journey, though it felt oddly gratifying to be among the bosom of her loved ones once again.

Stuart's apparent angst regarding her absence overnight delivered a finely tuned theory, to which Sandra nodded at relevant points as she tried to cushion her banging skull.

'I woke in the middle of the night and assumed you were on the loo. Then when I came down and saw you weren't here at all...well...I had to call Rose to see what had happened to you! I didn't want to wake her at two a.m., but I had little choice, did I?'

Suddenly Sandra's innermost fears returned in a flash.

But she need not have concerned herself.

A friend in need had again proven herself a friend indeed.

'And...what did Rose say when you asked about me?'

'Well, obviously she claimed that you had met up with the girls early, which I already knew because Laura had told me. But evidently you decided that last night was time for a bit of mid-week bender, did you?'

Sandra observed the crisp, clean un-ironed shirt draped over Stuart's forearm as the next question stumbled from her lips.

'And...where...did she say...I was?'

'On her sofa...comatose...absolutely sozzled! And by the look of you this morning I can say that she has my sympathy. Honestly, Sandra. A grown woman getting in such a state! Where is your head these days?'

Sandra swallowed dryly and kicked off her shoes in the hallway.

'I do feel a bit rough. Your shouting isn't helping!'

His tone softened a little as he kissed her tenderly on the cheek.

'I'm not shouting, dear. It's your hearing that's super sensitive. No doubt along with a blinding headache as well. You should know better at your age!'

She shuffled past her husband into the kitchen, to find Laura at the stove in the process of preparing cooked breakfasts and singing along to the radio. Sex Talk by T'Pau throbbed through the speakers as a coincidental if untimely backdrop.

'Hi Mum! You remembered where you live, then? Fry-up?'

Sandra almost retched on the spot at the thought of a greasy solution to her self-induced sufferance.

'No thanks, love. Just a coffee will be fine.'

Sinking herself heavily at the kitchen table, she hid her face in her hands as another distinctive voice resonated around her cranium.

'Hey…way to go Mum! Wait until I tell the lads at school! My mother got off her face again last night!'

Stuart had resumed his position at the ironing board and was quick to intercede against Daniel's enthusiastic appraisal of the matter.

'Er…I don't think your mother wants the whole school knowing about her embarrassing indiscretion…do you, son?'

Sandra's thoughts reverted to the incredulous events of the previous evening. She smirked to herself as she hid behind her fingers.

Indiscretion?

If only the world knew!

The final member of the Bancroft clan appeared and proceeded to make her presence known by clawing at Sandra's bare ankles.

'Ouch! Can somebody feed the cat, please?'

Stuart's muttered cursing as he attempted to press his shirt began to irritate Sandra into submission.

'Darling…do you want me to do that for you?'

'No. You just sit there in your own mess! We'll cope…won't we kids? We don't need mother do we, kids? We are quite capable of sorting ourselves out in the morning…aren't we…'

243

Finally, Sandra succumbed to her already aggravated temperament. She could take no more of the customary family banter.

'SHUT UP! FOR CHRIST'S SAKE! ALL OF YOU JUST SHUT UP! I APOLOGIZE…OKAY? I HAD A HEAVY NIGHT! YES! ONE HEAVY NIGHT IN TWENTY-ONE FUCKING YEARS! SO, SUE ME IF IT'S SO FUCKING HORRENDOUS FOR YOU ALL TO CONTEMPLATE! AND AS IT SEEMS YOU CAN ALL COPE WITHOUT ME FOR NINETY SECONDS, I'M GOING UP TO BED!'

The concise, considered and highly audible outburst instantly silenced the room, aside from the harmonious and incredulously inappropriate sounds now provided by Patrick Swayze.

Just as the man said, Sandra indeed departed the room like the wind.

Stuart stopped ironing.

Laura stopped frying.

Daniel stopped munching handfuls of dry cornflakes straight from the box.

And Miss Jones emerged from underneath the table, staring in disbelief at Sandra's vexed form, which trudged promptly away from the frenzied bustle of the kitchen and tenderly attempted to climb the stairs, promptly to be followed by the hopeful and hungry feline.

A parting shot echoed back through the hallway.

'AND CAN SOMEBODY APART FROM ME FEED THIS FUCKING CAT FOR A FUCKING CHANGE!'

A few seconds contemplation ensued among the remaining Bancroft clan members to allow the dust of hostility to settle.

Daniel quickly resumed his ingestion of dry cereal and turned to his sister.

'I suppose now's a bad time to ask Mum if she's seen the earphones for my Walkman…'

The dull sound of movement downstairs accompanied Sandra's drift into mild dormancy. Still unfed, Miss Jones opted to join her on the bed and purred in contentment at the return of her adoptive mother and chief nutritionist.

Sandra didn't hear anybody vacate the house that morning.

She had already subconsciously decided that she would not be in any fit state to go to work.

Her sleep was eventually disturbed by the sound of the letterbox clattering, which alerted her to the fact that it must be after nine a.m. Sitting up in bed, she tentatively cradled her head. The hour's nap had somehow reinvigorated her hangover to even more testing proportions.

Briefly stroking Miss Jones, Sandra pulled herself upward and adorned her pink nightgown and white fluffy slippers, before wading downstairs to retrieve the mail from the doormat.

Forking food into the cat's bowl, she then made a large sweet black coffee and assumed a peaceful posture at the dining table.

Regaining focus, she observed the surroundings.

To her confused amazement, everywhere had been tidied up.

Stuart had obviously finished pressing his shirt before successfully deconstructing and relocating the ironing board.

And the breakfast pots had been successfully washed, dried, and put away. No sign of any breakages either.

As her eyes fixed gradual attention to the table, Sandra discovered a hand-written note.

It read simply:

Sorry about moaning at you this morning, love.

See you later. Hope the head's clearing okay.

Love S.xxxx

All that remained for Sandra to do now was to shower, dress, make the bed and relax for the rest of the day.

Then she remembered.

It was Wednesday. She should be at work and needed to phone in to apologise for her unplanned absence.

Mick Turner sounded furious.

But Sandra cared little at that instance.

And besides which, there was no rest for the wicked.

Her mother would be awaiting the weekly delivery of groceries.

But she supposed it was better to attend to it as soon as possible as opposed to later that evening.

Resigned to resumption of the regimental timetable, Sandra sipped her coffee and thought of better things.

Of another land.

Of another man.

Of another her.

Of a rather different, infinitely preferable Sandra Jane Bancroft, that she never knew existed.

Until last night.

28

BOMBSHELL

Twenty-seven days and nights were counted by as Sandra grappled with her untameable conundrum. The sumptuous evening with Andy seemed an ever-distant memory as a steely cold remorse for her actions had set root, causing her every movement and thought to be ravaged by torment.

Guilt was an alien yet forerunning emotion that now enveloped her home life as the days began to lengthen, and spring affirmed its proud status with noticeably warmer weather.

The garden rapidly began to adorn swathes of foliage, giving Stuart optimum excuse to invest his spare time back into to the greenhouse and beyond.

His existence had not knowingly been altered or even lightly touched by the potentially destructive circumstances. In his ignorant bliss, he continued to hold the unchallenged view that all was fine within Number Twelve and that his wife was her normal, dutiful, contented self.

As an ironic complement to her finely honed public facade, Sandra was anything but okay. A persistent stomach cramp had accompanied her intermittently through the past month, which she tried to equate to the stress of committing a terrible act of treachery against the man she married.

She could not concentrate on the simplest tasks domestically or at work. Her brain had effectively adopted shutdown mode.

Everything she had previously accomplished with ease now appeared as an insurmountable task.

But the true origin of her consternation was not the lasting sting of infidelity.

The actuality of her despondency was even more painful to admit to herself, yet it seemed so obvious from the moment the black clouds had descended into her psyche.

She was missing Andy Ratcliffe more than ever.

So much so, that it hurt to think about him, even for a second.

She craved his presence every single instance of every single day, knowing that to gleefully reignite their flickering flame would be initially enthralling if possibly disastrous for her future.

She wished it could be otherwise, but the endless hours were persistently occupied by reminiscence in his continued absence.

The scent of his body.

The gravelled tone of his voice.

The sensation of inner liberation that he had instigated within her was both ominous and undeniably addictive.

And despite her knowledge that she should never return to that world where he resided, she knew her willpower was perhaps not strong enough to resist the calling.

The lack of Andy Ratcliffe in her existence was spiritually starving her to grim proportions.

And the desperate need for sustenance was becoming seemingly more urgent with every breath.

*****

Having informed Mick Turner that her increased hours were unworkable because of her commitment to her mother's supposedly unstable condition, Sandra had recently been allowed to revert to a four-day week.

Utilizing the opportunity granted, it was on the third Wednesday afternoon in May that she succumbed and decided on a whim to visit Andy at home again. There would be no prior telephone call.

She would not alert him to her intent or needs.

Sandra concluded that she would simply arrive, hopefully allowing the element of surprise to fuel the moment just as before.

Yet they had not uttered a word to one another since that incredible evening of a few weeks earlier. And even more irritating to bear was the fact that such silence was no accident.

The note she had left for him declared that *she* would eventually contact him. Andy being Andy, he had respected her wishes.

But how she wished he had ignored her request and visited her at work. Just once.

Just for a few golden minutes. Just to brighten her day.

To invigorate her once more.

To keep alive that wonderful untouchable thing which they had inadvertently and tenderly nurtured.

Yet there had been no communication at all.

As she travelled on the bus toward the outskirts of the city, a tragic and demoralising thought occurred. A stream of concern that was no longer unfamiliar.

That perhaps, just perhaps, he might not want to see her again.

But the fragmented nature of their relationship was deeply agonising, and her frustration had long since crashed its threshold.

And despite her recent misgivings regarding jeopardising her staid and uninspiring marriage, Sandra had little hesitation in submitting to her desire for Andy, so domineering had it become without him around.

On alighting from the bus, her path toward Trafalgar Gardens was bathed in warm sunshine. Dressed in a plain white t-shirt and blue jeans, she strode confidently, clutching her handbag to her side. The area appeared more inviting in broad daylight, and she felt at ease as she entered the road in question.

Yet almost immediately, she sensed something was amiss.

Step by step she neared the row of terracing that housed number Ninety-Four; the aroma of suspicion growing ever stronger.

Closing in on the hallowed destination, her pace slowed dramatically as the vaguely familiar frontage of his home honed into view.

Yet, somehow, it was different.

Drastically different from how she recalled on her previous two visits.

The blistered brown paint of the door and flaking window frames had been rendered with a sharp, clean coat of white. The paved area under the front sill had been weeded and the rubbish tidied.

249

And looming large overhead was an unwelcome symbol of foreboding.

A symbol that provoked Sandra's latent emotions as she wavered curiously underneath it.

She looked at the sign, disbelievingly registering the doom-laden phrase inscribed in bright red letters against a pale green background.

Two, almost hateful words that spat at her from above, pouring poisoned rain onto her long-held hopes.

FOR SALE.

A phrase that signified the possible commencement of dramatic alteration in the life of Andy Ratcliffe.

And quite possibly, the bells now tolled for the end of their intense and albeit minimal, affair.

Staring up at the wooden sign, she realised that this development could well signify the beginning of the end of her dalliance with paradise.

In her haste to discover more, Sandra sidled through the freshly painted gate and knocked on the door via several, frantic uneven raps.

Her heart now pounding in expectation, she waited for the door to open and Andy to poke his head through the gap to convey some mirthful comment to make her laugh.

Instead, the door opened almost instantly, and another familiar face peered from the shadows of the hallway.

It was Annette.

She did not smile with a natural inclination.

Her obvious surprise at seeing the unexpected visitor was evident for Sandra to fully absorb. Indeed, Andy's daughter was veritably stunned by the uninvited guest that hovered at the doorstep.

Her attempts to perform a greeting were stuttered and awkward in tone.

'Oh…hi, Sandra…didn't think you'd…erm…Dad's not here at the moment.'

Alarmed by the lack of warmth in the welcome, Sandra gulped nervously and shuffled her weight from foot to foot.

'Hello, Annette. How are you?'

The younger woman seemed strangely unsettled by Sandra's arrival.

Yet it did not make sense. Only two months earlier, Andy's daughter had practically begged Sandra to make amends with him.

But now, as they dodged and weaved discussion in the porchway, the scenario had been tarnished by a hidden progress.

'I'm…fine, thanks, Sandra. Good. Listen…Dad's just gone to hospital for his shots and check-up. I'm not sure when he'll be back.'

Sandra did not feel the need to beat about the bush.

Her quest needed accomplishment.

'How is your father? I haven't seen him for a few weeks. I just thought I'd drop by…and…but I can see that I've…jumped the gun.'

A look of ashen fear befell Annette's features as she struggled for an appropriate line of responsive dialogue.

Sandra continued to take the honour from her.

'I see that the house is on the market. Andy did mention that your mother was up for a quick sale. Leaving the country…isn't she?'

Annette simply nodded, not wishing to allow Sandra even the briefest glimpse of the activity behind her, back in the depths of the house.

The gap in the door remained at a firm minimum, which began to induce a mild annoyance in Sandra's approach.

'Hmm…she didn't hang about in giving the place a facelift, did she? Well…I can see this is a bad time. But I do need to talk to your dad at some point.'

Suddenly, an authoritative bark resonated from the gloom somewhere over Annette's shoulder, enquiring as to the identity of the caller.

The voice was that of another woman, which alerted Sandra to the cause of the apparent coldness in Annette's manner.

On hearing the call, Annette turned back and responded to the question with guarded caution.

'It's okay, Mum…just…just a canvasser…that's all.'

The voice from the background boomed once again, further stirring Sandra's already aggravated state of inner distress.

'Well, get rid! We don't need salesmen at the door. Not anymore, anyway!'

Annette reluctantly turned back to the visitor. She was caught in a no-win scenario. And Sandra's emotions were beginning to rise visibly.

'Look…I miss your dad…and really need to see him. Don't just shut me out of things. I'm his friend. The friend *you* wanted me to be. *Remember*?'

Annette tentatively stepped outside and pulled the door shut behind her, to prevent another potentially unpleasant interruption from her mother.

'Yes…I know…but things have changed…Mum wants it sorting sooner than we thought. So, Dad might be coming to live with me at my boyfriend's if she gets her way. She's in there now, scrubbing and cleaning everything. She's on a right mission.'

Sandra tried desperately to contain her growing upset as confusion descended on the scene. She wanted to storm the house and grab Annette's mother by the throat for being so harsh and dispensing.

Yet the startling and understandable truth of the matter quickly hit her squarely between the eyes.

Michelle Ratcliffe was in fact, living out her own particular dream.

Eventually going to visit her very own, newly discovered, and perfect world.

Leaving behind the past she no longer wanted, in order to fully embrace her future.

This was the exactly the same predicament that Sandra faced.

Only now, such a prospect suddenly seemed bleak and uninviting.

And completely untenable.

She looked to Annette with a forlorn gaze of acceptance, hoping that harsh inevitability would not draw its curtain on her ambition.

'Does…your dad…does he still…talk about me…often?'

The considerate reply was nonetheless unyielding in its meaning.

Sandra could barely listen to what she had requested to know.

Annette placed a gentle hand of consolation on Sandra's arm as she commenced explanation of what had recently occurred.

The mood became increasingly sombre as the story unfolded.

'I try not to mention it. It's his business. And yours, of course. He is so fond of you, Sandra…but he has come to realise…that…you and he…can never be…and since you haven't kept in touch…he's sort of lost hope within himself. His confidence has never been high since his diagnosis. I suppose he felt rejected all over again. I don't know. I'm just guessing.'

Sandra became alarmed at the fact that her tardiness in communication had possibly caused Andy to feel such things.

The notion seared her veins and jabbed at her heart.

She wiped her eyes and continued to search for some handhold on rapidly disappearing aspirations.

'No! I still need him, Annette! I can't just walk away and forget him. He's part of my life, now. Please tell him…I haven't forgotten about him. Please…let him know that I'm still here for him.'

Annette held Sandra as she became increasingly unsteady with the imminent release of her remorse.

'Sandra…you don't understand. He *knows* how you feel. That's why…he's decided to try and forget about you. It hurts him to think that you would give up everything for him. He doesn't want to be responsible for that. That's why he's not stood in Mum's way over the house. He's resigned himself to a future alone. That's up to him. No one can change how he thinks. He's his own man.'

Now becoming mildly distraught, Sandra's upset began to froth openly at the scene as she argued against the apparent futility of it all.

'I can *try*! I can change him! I can always be there with him! He doesn't need to be alone. Tell him! Tell him for me, Annette!'

Annette held Sandra closer to buck the welling tide of emotion.

She looked sternly into the older woman's eyes.

Her words acting as the final scolding resolution to the matter.

'You can't ever love him, Sandra. Not properly. Not the way you want to. Not the way he needs you to.'

The reaction was bemused, inflamed and irate.

'Why *not*? *Why* can't I love him?'

Annette sighed in sympathy.

'Because…he won't ever *let* you.'

'Well, you can tell him from me! I *do* love him! So, it's too bloody late isn't it! It's already *happened*!'

Finally submitting to destiny's call and her increasingly frail composure, Sandra withdrew from Annette's caring grasp and fled.

Desolation sullied the blue sky above as Sandra Bancroft walked quickly away, now knowing the reason for Andy's recent absence.

She had secretly feared that the gates to her once promised land might be closing all over again.

Now it was confirmed.

Her pathway to Eden was seemingly blocked forever.

29

A MOTHER'S IGNORANCE

Sandra did not respond to Phyllis Baxter's incessant beefing.

Instead, she shut her ears and consoled herself against recent, private loss. The Spring Bank Holiday seemed to endure forever.

Monotony and emptiness had been the sole inspirations behind Sandra's visit to her mother's house on that desperate Monday morning.

She repeatedly explained to Phyllis on at least three occasions during the previous three days on the telephone that she would be visiting today, as the bakery was closed.

But the message had not registered with the griping octogenarian, whose continual negative commentary simply droned as a background hum while her daughter stood pondering in the kitchen.

Looking out of the rear window of the bungalow, Sandra observed the lemon-yellow bed linen billowing in the spring breeze. The sunshine was endeavouring to act as a welcome remedy to the darkness she felt within herself.

It bathed all in the vicinity, splashing its vibrant colour upon lingering greys and accentuating nature's emerging pallet to the full.

However, the engaging scene beyond the window did not distract Phyllis from launching her verbal assault on the small selection of groceries amassed on the worktop.

With arms folded and her concentration centred elsewhere, Sandra did not involve herself with the inspection, instead continuing to stare aimlessly through the pane whilst catching only vague snippets of the inane referencing from the other side of the kitchen table.

As the supermarket was closed, the local Happy Shopper was the sole avenue for Sandra to acquire a few basic items.

If nothing else, it got her out of the house.

She anticipated the non-stop complaints as her mother approached the table to inspect.

Yet the reviews that emerged were astounding.

'Eggs are all looking good. Not one is cracked!'

'Yes……lovely. Bread's nice and soft. Unusual for a bank holiday, that is! You usually get it three days old on a Bank Holiday!'

'Oh! Strawberries! Oh…and cream! Oh, you do treat me, our San!'

'Cream of chicken soup? That's better! Can't stand that other rubbish you bought last week.'

'Peach toilet rolls! They'll match the walls!'

'Washing up liquid? Yes…I am about out of Fairy…'

'I went to get me feet done last week…did I tell you? Bloody foreign chiropodist! Like a friggin' butcher, he was! Mind…they don't hurt as much now!'

Finally, Sandra tuned to her mother and issued a stark order.

'Please…Mum…here's your drink. Just go and sit in the lounge. I'll put all this away and bring you a sandwich. Is your usual filling, okay?'

There was no argument from Phyllis, although even when back in the lounge she continued to convey regular opinion from her armchair, which duly carried along the passage and through the open kitchen door.

'I suppose that husband of yours is showing off his growths to some country gents today, is he?'

'I still haven't seen anything of that grandson of mine. Have you told him my lawn needs cutting? It's up to my knees!'

'Not much change judging by this till receipt, San. I don't know how I'm supposed to survive on my pittance of a pension!'

'Bloody Government!'

'Jimmy from a few doors up popped his clogs last week…did I tell you? Mind…he was a bloody misery guts…and he let his dog shit on everyone's gardens! I shan't miss him!'

'Hope they buried the bloody dog with him! Save me scooping the bloody stuff up anymore!'

'Can you just check if me washing's dry, San?'

'And if it is dry, can you bring it in for me?'

Sandra was no longer hearing her mother.

Phyllis continued to offer her well-meaning commentary via intermittent glimpses at the television screen.

Anything and everything that had happened in the time since Sandra's last visit had been mentally logged ready for her weekly report on the surrounding neighbourhood.

As she watched the TV with the volume turned down, her preoccupation with maternal rambling hardly allowed Sandra room for reply.

But Sandra would not reply, anyway.

Because she was incapable of replying at that moment.

As her mother ranted on about life's testing miscellany, Sandra buckled helplessly in the next room, finally wilting under the weight of long concealed trauma.

Struggling to confine her shredding distress, she clung to the kitchen table for support as the tears fell freely.

She did not register her mother's persistent monologue, as her attention had long since switched to another, distant person, in another, faraway place.

Sandra was adamant that the breakdown of her defences would not bear any witness.

Yet the sternest test of her feminine mettle was still ahead of her.

Phyllis' closing enquiry encouraged the final thread in Sandra's resolve to snap completely, in turn leaving her descending rapidly into a deep, black pit of hopelessness as she fought with her own emotions in the kitchen.

'Hey, our, San! There's something I've forgot to mention.'

'Went totally out of my head it did.'

The hiatus seemed eternal.

And Sandra's acute perception had guessed what was coming next.

'I say, our Sandra. How's that stallion of yours that you mentioned a few months back?'

'Sometime before Christmas, wasn't it?'

'Is he still knocking about the bakery?'

'Have you been out with him?'

'About time you traded in that useless husband of yours…'

In a final submission to her overwhelming upset, Sandra quickly retreated to the rear yard and began to collect the laundry from the line, hoping that the seasonal sun might also dry her tears forever.

And maybe, perhaps one day, help to mend her breaking heart.

'Bit warm for casserole, isn't it?'

Sandra chuckled as she watched Rose set the alarm and close the shop door. The early-June heat offered little respite from the engineered warmth of the shop's interior.

'Yes…well…it's a special request from our Daniel. You know what kids are like. They get these funny cravings from time to time. He must have had it at a mate's house sometime.'

Rose locked the door and glanced down to the shopping bag that swung from Sandra's side. She then affirmed the time to be approaching five-thirty.

'It won't be ready till ten tonight! That's if you get it in by six!'

Sandra shrugged.

'Nobody will be home until later, anyway. Stuart has a club meeting after work and Daniel's got cricket practice. So, I'm in no rush, to be honest.'

Rose moved closer to her best friend and lowered the tone of her sincere and caring enquiry.

'I've been very hesitant to ask, San. But…how are things…you know…at home? Are you…you know…getting over what happened?'

Sandra forced a half-smile, hoping to convince her colleague and ever faithful alibi that her feelings for Andy had been well and truly relegated to the past.

'I'm getting there…slowly. Listen, Rose. You know…you've been amazing through all this. I feel like I've been a silly, stupid little girl. I can't believe I put myself through so much and ended up with…well…a few nice memories.'

The firm embrace between friends was mutually gratifying.

They held one another under the blue skies, both secretly relieved that the ever-present unease created by the episodes of recent months had ended.

Sandra looked to her mentor in thanks, yet she still sensed an over-riding feeling of unfinished business.

The women stared at one another for a few seconds, both expectant of further words on the matter.

'I still think about him every day. I don't even know where he's living now. I don't suppose he thinks about me very much. I hope he does, though. I'll never forget him. Don't reckon he'll be seen in the shop again, anyhow...'

Rose wiped a tear from her eye before pecking Sandra on the cheek.

'Come on...you daft sod! You're getting me filling up! I'll take you home. You need to get that stew pot in the oven!'

*****

Miss Jones was the only occupant of the house and offered a suitable feline greeting as Sandra closed the front door behind her.

Circling the kitchen floor as though performing some practised pre-dining drill, which indeed it was, the cat looked up adoringly at her adoptive human mother and ever-reliable filler of the food bowl.

Sandra smiled and cradled her fur baby up from the floor, kissed her on the top of her head, and rubbed under her silken white chin.

Now purring like a car engine, Miss Jones jumped from Sandra's grasp, prior to an indistinctly flavoured variety of brown meat being upended from the tin and forked into her dish.

In turn of priority, Sandra duly switched on the radio, the kettle, and then the oven.

Gazing beyond the kitchen window onto her back garden, she absorbed the neat and ordered arena of greenery and shrubs that Stuart had carefully created over the past two months. The lawn was a picture of tidiness and was certainly looking ready for the long overdue onset of summer.

As she emptied the shopping bag onto the worktop, she imagined herself sitting reading on the patio.

Endless weeks of hot, hazy evenings relaxing with a cool glass of fizzy wine.

Or maybe two glasses.

Watching Stuart concentrate as he potted hither and thither in his quest for green-fingered excellence.

The thought was surprisingly enticing, and she found herself smiling with the spiritual contentment that only settled family life could supply.

Having battled with the tormenting residue of her dealings with Andy Ratcliffe, Sandra was again beginning to feel appreciative of the peaceful existence she was still fortunate to be blessed with at Number Twelve, Orchard Road.

The rest of the family had thankfully remained unaware and subsequently unaffected by the hidden drama of recent months. No detriment had been incurred to anyone.

On the face of it, all appeared very well with the Bancroft clan.

Sandra was relieved to have made a clean break from the ghosts of her recent history.

The knowledge that her pangs of selfishness had not been fully sated or even indulged beyond the briefest of physical liaisons, had gradually begun to sooth any unsettling disposition regarding her standing in life.

What she had supposedly failed to achieve aside her years of marital and maternal commitment suddenly mattered very little. Indeed, over the last few weeks, she had begun to see the light and smell the roses.

She could at last see the wood for the trees.

With a few occasional and hesitant recollections to etch the period securely into the back of her mind, Andy was now somebody that she could begin to try and forget; maybe once and for all.

And her enthusiasm for the future heightened as Rick Astley provided similar sentiment that echoed around the kitchen. Its positive message filled the room as Sandra emptied the diced beef into the casserole dish.

Miss Jones offered a cursory glance of gratitude as she quickly finished her dinner, subsequently licking her lips to the aroma of fresh meat up above her.

She positioned herself obligingly at Sandra's feet in the hope of a stray morsel.

'Not for you Missy…you've had yours. This is for your brother!'

Scraping carrots in time to the dance beat, Sandra began to hum along to the tune, causing a certain feline's ears to respond with an enquiring twitch of curiosity.

She reached over and flicked the kettle to re-boil, again glancing briefly beyond the window as the high sun showed signs of a gradual descent toward the distant rooftops.

She thought she heard the front door open as she sliced the carrots and dropped three or four handfuls into the pot. Daniel grinned from ear to ear as he poked his head around the kitchen door and observed his stomach's desires being created from scratch.

'Hi Mum! You, okay?'

A mother's eternal love for her son shone through as she endearingly beamed back at his increasingly handsome face.

'Hi, love! As you can see, I'm complying with this morning's request. Though it won't be ready for a couple of hours, yet. How was cricket practice?'

'Good, Mum. I might make the team. Even though the new season is already half-way through. I hope so, anyway. Alright if I nip to Jason's for an hour?'

'Yes, love. But don't go in your cricket gear, will you? It needs washing by the looks of the grass stains on the knees. Leave it at the bottom of the stairs. I'll do it tonight after tea. And put something nice on! Not that horrible baggy track suit.'

Daniel nodded before disappearing upstairs as Sandra removed the outer skin from a swede and began to cut it into large cubes.

Miss Jones had finally accepted that raw beef was off the menu so far as she was concerned.

All those uncooked ingredients would require far too much jaw work.

Retreating outside to the sun-drenched patio, she washed her face in full view of Sandra, who smiled before chopping three small onions.

Daniel had duly changed and descended the stairs, bringing his dirty laundry with him. Sandra watched admiringly at the fact her only son had listened to her for once.

The blue denims and black t-shirt suited his growing frame. Dropping his cricket kit in front of the washing machine, he opened the fridge door, removed the bottle of milk, poured himself a glass, and promptly swallowed a half pint in five seconds flat.

Returning the milk bottle to the fridge and placing the glass in the sink, he turned and smiled to his doting mother.

'Okay, Mum. I'll be back for eight. Is that alright?'

He glanced in curiosity across to her. She now faced away from him as they both stood next to the sink.

Seemingly preoccupied with her task, she did not respond to Daniel's comment.

'Mum?'

Moving his position he entered her eye-line and studied her face. Daniel immediately detected that his mother was crying.

He duly became extremely concerned and placed his arm over her shoulder.

'Mum? Mum…what's the matter Why are you upset?'

Sandra wiped her eyes and looked to her son with motherly affection.

He was so caring; so handsome; so entirely hers.

Putting down the chopping knife, she turned to face him and without further word, held out both arms. Daniel responded in kind, now beginning to panic a little about his mother's undue distress.

Pulling her closer into his embrace, he conveyed his worry.

'What's happened, Mum? I've never seen you like this before. What's the matter? Tell me.'

Pulling back slightly, she looked to him squarely and engaged with his natural and justified consternation.

She wiped her eyes again and cradled his reddened cheeks in her palms.

'Daniel…you do know that I love you…don't you?'

Puzzled by the sudden declaration, his brow furrowed.

Now Daniel was deeply perturbed.

He wasn't even sure how to respond to such an odd statement.

'Well…yeah of course…you're my *mum*. But I don't want to see you like this. You're not ill…are you? Is it Dad? Is he okay?'

She shook her head, gulping back her inner anguish as she observed Daniel's wide-eyed expression.

'Mum, tell me. Why are you crying?'

The response from Sandra was timely, with the evidence on full display to back her claim.

Her son would never need to know the truth behind her tears.

Sniffling in maternal relief, she slowly smiled and kissed Daniel softly on the nose.

'It's the onions, love. That's all. It's just the onions. So don't you worry! Get yourself off to Jason's. I'll see you later.'

Seemingly appeased by her feeble alibi, he smiled back at her before pulling away from the mildly embarrassing cuddle and reached for his trainers from under the table.

'Bye, Mum!' he called from the hallway.

Listening to him depart with the requisite slam of the front door, Sandra poured the casserole stock into the pot and slid it into the oven as her mind pondered life and all therein.

Evidently, to her mild dismay, her feelings for Andy Ratcliffe were not quite a thing of the past just yet.

31

ENCOUNTER

Sandra had become happily accustomed to spending her Saturday afternoons in the city High Street with Laura. However, with the onset of warmer weather, her daughter had begun to cry off from the ritual retail therapy sessions, preferring instead to meet up with her boyfriend, Craig.

Having recently passed his driving test, the offer of a spin in the country seemed an infinitely more attractive proposition than traipsing the shops with her mother in search of the elusive perfect garment or outfit.

In truth, Sandra was fully understanding of Laura's growing disinterest. After all, she was now eighteen. She was growing up fast and becoming increasingly independent. A-level results were pending. It was an exciting period of her life in all manner of ways.

Anyhow, Sandra still shopped alone. Secretly thankful for the time it afforded her away from the work and family environment. She had begun to relish the opportunity to wander freely at will.

Stuart's horticultural pursuits were now back in full swing and were keeping him fully occupied most weekends, so Saturdays officially became Sandra's day.

In recent conversation with Rose, she jokingly referred to it as The Alternative Mars Bar Day.

No work; a lot of rest; and a little play.

The sun was again high and warm with temperatures touching the mid-twenties by July.

Sandra ambled along her usual trail of outlets, casually scanning through windows for discounts and generally being absorbed by the throbbing mix of shoppers and the quest for a bargain.

In her respectably short, light blue summer dress and colour coordinated wedge heels, it was nice to feel the heat on her legs and arms, which added to a steadily deepening tan augmented during lazy late afternoons on the back patio.

After an hour or two, she was ready for a break from the hustle and bustle of the retail scrum.

Purchasing a can of pop and a fashion magazine, she ventured over to the market square and perched herself on a bench.

The area was amassed with groups of teenagers, either standing in groups laughing and talking or racing around the edge of the fountain on bicycles and roller skates.

They provided a pleasant diversion from the absolute seriousness of shopping. Infants splashed in the spurting water as the backdrop of juvenile excitement offered genuine entertainment for the onlooker.

Browsing through her read with a fair amount of disinterest, the cold drink felt refreshing as it fizzed and trickled down her throat. It was contenting to be at peace once again. Her life felt like her own once more, and the dual relaxation of mind and body was most welcome.

She was part-way through the agony aunt section when the thunderbolt crackled from the azure heavens on high. It landed next to her just as she was intrigued by a dubious account concerning the perils of double dating.

When the lightening hit, time stood still.

'Hello, gorgeous. Keeping my seat warm for me, are you?'

The voice was readily familiar, instantly breaking her attention from the page of fictionalised trivia. She looked up, squinting at the silhouette standing above her.

Shielding her eyes from the sun's glare with her hand, she immediately confirmed the identity of the man that had spoken in those low, seductive, gravelled tones.

'Oh…my…God…Andy! Oh my God!'

Sandra stood up, instantly overpowered by uncontrolled, intense excitement. In her haste, she tipped over the can of pop, which duly began to spill onto the floor through the slats in the bench. Her magazine fell from her lap to her feet, the pages flapping in the light breeze.

Without hesitancy or concern for possible witnesses, she leaned toward him and offered an embrace of genuine pleasure.

266

She was airborne once more.

In that split-second of wondrous proximity, the memories she had tried so hard to bury so deeply came racing back to the foreground.

That voice of pure velvet. The aura of implied passion.

His very presence immediately invigorated her beyond anything or anyone else she had ever known. Her expression altered to carry an edge of shock as she noticed his singular crutch, which he partially hid along the length of his body.

As ever, he was ready with the quick-fire assurances.

'Yes…the walking stick had to go. Need a bit of extra support now. They've changed my medication…again! So, I'm struggling a bit. But hey…with these looks, who's going to notice a long metal pole that helps me stay upright all day?'

She wanted to laugh along with his endearing self-mockery, but instead placed her hand to her mouth in disbelief. Her doe eyes moved upward once more and glazed over as she lost herself all over again in his perfect image.

His skin was naturally tanned, but the recent sunshine had increased the attraction of his dark, brooding visage. The crisp white t-shirt and black denims showed off his colouring to perfection.

'Crutch or not, I'd still fancy you! Andy. How's life, then? Apart from the obvious, obviously…'

He chuckled before nodding across the street.

'I'm good. The house went a few weeks back. I'm living with Annette for the time being. At her boyfriend's place. He's a good bloke. She's here with me now. She's just nipped into C & A for a five-minute half-hour browse!'

Sandra giggled knowingly.

'Yes…I understand…I've got one of those daughters, too!'

Andy glanced along the bench beside her.

'Where is your baby girl then? Not shopping with you?'

'No…I'm on my own today. Laura's gone out with her man for dinner in some luxurious country pub somewhere.'

He stared into Sandra, obviously enamoured by the chance meeting as much as she was.

'I spotted you across the square. I tried to hurry over but thought it'd take forever on this bloody thing!'

She chuckled again as he waved the crutch aloft in frustration.

'So, Sandra…how long you in town for?'

'Oh…I don't know…I've about had enough today to be honest. It's a bit hot and overbearing for intensive retail! Another half-hour…maybe? Not sure, yet.'

Displaying gleaming white teeth through a spellbinding smile, he moved closer to her, drawing her back under his spell just as before.

Her anticipation of his next words was all-consuming.

The actual proposition could not have proved to be more innocent.

'I wondered…'

'Yes, Andy…'

'…if you fancy joining an old friend for an ice cream?'

She nodded eagerly, pleased that his sense of humour had not diminished. Andy wavered before her. He seemed more unsteady on his feet than she had previously noticed. His movement seemed more awkward, as though he was unsure of direction.

But the simple invitation was accepted without hesitation.

'Yeah…I do fancy an ice cream. Where…here in the square?'

'Why not, indeed.'

As they talked, Annette eventually appeared carrying a bag containing a new outfit. She seemed initially surprised to behold Sandra, but quickly warmed to the idea of her father seeing someone familiar who made him so visibly positive.

She shook Sandra's hand, perhaps a little coyly after the upset that had elapsed during their previous crossing of paths at Trafalgar Gardens.

'Hello, Sandra. It's good to see you again.'

'And you, Annette. You look lovely.'

Andy's daughter blushed slightly and looked down to her feet, wanting her father to rescue her from her understandable if ever so slight unease in Sandra's presence.

The ever-reliable Mister Ratcliffe duly took the mantle.

'We were going for an ice cream. Want to join us?'

Annette checked her watch and scanned the heaving scene all around her.

'No thanks. I'll drop you off if you want to go somewhere else, though.'

Andy winked at Sandra and nodded his head.

'Great idea. I know just the place. Come on. Let's get away from all these nutcases. Get us some peace and quiet for a while.'

Sandra was curious, yet happy for the destination to remain a surprise.

'Not telling me where then, Andy?'

'You'll soon find out. Somewhere we both know quite well... somewhere...nice.'

*****

Bradham Park in the summertime.

A glorious exhibition of natural, consoling beauty.

Annette navigated the car into the vacant space and pulled on the handbrake before opening her door. From the rear seat, Sandra got out and was slightly alarmed to see Annette help her father to his feet.

'I'll come back for you in an hour, okay Dad? Or do you need a bit longer? Its nearly three o clock, now. I'm off to the garden centre.'

Andy looked at Sandra to gauge the mood.

'No...I think an hour will be fine. Thanks love. See you later.'

Annette kissed him tenderly on the cheek knowing that he was in good hands, before getting back into her car and winding the window down.

'Have fun! I'll see you both later!'

Sandra and Andy observed her car disappear through the main entrance and merge with the main road traffic before they finally turned to face each other.

269

The look they exchanged might have spoken a thousand words.

Yet the uncertainty between them belied an undercurrent that required exposure.

Not having satisfying closure to their unorthodox acquaintance was proving greatly unsatisfying for both.

Sandra had suffered due to her feelings for the man standing beside her and she had never expected to be in such a position.

Yet there they were, together once again.

The mixed feelings of the moment tormented her. It was almost as though life had never suggested a motive for their worlds to collide at all.

Andy gestured toward the centre of the parkland and gingerly began to walk.

'So…how's things at the bakery? I presume you still work there?'

As always, Sandra decided that honesty was the best policy.

She felt no need to be on her guard when talking with Andy.

'It's certainly not the same without you to look at! But I suppose it's for the best you don't come in anymore. I don't think the boss would appreciate seeing his staff man-handling customers!'

Andy's laughter resonated upward into the tall swaying poplar trees. They hissed an approving response on the gentle breeze.

'And the family? Stuart? Kids? All doing well, are they?'

Sandra was quickly becoming disenchanted with skirting the real issue. She did not want to talk about her husband or her children. She wanted to talk about her and Andy. And what was possibly left of their unpredictable, remaining time together.

She glanced along the narrow avenue of the parkland to the whispering foliage that gleefully flanked their path. Children could be heard shouting from the distant playground. Parents and kids on bicycles guided their young ones from in front and behind. Dogs chased balls and sticks as young couples shared picnics around the cricket pitch.

It was the quintessential summer scene.

A place of true peace; a place to think clearly.

Yet it failed miserably to stir the souls of two people.

As they ambled side by side, still unaware of fate's plans, they struggled to continue with the exchange of banter.

The hiatus in conversation finally forced Sandra to confess her long held feelings.

'That last night we shared. You know, it was...always will be...unforgettable.'

Seizing his opportunity, Andy tentatively probed her sense of humour, just to check she still had one.

'Yeah? Which night was that, then?'

She grinned reluctantly but did not look at him, continuing to stride purposely as he struggled to keep up with his singular crutch.

'I'm sorry, Andy. I'm going too fast.'

'No...not at all. It's me...I'm just not used to this bloody thing yet.'

Their stroll carried them across the footbridge that arched over the clear, gurgling stream below.

'That day...when I came to see you...and your wife was there...sorting your things out...it hurt me. I felt so sorry for you. In fact, I should be thankful that Annette was there to prevent any...well, confrontation, I suppose.'

Andy motioned with his free hand on spotting the ice cream van through the trees and they altered direction slightly.

'Why would there be confrontation, Sandra? Michelle hasn't got any feelings for me. She wouldn't get jealous or anything. She's not that sort of woman.'

They joined the queue that flanked the red and yellow van.

Sandra engaged meaningfully with his brooding gaze.

'No, Andy...but I am. I wouldn't be able to avoid getting jealous about you.'

The conversation stuttered again.

Armed with a vanilla ninety-nine apiece, they positioned themselves at the edge of the lake in the same seats as their visit a few months earlier.

Both scanned the water as they thoughtfully licked their cones.

The swans were still in residence yet sheaths of beautiful white feathers had almost completely eclipsed the brownie grey, unkempt plumage of their infancy.

They would soon be evolving into near replicas of their parents.

They were so graceful. And so unconcerned.

So untouched by the human world and its persistent, futile troubles.

'Well, Andy…what about you?'

He observed her warily, as though reserved about disclosing his opinions on a somewhat limited future.

'What about me?'

His reply induced mild irritation in Sandra, who changed her angle.

'Well…okay…what about *us*, then?'

The discomforting quiet duly resumed.

Emotional barriers had evidently raised themselves during their estrangement from one another and were not yet ready to drop.

He continued to watch the birds on the water, striving to try and allay her understandable curiosity with some form of appropriate answer.

Still Sandra continued to press the issue with growing impatience.

'Annette said something to me when I last saw her. That you wouldn't let me love you. Is that true? Is that what you really felt about us all along? Does commitment really make you so fearful?'

Now disgruntled with the stunted dialogue, Andy tossed what was left of his cornet into the pond, resulting in a frenzied inspection from the family of swans.

Sighing heavily, he pushed his fingers through his black hair, which had been allowed to grow considerably longer over the weeks.

He switched his attention to Sandra to try and address her demands but seemed outwardly nervous as he spoke with painful reticence.

'Sandra…you won't ever understand, what it's like for me. Living with this…problem. I can't be a normal bloke anymore. I can't do normal things. Have normal feelings. I know that's not the case for most sufferers, but I'm me. I can't help being…me. Call it self-indulgent. Call it what the hell you like. But here I am. That's it.'

272

Sandra duly finished her ice cream and crossed her legs.

Maybe as an instinctive gesture.

She wasn't even sure, herself.

'But Andy…I grew to like you…for *who* you are. Don't you get it? Your illness doesn't matter to me. You don't have to change for me. Never.'

He looked across to her. The stern glaze of his blue eyes and grimace of reluctance belied the warmth he truly felt for her in his heart.

Yet reality would not allow any light into his standpoint.

'But Sandra…I'm going to change whether I want to or not. It's unavoidable. I won't be like this forever. And you'll have to adapt to that change…and you'll have to change yourself…and I could never ask you to do that.'

Her hand rested on his knee as her tone increased in urgency.

'But I could change for you, Andy. If I needed to…I could!'

He shook his head and took her hand firmly in his.

'I think…we've been over this before…haven't we?'

The hard edge to the exchange had reduced again.

Now he conveyed his beliefs in a soft, tender tone that conveyed genuine care for the beautiful, reckless woman sitting beside him.

'Sandra…you're…perfect…just as you are. You wouldn't be who I fell for if you changed…would you? Do you understand, Sandra? We're just not…just not meant to be…'

She was not emotionally upset by his persistent dismissal of their relationship's potential.

Instead, Sandra felt an inner fury erupting deep within her.

Because she finally realised, that he was entirely correct in what he was saying.

There was no foundation for her to offer up any argument.

And his opinion was forged from firm logic and grim truth.

All angles she had considered fell by the wayside when drawn against Andy's common-sense approach.

No, she would probably not be prepared to care for him.

No, she did not wish to leave her husband of over twenty years, only to stand by and watch Andy deteriorate before her eyes.

Indeed, such a prospect filled her with unease and would ultimately prove more heart-wrenching in the long run.

She suddenly realised that the harsh facts were indisputable.

And that their brief, intoxicating, blinding love affair was truly concluded many weeks ago.

*****

Sixty minutes had seemed like sixty seconds. They walked slowly back through the parkland, along the central pathway to the main entrance.

Both being aware they now faced a painful if positive separation.

Annette was waiting patiently in her car as Sandra tried to hold off the moment of finality.

For the first time, Andy seemed racked with guilt over the inevitable end to their friendship. He could barely face her as she stood radiantly before him against the backdrop of the park.

Finally forcing himself to address Sandra's sorrowful gaze, he muttered what, unbeknown to them both at that moment, were to be his final words to her.

'Sandra…I'm sorry…okay? I don't know where life will take you…but I hope I'll always be with you…in here…somewhere.'

He gestured to his chest with a closed fist before turning toward Annette's car.

But Sandra was not quite willing to relinquish him just yet.

Succumbing to unbridled physical will, she pulled him into her arms. She squeezed her eyes tightly shut as she squeezed his body even tighter.

Not wanting to let him go, yet knowing that this would probably prove to be her last ever chance to touch him at all.

She lost herself in his manliness.

The feel of his limbs around her.

274

The fragrance of his aftershave.

The warmth of his breath.

Yet, as with most aspects of fate, their parting was unavoidable and pre-ordained.

The decision to follow different paths was not theirs to make.

Annette poked her head through the car window, respectfully observing the moment of tenderness before leaving the car and walking slowly toward them.

She watched as her father solemnly retracted from the tender union with Sandra.

Now by her father's side, she linked her arm into his. The offer to Sandra of a lift home was politely declined.

Sandra needed the walk to clear her head once again.

Annette held out a hand of farewell.

'Goodbye, Sandra. It was a privilege to know you. Maybe we'll see each other in town...sometime...'

Sandra kissed Annette on the cheek and wished her well as Andy looked disconsolately into the distance.

'Annette...'

The younger woman waited for Sandra's instruction, which was simple and earnest.

'...please...look after him for me.'

The girl looked to her father's best friend and nodded quietly.

'You bet.'

Watching Andy being helped into the car, Sandra fought to remain still and stoical.

Thankful for the absence of open emotion at that moment.

There was no song and no dance.

No final word of hope.

Any remaining wishes or regrets were now rendered immaterial.

Andy and Sandra stared at each other; both seemingly lost.

Now separated by the glass of the car window.

And separated by their destinies.

There were no tears.

And no joy.

Just a mutual, frustrating acceptance of things.

Life and it's confusing, if occasionally exhilarating plan.

Sandra watched in dignified silence, as Annette's car pulled away and departed Bradham Park.

Through those wrought-iron, rusting gates.

Taking with it, the only real dream she'd ever had.

32

LIFE GOES ON

A new Millennium dawns.

A dozen summers and winters had elapsed since that final goodbye at the edge of Bradham Park.

Twelve years that had naturally incurred certain changes to the Bancroft household, both by external circumstance and through choice.

Now at a buoyant fifty-five years of age, Sandra had stayed loyal to and had progressed at Turner's.

In itself, something of a minor miracle, as the business had been rendered vulnerable to closure at least four times during this period.

With her faithful mentor Rose Riley having retired some three years ago, Sandra had graciously accepted the vacant role of shop manager.

But another development was in the pipeline. Mick Turner himself was more than ready to hang up his rolling pin and put his feet up in older age, and in consideration of this plan he had supplied something of a generous clause.

Sandra and Stuart had been offered first refusal on taking over the reins of the bakery as all-out proprietors.

It was a very tempting offer. One which would provide certain securities for their family's future. Indeed, acceptance of such a sensible and courteous proposition was not beyond the realms of reason. Stuart had concluded a successful banking career twelve months ago and turned his attention to horticulture as a full-time if barely paying hobby.

Yet he acknowledged that there was some scope in assessing the possibility of taking over a still-thriving town centre concern.

But as with most families, other more pressing issues had presented themselves. The Bancroft clan had also altered.

New arrivals had descended upon the family unit.

New arrivals that demanded love, care, and consideration.

*****

277

Laura let herself in through the front door of Number Twelve, Orchard Road and hollered through the hallway.

'Hi Mum! Dad? We're here!'

Sandra emerged from the kitchen, a beaming smile adorning her features as she hugged her daughter.

'Hi-ya, love. Where's Craig and my little soldier?'

'Just locking the car. Thomas is with him.'

Standing with her arms folded in the doorway, Sandra felt her inner pride swell as she watched her son-in-law walk up the driveway, whilst holding the hand of her five-year-old grandson.

On seeing his grandmother, the little one squirmed from his father's grasp and eagerly scampered toward her, his blond hair glistening in the midday sunshine.

Naturally, Sandra erupted with sheer delight.

'Hello, little Tommy! And how's my grand baby boy today?'

Flashing eyes of brightest azure, the cherub readily jumped into her arms and gave her a sloppy kiss full on the lips.

'Oh…your grandma has missed you! Yes, she has! And who have you come to see today?'

Resuming terra firmer in the hallway, Thomas eyed his grandmother with curiosity as he thought long and hard about the question. He placed a finger to his lips, frowned slightly and held Sandra's gaze, which in turn encouraged her to offer a little clue.

'Come on Thomas! Who have you come to see, today? He's small…furry…has a tail…'

Having an answer materialise in his head - albeit the incorrect one - the youngster jumped up and down with excitement.

'GRANDAD!'

Sandra clapped her hands in pleasured hilarity as Craig entered the fray and closed the front door behind him.

'Laura hasn't shut up about this all bloody week!'

With the family finally convened in the lounge, Sandra opted to lead the introduction ceremony.

'Okay…everybody be quiet…because today…I'd like you to meet someone for the very first time. But remember, he's still very, very shy. So…Thomas…and Laura…no shouting or screaming! Just sitting and watching…okay? You don't want to frighten him, do you?'

Thomas shook his head, grinned excitedly, and clasped his hands on his lap as expectation grew.

Laura perched on the edge of the settee next to her father. Brimming with anticipation, she clutched mischievously at his kneecap, causing him to yelp and giggle.

With Craig crouched at the lounge door, the time was ripe for Sandra to unveil the newest member of the household.

She slowly retreated into the kitchen and carefully pulled open the conservatory door. The silent throng waited with bated breath, as Sandra returned to the living room and stationed herself in front of the hearth.

Again, she pressed the need for everyone to be quiet and whispered a commentary to accompany the suspected movements of the latest family addition.

'Here he comes…hush now…be still…'

All eyes focused on the kitchen as a vague and shadowy movement could be detected on the shiny tiled floor next to the fridge. Then in tandem with the unfamiliar presence, an inquisitive meow emitted from behind the door.

Soon to follow, a tiny white paw appeared in the gap between the door and frame, frantically grasping for a way through to the next room.

Having successfully navigated an entrance, the little ball of ginger and white fluff peered through two enormous green eyes at his captive audience.

With ears and tail pointing straight upward, he scanned each face in turn before emitting another barely audible call for his adoptive human mother and vastly experienced filler of food bowls.

Responding to the kitten's cry of curiosity, Sandra carefully shifted her position and cradled the unkempt fusion of claws, whiskers, and fur in one hand.

Slowly offering him up for closer inspection to the wide-eyed and admiring audience, she proudly boasted of the most recent inhabitant of Number Twelve.

'Ladies and gentlemen, boys and girls…I present to you…my new little friend…'

Laura squealed with delight at the sight of the adorably cute newcomer, who continued to stare bemusedly at the gathering of strange spectators, whilst gripping onto Sandra's right index finger with both front paws.

'…one and all…please welcome…Mister Jones.'

On seeing the endearing little face of the kitten, Thomas jumped from the sofa and ran directly to his grandmother.

To his eternal credit, Mister Jones endured ten seconds of severe stroking, kissing and ruffling from the five-year-old, before leaping from Sandra's grasp and escaping back into the conservatory.

*****

The afternoon sunshine successfully enticed the family onto the back garden. Drinks were served and the patio and lawn were vibrantly occupied amidst a warm, golden glow.

Stuart invited Craig for a tour of the garden and now fully extended greenhouse which, from a distance, surprisingly appeared to generate more than a semblance of interest from the son-in-law even though he'd seen it all before several times.

Thomas managed to encourage Mister Jones onto the lawn in a game of chase the string, leaving Sandra and Laura to recline together on deckchairs and enjoy the entertainment.

'Oh, Mum. He's so gorgeous! How old is he?'

Sandra chuckled at the affectionate scenario playing out before them.

'Six weeks. I know I said I wouldn't have another cat, but the house seemed to lack something after we lost Missy.'

'I know, Mum. She was a great pet. Losing her hit you harder than *Dad*.'

'Well, I wasn't planning on it, but I just happened to pick up the local free paper one day and a breeder was advertising a new litter.'

Laura observed her son as he uncontrollably laughed out loud at the frustrated feline frantically clawing at fresh air and shadow.

'She only lives in the next village. They were all so lovely, but that one kitten was the *only* one that turned and looked at me when I visited. The others just carried on feeding as though I wasn't even there!'

Laura leaned forward in her chair.

'I *love* the name, Mum. It's a touching tribute. I've always wanted a cat. But we had Thomas instead!'

Her mother laughed.

'Yes…cats and babies don't often mix! Actually, I'm sure I've still got *this* week's local paper somewhere. Hang on.'

Laura sipped her drink as her mother disappeared into the kitchen and returned in a matter of seconds.

'She might still be selling the rest of the litter. I'll have a quick flick through…see if I can find the advert for you.'

Laura watched the activity around her as her mother began to scan the pages of the free journal through the lenses of her bi-focal spectacles. Becoming quickly disenchanted with her search as she studied the classified section, she quickly cast her eyes over the obituaries.

'Have you found it, Mum?'

'Not yet. I'm just checking I'm not among the deceased! Always good to know. Offers peace of mind when I know I haven't croaked it yet. Strange habit, eh? I'm not quite ready to join the dead just yet!'

Laura nodded and chuckled at her mother's slightly sick sense of humour. But as she continued to absorb the aura of contentment that occupied the back garden, Laura would not have realised that a full minute had elapsed without another word being spoken by Sandra.

Or the reason behind her mother's involuntary silence.

Sandra's heart almost stopped as she spotted his name at the bottom of the column.

Surely it couldn't be him?

Not the same man she knew so intimately and so briefly from all those years ago.

Even with the progression of his illness, he was surely still too young to have paid the ultimate price.

Sandra read the entire tribute over and over in her head.

The evidence was all too damning, as she disbelievingly analysed the short yet painfully cutting notice.

RATCLIFFE,
ANDREW IAN
LOVING FATHER TO ANNETTE
DAD - YOU WERE THE BEST!

PASSED AWAY SUDDENLY
TUESDAY 8TH AUGUST AGED 53.
FUNERAL TUESDAY 22nd AUGUST 10am
CITY CREMATORIUM

'Mum…have you found it, yet?'

Sandra did not even hear her daughter speak.

Her mind had been swiftly transported from the rear patio in Orchard Road, to another, presumably long forgotten world.

To a distant, fantastical place where she had reluctantly left her dreams behind many years ago.

She quickly read the notice once again as her heart slowly regained a regular beat. The sudden shroud of sorrow was matched only by her over-riding bemusement.

Her thought process began to whirr in a madly confused debate with itself.

He was only a couple of years younger than she was. No. It couldn't have been his illness. The disease would have advanced, but surely it couldn't have caused his passing so prematurely.

He must have had an accident.

Or worse.

Staring blankly into space, she closed the newspaper, much to the concern of her daughter, who furrowed her brow at Sandra's trance-like state.

'Mum? Did you find the advert for the cat breeder?'

Finally, Sandra re-registered the identity of her surroundings.

She looked at her husband and son-in-law by the greenhouse.

She watched her grandson playing with Mister Jones.

And she eventually engaged with her daughter's understandably bewildered expression.

Sandra felt an urgent need to depart from the scene for a moment of personal tranquillity.

A minute to contemplate.

To be alone with her thoughts.

To conjure the memories of a man she knew once upon a time.

A man she truly believed she may have loved.

A man who was now gone forever.

She turned to Laura, trying to remember the question her daughter had asked before searching vainly for some kind of answer.

'Erm…cats…no, love. The advert isn't in this week's edition. Please…excuse me…'

Promptly leaving her deckchair and entering the kitchen, Sandra knew instinctively that she would attend Andy's funeral.

This reflexive decision was rapidly followed by the frantic notion that she may be too late. Checking the calendar, she confirmed with immense relief. Today was Sunday the twentieth.

The cremation would be taking place in two days' time. The knowledge that she had not missed his final farewell swept through her, cleansing her heart with misplaced relief.

She supposed that upset should be the correct reaction. Yet, she could not feel sad. Observing the endearing exhibition of family contentment beyond the kitchen window, she folded her arms and smiled.

She smiled out of pride for what she had achieved.

And despite great personal misgivings at the time, pride in herself that she had opted not to throw it away all those years ago.

Sandra felt intensive appreciation for what she saw in the garden at that moment.

She exuded genuine love for the people in her fold.

And then her conscience again revived thoughts of Andy.

The supposedly parting of ways at Bradham Park twelve years ago was evidently, not quite, the last goodbye.

That was now still to come.

Bloody typical of Andy Ratcliffe.

Teasing her to the very end.

She was still lost in pensive reflection when another familiar voice disturbed her moment of whimsy.

'Hey, Mum! How's things? Where's the kitty, then?'

The loud tones boomed through the kitchen doorway breaking her concentration. Daniel had just arrived with his girlfriend, Louise.

As the latest visitors instantly eclipsed the lingering vision of Andy, she carefully filed her thoughts of him to the back of her mind.

'Any beer in the fridge, Mum? It's roasting! Come on! Where's this pussycat, then?'

Sandra kissed her son and Louise in turn before escorting them outside.

Back into the summer sunshine.

Back into the bosom of her family.

Back from that distant, mystical place of eternal longing that time had now almost fully erased.

33

GOODBYE, FAREWELL, AMEN

Tuesday the twenty-second of August. Year Two Thousand.

It was always due to be a relatively normal day.

The typical routine of home, then work, then home again.

At least, that was the original plan.

Until forty-eight hours ago.

When Sandra had inadvertently stumbled upon the public notice for a friend's final departure.

Mick Turner had understood implicitly.

He fully grasped the importance that the day carried for the manager of his bakery come cafe.

But then, he always had been a very considerate and discreet boss.

Besides which, it would provide the apt opportunity for the new serving assistant at Turner's to prove her worth under increased pressure.

Mick privately sympathised with Sandra's cause as she exited the shop's rear fire door to head for the crematorium.

Out of necessary caution, she had taken her change of clothes to Turner's to attire in the staff room. Dressed in a black skirt and jacket, she did not feel at all discomforted about the imminence of the occasion as she climbed into Rose Riley's new car.

Ever the friend in need was Rose. Even though she had retired, she was still the reliable alibi. Of course, she would take Sandra to the funeral. The secret was still safe and would forever remain so.

Yet strangely, the journey for Sandra became gradually fraught with personal doubt as to whether she should attend at all.

Aside her trusted confidantes, nobody even knew she was going to the crematorium that day.

Not her own family.

Not Andy's family.

No one.

But she knew she had to be there.

The last gesture to a man she still cared so deeply about.

Initially, Sandra didn't even wish to know the details of his passing.

The simple fact that she could be present for his ultimate bow was partial consolation for the years during which she so wished to set eyes on him once again.

Her personal sense of loss was not so much one of emotional hurt.

More a primitive aching from deep within her core.

But she hoped this anguish would soon be over.

And as she alighted from Rose's car outside the crematorium entrance, the amusing thought occurred that she might just meet Andy again one day, and they might fulfil their once very potent yet strictly forbidden promise.

Up there somewhere.

In that special place where dreams surely must come true.

*****

The morning sunshine already blazed high against a deep blue backcloth.

The ominous appearance of the single storey red brick construction honed into view as she strode along the delicately landscaped pedestrian approach.

Stepping tentatively through the carefully tended surroundings of the crematorium complex, she could observe a small throng of mourners outside the chapel.

Sandra re-assessed the time with her watch.

It was nine minutes to ten.

The group were evidently in waiting for Andy to make his grand entrance.

Strangely, after arriving at the venue, Sandra's nerves had settled.

Nor did she yet sense any emotional upsurge typically associated with such an event.

She was now driven by an overwhelming sense of justification.

Her misgivings during the drive there had thankfully subsided.

286

She had every right to stand with Andy's circle and wish him on his way.

It was again as though she were following some loyal ordainment.

Sandra would never let Andy down. Especially now.

She positioned herself to one side of the gathering. She listened politely as voices emitted the usual cursory mutterings at regular intervals.

Individuals offered a brief and curious glance in her direction from time to time. Appropriately, there was a suitable dosage of laughter in the air.

The atmosphere was positively upbeat, just as Andy would have wanted.

But naturally, Sandra recognised nobody.

And naturally in turn, she was unknown to anyone present.

Then another amusing thought occurred.

That Andy might just have set the whole thing up.

So that he could jump from the hearse when it pulled up. She envisaged him, flipping up the lid of the box and having a good giggle at everyone's expense.

But sadly, this was no charade.

And the hush that immediately descended at first sight of the funeral cortege, brought the upsetting fact of the matter to the forefront of all minds.

Two silver limousines wound their way steadily along the path toward the expectant party. Sandra remained apart from the main group, preferring instead to reside in the shade of a tree, out of view from most.

To see the hearse at close quarters immediately crushed her well-intended sense of composure. Her heart raced and body perspired as her moistened gaze settled unavoidably on the primed white coffin that lay peacefully in its cradle of blue flowers.

The hearse came to a halt under the entrance veranda. Four appointed mourners appeared, standing in wait for the second car to station close behind.

Sandra watched the second limousine in fragile silence as it pulled to a stop, allowing the passengers inside to gradually emerge from behind the tinted glass doors.

Twelve years had altered appearances.

Annette looked visibly older, yet even more beautiful for the fact.

Her previously shoulder length hair was now cropped stylishly short, and she looked every inch the doting, grieving daughter.

Andy would have been so proud to see her at that moment.

Beside her, a tall and handsome-looking man positioned himself behind the hearse. Dressed in a black suit, his determined and fixed expression suggested that he may have been Annette's boyfriend.

Evidently, he had been appointed as pallbearer.

Reaching for the coffin as it was gently extricated from its cradle, he removed the wreath laying on top, which had been created from a circular arrangement of red roses.

Sandra's determination to hold firm began to falter rapidly, as she saw the word that those most regal of flowers had formed.

It simply said:

DAD.

Sandra struggled to focus on the other two members of the group that had accompanied Annette in her car.

An elderly couple. Presumably married.

Both with grey hair. Both walked with a stooped gait.

Both perhaps in their late seventies. Maybe older.

And then Sandra was distracted by a vaguely familiar face that approached the desolate scene.

Michelle's appearance had hardly changed from the photograph Sandra had briefly spied on Andy's bedside drawer all those years ago.

The woman offered little in the way of emotion.

Maybe a hint of a smile acknowledged the waiting group.

Annette's mother.

Andy's first, and only wife.

Together with the man she abandoned him for.

Tanned, sharp-featured and stern, she stood by respectfully with her presumed new husband and casually observed the sympathetic crowd.

Sandra's inner response was one of dismay.

The Ex quite rightly hid her suspect expression behind a pair of large sunglasses, whilst paying polite greeting to the faces that gathered ever tighter around the entrance.

Her daughter Annette on the other hand noticed nobody and spoke to no one as the ceremony commenced.

All present duly observed her father's coffin as it was lifted to shoulder height and paraded slowly into the chapel to the sound of a soft organ accompaniment.

By protocol, Annette followed next.

She gently ushered the elderly couple to walk with her into the chamber, which then encouraged a steady procession behind them.

Deep solemnity hung in the air.

Complete silence again resumed upon the incomers, allowing the many attendees to make their entrance and take their preferred positions.

Out of courtesy, Sandra decided to wait until last of all, filing in behind as the sorrowful procedure ensued.

She sat quietly in the back pew.

Separated both physically and emotionally from the main group.

Content to be alone with her own personal recall.

And now alone with her own sudden, intrusive, intensive remorse.

She listened as the deafening quiet endured, whilst maintaining her attention on the ivory-coloured coffin that now lay plinthed in the corner, ready for its final curtain call.

She observed Annette replace the wreath of roses on the casket lid before sitting next to the elderly couple on the front row.

And Sandra then offered deep scrutiny to the woman behind Andy's daughter who, almost as though she detected the look of scorn from the rear of the room, turned to glance briefly in Sandra's direction.

Her features still partly masked by the large sunglasses.

Finally, the celebrant made his subtle entry on to the podium.

Visually absorbing the room for a few contemplative seconds, he began his address to the despairing congregation.

With immediate effect, the emotive content of the tribute began to infect the fragile stillness within those present. As he opened his verse, unavoidable tears became increasingly audible.

The reverend was a thin, pleasant looking man in spectacles. With a soft yet affecting tone. He smiled as he talked, gesturing with his hands, inviting the gathering to appreciate his earnest words of appraisal.

Sandra wanted to hear every single syllable of the homage to a man that still occupied an unspeakably large place in her heart and soul.

And always would.

Yet that same heart how it now wrenched, as the foreboding, inevitable conclusion to their brief liaison advanced ever closer.

'Dearly Beloved.

Whilst today we convene through our rightful sense of compassion, our feelings of loss and the weight of our grief, we are also present here today to pay our final respects to Andrew.

For comfort and for hope, let us centre our thoughts to the presence of God.

Amid such sorrow, we turn to his words for strength. God is adequate for each situation and circumstance of life.

He is a God of sympathy and understanding. He knows of our hurt and our loneliness. He understands how we suffer. The Bible tells us that he mourns our sorrow and records our tears.

Today we commemorate the instance that will affect us all. When we are face to face with the two greatest mysteries of the universe.

Life.

And death.

Death is a certainty. Life, sadly not so.

Let us again look to God in prayer.

Eternal God, our Heavenly Father, from whom our souls have derived, and to whom our souls must eventually be returned.

Dear God, help us to journey before you with reverent and submissive hearts, that as we listen to the scriptures beautifully written and meaningfully read, we may be lifted above our darkness and distress and reside within the comfort and protection of your presence.

Death forces us to trust in the Almighty's boundless love. At death we come to the end of human knowledge, human power, and human sustenance. We are left to the mercy of God.

God is love. And this is a glorious fact to lean and rejoice upon.

God's promise is to never leave us nor forsake us.

We are taught not to fear that which destroys the body only. Rather, he said fear him who can destroy both soul and body. Man is primarily a soul. Physical bodies are mere conduits for the spirit.

Finally, we are taught that death is a doorway to the future. Without death, we could never know the future. Death is something planned and necessary in the eyes of God. It is an appointed event that will unavoidably come to each of us in turn.

We are quite naturally saddened by death because of our fears, our uncertainty, the personal loneliness that it brings, and by our lack of faith.

We are naturally reluctant for death to invade our families, our circle of friends and our loved ones.

Today we mourn Andrew because of the fond memories. Such memories are a blessing to us. They bring tears now, but subsequently they will bring joy.

As the only son to David and Caroline, and as doting father to his only daughter, Annette, Andrew faced the daunting prospect of physical adversity from the age of thirty-five, when the diagnosis of Multiple Sclerosis was confirmed.

Despite the affliction to his health, he has been described as a consistently humorous man, who would always take the opportunity to create laughter when sadness abounded.

A man who would readily mock himself first, rather than amuse at the misfortune of those around him.

291

Also being a quietly spoken character, Andrew never once bemoaned his ailing to witnesses.

Never once was it recalled that he did place his own needs before those of others even though, in later life, the quality of his existence diminished significantly.

He enjoyed the great outdoors immensely, despite his increasingly limited capacity to independently seek such natural pleasures.

He enjoyed the company of people and found them to be an endless source of fascination throughout his younger life and especially in his remaining days in residence at St Johnston's nursing home, where he found several companions to converse with daily.

But the greatest love of his life was the aforementioned Annette, who whenever possible, bravely assisted her father through the latter days of his illness, before his condition required more advanced, professional attention.

In similar fashion, he remains the love of her life also, and it is with this sentiment in mind that we have agreed to Annette's request to alter the orthodox order of service today.

As you will already be aware, hymns and prayers have not been requested to accompany Andrew's final passage onwards into the netherworld.

Instead, we have a song.

A song of Andrew's personal choice; from his own favourite artist.

Not only in commemoration of his relationship with his daughter, but also in reference to a very special friend, whose love and loyalty it is claimed, served him great solace during his final days.

And so, we must now join the grieving family, in helping them adjust to their considerable loss.

In accordance with Annette's wishes, could the congregation please be standing as the Lord receives Andrew.'

*****

Sandra watched as all around rose to their feet, wiping the grief from their eyes as the music began to linger across the room.

She felt numbed, wondering, hoping, that the un-named person in the service could possibly be her.

Stupid, selfish, and inappropriate thoughts cursed her fitful concentration.

Or did he refer to *another* special friend?

Did Andy perhaps meet somebody else after her?

As the coffin began to glide gently into the darkness, the guitar's introduction to the song provided immediate confirmation.

That Sandra was indeed that cherished, unidentified confidante.

Wonderful Tonight. The anthem for lovers.

The song they danced to in his lounge at Trafalgar Gardens.

And Sandra's longing had endured with this piece of music as the eternal soundtrack. But no longer could she uphold the pretence.

Her excruciating stoicism gave way to her tears, as the torturous seconds of finality brought the unbearable truth to all present.

Enveloped in the tender atmosphere of the occasion, the throng's audible and visible display of sorrow was unbearable to digest. Andy's coffin disappeared behind the navy-blue drapes, forever lost.

To another, hopefully better world.

The intimate beauty of the music was so ruthlessly devastating.

Filing from the chapel pew by pew, the group slowly amassed outside to express condolence to Annette.

Sandra again waited at the back of the line, not wishing to make her presence obvious to strangers. One by one, Annette thanked the attendees as the procession of remorse dispersed into the welcoming summer sunshine.

Until, finally, Sandra came face to face with Andy's daughter.

The joy of recognition, of sadness and of mutual loss engulfed the pair as they joined once more in a trembling union of acknowledgement.

Annette wailed into Sandra's earnest embrace, who also conceded to her upset once more.

The moment lasted for a full minute before both felt suitably able to acknowledge one another with renewed composure.

With the words sticking in her throat, Sandra stammered her sympathies as Annette's angelic features again became etched with grief.

Finally, the daughter spoke, in calm, measured tones.

'I'm so sorry, Sandra. I didn't know whether to tell you he'd gone. I'm so pleased you're here. He never forgot you. Right to the very end…he never, ever forgot about you.'

Sandra smiled and nodded as the saltwater fell from her eyes.

'I know.' she mouthed.

Annette gestured with a forefinger.

'Don't go just yet. I've to thank the reverend. Then I still need to say things to you.'

Sandra moved from the building and into the welcome warmth beyond. The sun bathed her in an uplifting light, somehow erasing the downbeat intensity of the previous minutes. Annette quickly returned to her side and the two walked with arms linked around the burial grounds of the crematorium.

With a soothing air descending over them, a conversation began.

'I can't come to the wake, Annette. I've got to return to work. But I've got to know one thing…did he go peacefully?'

Cleansing her face with a tissue, Annette took a deep breath before supplying her ready response.

'He was coping well with the illness. His mobility was increasingly restricted, but he was still getting around with support. But he was the same old Dad, really.'

Sandra touched Annette's shoulder with a steadying, reliable hand.

'How long was he in care for?'

'About…the last five years. Until then, he stayed with me and James, my boyfriend. But, with us both working, Dad eventually needed that little bit more hands on help. What he got from the house sale was used for that. Hung onto it all those years he did. Just for the purpose.'

Sandra looked deep into Annette's blue eyes, searching for the knowledge that still eluded.

The knowledge that her head did not wish to digest, but her heart pleaded to discover.

'So…how? If he was coping well with things…what happened?'

With a renewed burst of emotion, Annette struggled to stay assured, yet remained determined to supply Sandra with history's tale.

'He was in the gardens of the care home. Just reading a magazine, I think. Nothing strenuous, as normal! Anyway…he suffered a massive stroke. Right there on the bench. He never came out of the coma. He never knew a thing…just as though someone flicked the off switch.'

In a futile attempt at consolation, Sandra welcomed Annette's crumbling form back into her arms. Holding her close, she looked to the intrigued onlookers who were evidently curious as to the identity of the woman who had engaged Annette's attention in such an informal and integral way.

In particular, the elderly couple who had entered the funeral arena with Annette. They stood close together, bemused by the impassioned scene in the short distance.

Drawing her head up once again, Annette forced a smile and looked deep into Sandra's equally torn gaze.

'The song we played…it was for you. *Just* for you. Dad told me about it years ago. He said you'd get it….'

Sandra's features became inscribed with desolation.

Yet she was inflated by memories of that secret evening long ago.

Of that special dance.

Of that incredulous, singular union in the shadows of the night.

'Yes…I get it. Thank you, Annette. It means so much.'

The elderly couple still scrutinized from the end of the driveway, peering, and pointing for advice from others who had joined them.

Sandra felt the compulsion to confirm her suspicions.

'Just one more thing, Annette. The lady and gentleman who came with you…who are they? Neighbours?'

Annette turned slowly and waved to the subjects of the question.

Their responsive gesture led her to face back to Sandra.

Her eyes lit up, no longer tainted with the sadness of earlier.

'Don't you know?'

With raised eyebrows, Sandra shook her head.

'They keep looking at us, that's all…thought they might be wondering who you are talking to.'

Annette chuckled and placed a hand to her mouth.

'That's Dad's parents. It's Grandma and Grandad! Didn't you know about them?'

Along with the sensation that she had somehow already known the previously unspoken answer, it still came as something of a surprise.

'No. He never once mentioned them. How are they coping?'

'I don't think it's quite sunk in yet. They aren't as alert as they used to be. Old age and all that.'

There and then, Sandra felt sated. There was little else to say.

In that instance of finality, she pledged in her own mind never to see Annette again. Kissing her goodbye, she wished Andy's daughter well for the rest of her life.

As she watched the younger woman return to her family, Sandra turned on her heel and made her way to the entrance gates, where Rose Riley awaited to take her friend back to work.

It had been long-awaited closure to a chapter that had occurred exactly thirteen years earlier.

Through her upset, Sandra had finally acquired a positive perspective that enswathed her amid the reality of Andy's passing.

Yet now, she finally accepted that Andy was never really hers.

And that she was never truly his.

Yet the knowledge that she had remained in his heart was so gratifying.

As she departed the scene, Sandra's underlying pleasure was for the fact that despite the nature of her fractured friendship with Andy Ratcliffe, she would remain ever thankful.

Thankful that her life, just for that brief, enticing period, had been touched by the potential of an incredible adventure.

A short-lived journey she had taken, that lay beyond her wildest previous imagination.

But that was just it.

It was mostly imagined.

It could never, ever have become real in the fullest sense.

And Sandra was content to accept that dreams don't come true.

After all, they aren't supposed to.

Are they?

'Mister Jones! Come out of there! Look…din-dins…come on…'

Stuart entered the kitchen to discover Sandra on her hands and knees. Her head and shoulders were concealed however, due to the fact that her top half was positioned in the cupboard underneath the sink.

He smiled knowingly, seizing the opportunity for mild ridicule.

'I said you were too old to run around after pets! It took us twenty-five years to get rid of the kids! Never mind chasing bloody kittens now! Where's he got to?'

Sandra's muffled response echoed from the depths of the bleach cabinet, leaving Stuart struggling to decipher Mister Jones' exact whereabouts.

'Where do you say? Behind the washing machine?'

'Yeffmmph!' Sandra barked from the gloom.

His amusement at her latest attempts to rescue the new arrival from a fate worse than death was interrupted by the shrill tone of the telephone in the lounge.

Still smirking, he maintained focus on the episode in the kitchen as he moved to answer it.

The familiar voice of the caller served to disperse his smile immediately as he placed a cautious hand over the mouthpiece.

'Sandra! It's the dragon! What do I tell her?'

Resigned to temporary defeat, Sandra reversed from her uncomfortable posture and clambered gingerly to her feet, rubbing her aching knees.

Red-faced and mildly angered, she snatched the handset from Stuart, who was now embarking on a fit of the giggles.

'Oi! Smart Alec! You see if you can get him from out of there, then! There's cables and water pipes and all sorts down there! The little bugger's bound to chew on something! Hello mother!'

Moving back into the kitchen, Stuart ascertained his options as he scrutinised the available evidence.

For a start, the cat's food bowl was empty.

The logical step in enticement of a feline was surely to fill it.

No sooner had the task been achieved, than Mister Jones' inquisitive furry head appeared from the shadows of the cupboard.

With a twitch of his pink nose and silken whiskers, the maturing kitten leapt to the side of the bowl in one graceful bound and proceeded to dine with customary enthusiasm. Stuart pulled back the kitchen door to allow Sandra full view of his instant success.

She pursed her lips in frustration as Phyllis Baxter ranted incessantly in her ear. Much to his amusement, Stuart listened to his wife fend off each of her mother's requests with accomplished ease.

'Yes, Mum.'

'Yes, we'll bring Tommy round tomorrow.'

'Yes...with your shopping.'

'No don't touch the bandage...don't pull at it.'

'The scab will come off on its own.'

'Listen...I've got to go to work now.'

'Well, do you want me to send Stuart round to see to it?'

'No...thought not.'

'I'll see you tomorrow, then.'

'And don't worry.'

'And don't pick at that bandage!'

'Yeah...see you tomorrow, Mum.'

'Love you too! Bye!'

Stuart watched his wife place the phone back on the hook, a little relieved that he had avoided secondment to assist his mother-in-law.

'Now what's up with the old battle axe?'

Sandra shook her head, making sure she secured the kitchen cabinet, which was being casually inspected once again by a fully engorged ginger and white kitten.

'Oh...she's just moaning that scab is itching on her arm from when she fell over a couple of weeks back. Just being a nuisance as normal. Right, I'm off to work. See you tonight.'

Stuart escorted her to the front door.

'You sure you don't want a lift, love?'

'No…it's okay. I've used the bus for that long. I quite like it now!'

He kissed her on the lips as she stepped onto the driveway.

'By the way, Sandra…make sure you tell Mick about our decision.'

'Yes, dear.'

'And tell him why we've had to say no.'

'Yes, dear.'

'But thank him for thinking of us, anyway!'

'Yes, dear.'

'And have a good day!'

'Always do, dear. Byeeeee!'

Appreciative of Sandra's ever-reliable sense of humour, Stuart watched her walk round the corner to the bus stop before shutting the front door.

*****

As she stood waiting patiently in the early September sunshine, it suddenly occurred to Sandra how passing time fails to alter certain aspects of daily life.

The bus pulled up and hissed to a stop, revealing the grizzled features of the most unsociable bus driver in the northern hemisphere.

The thought occurred that surely he should have retired by now.

As ever, she prepared herself for the battle of wits and adopted the practised air of feigned civility.

'Morning.'

The grump grunted in response as he checked her pass for the ten thousandth time in his career, before shutting the doors with an affirming slam. Sandra steadily stepped down the aisle to her usual seat, keeping a firm hold onto the safety bars as she did so.

And as was completely predictable, the driver dropped his foot down onto the throttle, causing the vehicle to lurch forward.

And its contents to be thrown backward.

Eventually, having finally secured her backside into the seat of choice, Sandra returned her purse to her handbag and stared into the driver's rear-view mirror.

And for the first time in many fruitless years of trying, she finally caught his gloating, leathery face, gurning back at her with a gleeful grimace.

She smiled at his amused reflection, before straightening her lips and mouthing the one word that had remained unspoken for over two decades at the hands of this uncaring, unsociable, miserable bully.

'Bastard!' she whispered, watching his embarrassed glare rapidly avert from the mirror and back out front.

Laughing inwardly at such a well-earned if small victory, she rested her attention beyond the window and enjoyed the passing late summer scene far more than she could ever previously recall.

*****

Turner's was in the middle of the usual dinner time rush.

And the shop seemed busier than ever before.

School children were back at school. Pensioners had collected their pensions. Single mothers had collected their tots from nursery. Market traders sneaked a break. Traffic wardens hid from their victims…

All formed in a disorderly queue, eager for a taste of the local delicatessen's wares. Julie, the recently appointed new apprentice was in fact doing a sterling job at the till in keeping the waiting throng at a minimum, whilst Sandra flitted between the kitchen and the serving counter.

For half an hour she alternated between fetching fresh produce from the ovens and assisting Julie with orders.

'Sandra…where are the little plates kept? I'll need a new stack warming.'

Sandra nodded and reached for the cabinet door where crockery was stored.

301

Rummaging for the requested plates, her attention was diverted by a voice from the other side of the counter.

She withdrew from the hot cupboard and closed the door as the words registered amid the clanging chimes of history.

Inexplicably, her heart raced, and adrenalin began to flow through her veins.

Drawing quickly upright, she became fixed to the spot, analysing the possible source of the ever-familiar order for tea and toast.

Yet…it was a calling that compelled her to turn around, all the same.

All signs were there and begging for her attention.

The calming, gravelled tone.

The distinct, enticing aroma of aftershave.

The masculine presence.

Sandra slowly faced the front counter and took a deep, expectant breath.

Yet, to her bemusement, nobody was waiting in line.

Every customer had been attended to.

Julie was wiping tables on the other side of the room.

Sandra stood silently, rooted to the spot.

She waited and watched, rubbing her clammy palms on the front of her tunic.

Assured in her overwhelming belief that he had been there.

Watching her; wanting her to see him.

It may have been a trick of the mind.

Then again, maybe not.

She quickly scanned the scene beyond the window.

The myriad of shoppers in the High Street.

The bustle of another, ordinary, busy day in town.

She then felt a warmth surge through her.

She was convinced of his visit.

Yes. She was sure he had briefly been there with her.

Secretly observing her from his new world.

302

Where dreams definitely became reality.

Perhaps waiting for her to join him there.

And Sandra knew that Andy always kept his promises.

He pledged to her all those years ago.

That he wanted to stay with her forever, even though such a prospect could never be realised.

Yet in truth, he *had* remained with her since the first day they met.

And even in his passing, Andy Ratcliffe had never truly gone away.

He had inadvertently lit a beacon in her heart that had remained bright for many years.

And as she fondly contemplated his memory, Sandra knew that the fire he had ignited within her would continue to burn forever.

ACKNOWLEDGEMENTS

I wish to thank the following people for their invaluable expertise and support in helping this book gain wings:
Samantha Thornton; Hannah Bliss; Charlotte Wilson; Robbie Wilson; Carole Thornton, Chris Bliss; Charlotte Bliss; Jeanette Taylor Ford; Sue Hayward; Ford Wood; Beverley Latimer; Yana Z, and last but certainly not least, David Slaney for his superb cover design.
I couldn't have done it without any of you.
I am forever indebted.
RJT

Also Available on Amazon
by Richard John Thornton

thrillers

DELIVER US FROM EVIL
AT HELL'S GATE
THE SWANS AT CLEARLAKE
WITHIN THESE WALLS
A PRAYER FOR MARTIN
IN PLAIN SIGHT

the 80s trilogy

LAST OF THE OLD SCHOOL

Printed in Great Britain
by Amazon